Lying in Bed

Lying in Bed

a novel by
J. D. LANDIS

· Algonquin Books of Chapel Hill
1995

Published by
ALGONQUIN BOOKS OF CHAPEL HILL
Post Office Box 2225
Chapel Hill, North Carolina 27515-2225

a division of
WORKMAN PUBLISHING COMPANY, INC.
708 Broadway
New York, New York 10003

This is a work of fiction. Names, characters, places, and incidents are either the product of
the author's imagination or are used fictitiously. Any resemblance to actual events or locales or
persons, living or dead, is entirely coincidental.

Library of Congress Cataloging-in-Publication Data
Landis, J. D.
    Lying in bed : a novel / by J. D. Landis.—1st ed.
        p.   cm.
    ISBN 1–56512–068–X
    I. Title.
    PS3562.A4767L95   1995
    813'.54—dc20   94–43078
                                                                 CIP

10   9   8   7   6   5   4   3   2   1
First Edition

For
DT
My wife
With love
JD

What is the greatest experience you can have? It is the hour of the great contempt. The hour in which your happiness, too, arouses your disgust, and even your reason and your virtue.

—Friedrich Nietzsche

Hamlet or a Beethoven quartet is the truth about this vast mass that we call the world but there is no Shakespeare, there is no Beethoven; certainly and emphatically there is no God; we are the words, we are the music, we are the thing itself.

—Virginia Woolf

Lying in Bed

8 P.M.

I am lying in bed, waiting for Clara.

Actually, I am not lying in the bed. I am lying on it.

I am lying on the Double Wedding Ring quilt that was Clara's gift to me when we married just over four years ago. For so common and popular a pattern—with its circles within circles, a happy emblem of the willing commitment and submission of newlyweds to the gyve and take of marriage—it is an unusual example of the craft.

Huge for a quilt from its time, the Civil War, it is actually large enough to cover our bed, which was custom-made for us, as was most everything else in this vast loft, aside from the antiques, before we moved in on our wedding night.

It is a larger bed than what is called king-sized. So we call it emperor-sized, not to celebrate our condition of sovereignty in our secluded home up here atop the city but to make a private musical joke. It was in Beethoven's Emperor Concerto that the cadenza was first written out, and this bed has been the rebellious site of our endless improvisation as Clara and I have played

1

upon the flesh of one another in the deepening nights of our marriage.

Like the Great Bed of Ware, ours is square and consequently so is the quilt, as if it were from the century before its own. It is also unusual in its provenance and condition.

It is Amish and yet vastly more colorful than those enviably simple people were allowing themselves to produce at that wretched time. I imagine it being made in secret by one ambitious and beautiful young maiden who found its colors in the innocent blue of the sky and the promiscuous red of the blood that saturated the black Pennsylvania soil as this beloved nation sent an axe through its own neck.

The Double Wedding Ring design had appeared very little before that civil war and even then was not widely dispersed until the first few decades of the present century, which, appropriately, has run completely out of decades now and approaches the open mons of the millennium deadened by the safety on its senseless glans.

Like most Amish quilts from that time, this one is made of wool, though the wool has softened to an almost silky texture. Yet it sustains itself in defiance of the disintegration visited upon virtually every other quilt of its age and fabric by what is called the "burning" rendered by the natural dyes.

It is that survival, more than the cherishable but trite symbolism of the interlocking wedding bands (which the Amish, like Clara and me, do not choose to wear), that renders this quilt precious to me. Marriage has become the most disposable of our American institutions, as desire is discarded like some withered membrane from its flesh. But I am determined that ours will escape the disintegration of familiarity and will last beyond its own time, beyond death itself.

I am in love with marriage and find it even as mysterious as I hope always to find my wife. At the same time, I am forever attempting to solve its mystery, and hers. I have always wanted to know the truth of things, though I am aware, as Nietzsche said, that it is a condition of existence that those who lift the shroud from truth shall perish.

But I have perished before.

I AM LYING in bed, waiting for Clara.

Actually, I am not waiting for Clara. Clara left not twenty minutes ago. It is much too soon, and too early, for me to be waiting for her to return.

In fact, I had been waiting, with some impatience, for her to leave.

We have not been apart often enough in our marriage, not at night. It is true that we spend every day apart, she at her shop, I here, listening to my music, thinking my thoughts, pursuing my job, which I take delight in describing to the Internal Revenue Service, who are the only people I am obliged to tell what I do, as repairman, that great fixture in American life. (I got the idea, I must confess, from my father, who had called me a born diaskeuast, which has come to mean someone who fixes things. And while I've never been a diaskeuast, the Greek root of that word—*skeuos*, meaning *tool*—brought forth the image of the repairman, to mention nothing of its vulgar invocation of the male member. Words are so seductive!—is it any wonder I was ravished by them to the point of total surrender and virtual eradication.)

I have been audited but once, for I am immaculate in the handling of my finances, which are considerable, though through no effort of my own unless inheritance might be considered an endowment; and the audit was indeed occasioned by my reporting of this bequest. On that singular occasion I was rather disappointed that the agent assigned to my return did not ask me just what it was I repaired. I wonder how much more deeply she

3

might have probed into my ultraconservatively invested, slowly compounding tower of Treasuries had I been able to give my answer to her unasked question: "Myself."

Just what sort of repairman did she think I was, sitting before her in my daily uniform of tweed suit (trousers cuffed; poplin come July), Oxford shirt, club cravat (unlike Wittgenstein I am perpetually betied), sturdy brogues that might as well have come with a lifetime guarantee, aristocratic sandy hair, horn-rims from behind which my print-betrayed eyes gazed at her with the knowledge of how everything worked except the actual things of this world and, of course, me?

I like to think that what fooled her were my muscular build, courtesy of my father as my money had been the hereditament from my mother, and my hands, which are so large and architecturally veined and fiercely jointed that they frighten even me.

It is as if from birth I knew there was no place for me here. I had been born with the body of an athlete and the face, as my late mother used to call it, of a matinée idol, but I refused to put either to use and would not have known how to do so even had I been so inclined. I did not want to "do" anything. I did not want to "make" anything. I did not want to "move" anything. I did not want to "influence" anything. I did not want to "change" anything. I did not want to "teach" anything. I did not even want to "have" anything.

I was a bad American boy. I could find no local heroes (not among the living, certainly, but also not among such contenders as Jonathan Edwards, Emerson, any of the James boys—and I include Jesse and Frank, William and Henry—and Santayana). I could keep no friends, for the boys always wanted to explore the world and the girls my feelings. I knew no love.

I knew no love until I found Clara.

And while Clara and I do spend each day apart, and she tends to come home rather late from her shop, we are so locked together at night—in conversation, in the sex that must be every marriage's interbastation, in huddled sleep on this huge bed in this one boundless room that is our home—that I have been looking forward to this time alone ever since Clara told me this morning that she had a dinner date for tonight.

It is hardly unprecedented for Clara to be out at night, though rarely for dinner and then typically to meet with one of her sources who has trucked or vanned in from Kentucky or Indiana or upstate New York or somewhere else in that other America with what usually turn out to be unworthy pieces anyway, according to Clara, who will always ask me to undress her myself after one of these frustrating get-togethers, as if to affirm a need for me so great that she could not even step out of her clothes were I not there to undo and catch them, or to challenge me to find upon her the excoriations of another's touch.

More commonly when she is out at night, she is catching up with the things that most people, who don't work as hard and as independently as Clara, find time for during the day: seeing dentists and doctors, who I sometimes think only pretend to keep evening hours just not to lose so charming a patient; hectoring her accountant, who persists in telling Clara that she is merely lucky to be doing so well, particularly in so volatile an economy, and that therefore she should be putting more money aside for old age instead of tying it up in inventory; and on irregular but not infrequent occasions going for a workout and massage to her health club, from which she returns burnished and avid.

Usually Clara goes to wherever she is going directly from work. It is rare for her to come home and change, as she did tonight.

Perhaps that is why I was so eager for her to leave. But I could hardly express my enthusiasm for her absence. That would be unkind and open to misinterpretation.

So I put my arms around her and drew her to me. "I'll miss you," I said.

She rested her head on my chest. We are the perfect height for one another. "It's not as if I'll be gone all night."

It had never occurred to me that she might be gone all night. It was a most provocative thing for her to say.

"I'll miss you if you're gone for five minutes." That was the perfect thing for me to say. But, then, it has been Clara who has taught me how to speak.

But I do not miss her.

I am lying here, as I had known I would, luxuriating in solitude. Darkness is now falling on this late-summer evening. I watch it while it eats the light as it spreads down my body on the bed and slides off my shoes on its way across the loft.

I am alone again and silent in the night.

But there is no pain now, as there has been pain so often in the past.

I am married. Nothing can hurt me.

I HAVE NEVER been married before. Neither has Clara. We entered one another without the nearly requisite modern encumbrance of an ex-this or -that.

There are no in-laws either. Clara claims to be an orphan, by fiat. She banished her parents from her life for the cruel trick she feels they played on her the day she was born. I have made no attempt to get her to reconcile with them, not out of fear they won't like me, for Clara likes me well enough, but because their absence from our lives allows me to be that much more alone with her. Also, I cannot bear the idea of looking at two people and being forced to realize that Clara got her purple gaze from this one and the twilit incandescence of her hair from that, her forthrightness from him and her lenocinant smile from her. I detest echo and reflection, replication and even semblance. I repudiate the tyranny of gene. I do not want to see her in anyone else. I want her to exist as if she had sprung into being directly from the touch of the power she judiciously calls It.

I am a literal orphan on the maternal side and might as well be on the other too. My father and I have not spoken since the reading of my mother's will. This is not to say he was unhappy with the will. In fact, he had devised it with her. It was me with whom he was unhappy. It was me with whom he had always been unhappy. And so he had arranged with my mother to provide for me for life. That done, he left my life.

Clara, who has never met him, detests him on my behalf. While I sometimes wish he could know how I am finally content (with her, of whose existence he is not even aware; with myself), I cannot betray her by calling him. And I believe he would rather cut off his hands than use them to pick up the phone to call me, though that does not stop me from imagining now and then when the phone rings that it is he. But that could not be: our number is unlisted; I have not answered a phone in what must be nearly five years now; and he believes I live a continent instead of merely eighty blocks away, for Clara arranged to have him mailed from San Francisco a mawkish printed card, signed by me, four Christmases ago.

And we have no children, Clara or I. "Or at least none that I know of," I joke of myself. It is, obviously, not a joke a woman can make. If a woman has a child, she knows it. A man might never.

But I have no reason to suspect I have a child somewhere. My sex life had been severely limited before Clara, and I had insisted, on its one manifestation, that I wear what I knew then only as a safety.

That singular time, when I lost my virginity to a girl who sat next to me in my freshman philosophy course at Yale and who in fact introduced me to Nietzsche by mockingly calling me an ascetic priest until I finally gave myself to her, I proudly produced said safety that I had bought in a pharmacy on Church Street and like nearly every other American boy carried around with me "just in case," though in my pocket, not my wallet, for even then I never went out in the street with a wallet, having realized, prophetically, that New Haven was a miniature Manhattan and that the races played a game my father called, quite wittily though with the utter disgust of the righteous, Involuntary Socialism. "What's that for?" asked the girl, whose name was Cosima, of all things, or at least she called herself Cosima, after the Cosima with whom more great men have been in love than perhaps any woman in history. (I never did learn her real name.) "Birth control," I answered. "I'm on the pill," she said and waved the thing away. "I still need it," I said, though I had no logical reason to say so, for this was 1978, and AIDS, while it had by then entered our bloodstream, was unknown. She took the little packet from me and held it by its silvery edge between her lips as she proceeded to unbuckle my belt and unzip my fly and lower my tweed trousers and then my boxers. "Look at you," she said, which I didn't realize then might be a common female expression at such a moment. And so I looked at me. As I did, Cosima expertly ripped open the packet using her teeth and the fingers of one hand while the other hand held me upright. Then she fingered the safety by its edges like some rare coin and began to unroll it upon me, seeming to urge it along with the flitting tip of her tongue. And as she left the glans behind and headed down the helve toward where her other hand was redundantly holding me straight up, I felt my whole body rise from her dorm-room squab and a great bolt of feeling ascend from my groin through my stomach and chest and throat and into my brain, where it horrified me by obliterating all my thoughts and did all it could to burst open my skull. I had closed my eyes involuntarily, quite as if I'd sneezed, and when I opened them I saw the reservoir of the safety tipped over along the side of my penis, bulgingly awash

8

with my semen. Cosima was staring at it. "You came," she said glumly. "But that's okay. It happens." Her fingers had not left the bottom of the safety, and now she removed it from me, not rolling it up but gently pulling it until it came loose with a succulent pop and hung morosely from her fingers like a torpid windsock. "No need to apologize," she said, which made me realize, like some naïf Adam, that an apology might very well be what was required of me at this moment. "It was very exciting," she added. "One minute I was hardly touching you and the next minute you got even harder and I literally thought you were going to explode, I mean your whole thing, your whole cock, I thought it was going to explode in my hands. But all it did was come. Thank goodness. I never saw so much come in my life." She hefted the safety as if weighing it. "Of course," she went on, "I never saw anybody shoot right into a rubber before. But it was still prodigious. You must not have come in a long time." She seemed to expect me to say something, but I did not. "How long has it been since you came?" she persisted. "A long time," I said. She smiled. "I thought so. I can tell. Not just by this"—she waved the safety above me before releasing it so it fell to the floor—"but also by this." She reached down with the other hand and took my penis in her fingers. However much it might have fallen off, it now stood straight again, not because she was touching it, I realized, but because of the words she had been saying, the language she had used that had aroused me once again. "Look at you. I'll bet you last a lot longer this time, though it's all right if you don't because I don't care, I really don't, I just want you inside me and you can come if you want to, really, you can come whenever you want, I just want you inside me." As she spoke, she kept hold of me with one hand while she rose on her knees on the thick cushions and put her other hand up her skirt and wiggled her hips above me and finally got her undershorts down to her knees and bent over to push them toward her feet. She sighed when she

9

removed the drawers over her bare feet and brought them up in her hand. "Do you like them?" "Beautiful," I said, for they were indeed, not for their soft fabric or their lacy trim but for their very form and what they signified and where they came from and how they fluttered in her trembling fingers. She let them fall onto my tie and lifted her skirt with both hands and stuck its hem between her front teeth and placed her hands open and flat, palm down, on her stomach and rubbed her way slowly down until the tips of the first two fingers of her right hand disappeared between the lips of her vagina, which she then spread open with the fingers of her left hand so I could see. I could see, and I was seeing something I had never seen before. "I'm so wet," she lisped from the hem of her skirt in her mouth, "so very wet," and, in my innocence, I thought of rain, sordid yet soterial, falling down on both of us, she with her head back now, in her ecstasy, I somehow watching her fingers move and seeing the vulnerable curve of her throat at the same time. She came forward on her knees over my thighs and adjusted her body so she was on the flats of her feet, squatting above me. Then, as she released her skirt from her teeth, she started to come down upon me. "Wait," I said. Her eyes returned to mine. "Are you going to come again?" she snarled solicitously. "No," I answered, "but I need one of those." I pointed down to where I thought the spent safety must have landed. "You must be kidding," said Cosima. "No," I confessed. "Why?" she pleaded. "Birth control," I repeated. It wasn't enough she was on the pill. I would do anything to keep from replicating myself on this earth. I wanted to be alone in my desolation, not bequeath it. "Well, did you bring another one? Tell me you brought another one. Please tell me you brought another one." "No." "Then how are we going to . . ." She sounded as if she might burst into tears. I took her hands in mine by putting my fingers between hers, whose bones, I realized—for this was the first time I had ever held hands with a girl—I might easily have snapped in half. But I merely straightened my arms so she rose in the air and I could wiggle out from beneath her. "Wait here," I said. Cosima fell back against the arm of the squab. "Where are you going?" I pulled up my underpants and pants together. "To buy another one. Don't worry. I'll be right back." "You must be nuts," she said angrily. Then she started to laugh. "You must really be nuts. Remind me not to get involved with freshmen ever again. I mean, don't bother. I can get myself off. I hate rubbers anyway. I'm on the pill, for God's sake. My roommates are coming back any second. Don't bother. I won't be here when you get back." I ran down the steps of her Vanderbilt Hall entrance and raced across the Old Campus and fled out the gate and dashed into the pharmacy on Church Street. When I got back to the Old Campus I realized I could as easily go to my own entrance and my own room as to her entrance and her room, but I went to hers. I knew she would not be there, or if she were there, her roommates would be gathered around her, and they would be laughing, and when I stepped back in and she pointed at me and threw her head back in even greater laughter so that she once again exposed her throat to me, now not in passion but in derision, they would all laugh even harder and I would be forced to join their laughter, for it was indeed funny, it was like something out of Molière, I realized, whom we were reading in French. And it must have been my thinking about being a character in *L'École des femmes* that had me laughing, instead of envisioning the breaking of her delectable neck, when I reached her door. I had expected it to be closed, locked. But it was open, just as I had so discourteously left it. And there was Cosima, on her back, sunk deeply among the pillows. She had taken off all her clothes. She had lit a candle against the fading light of this springtime freshman day. "C'mere," she ordered. "I didn't think you'd be here," I said in my surprise, "or else I thought your roommates . . . I don't understand." "I don't understand you either. I don't want to have to understand you. I just want to have you inside me." So she did.

I did not make love to Cosima ever again. Nor did I make love to anyone else during my remaining undergraduate years, or during the numerous years of my formal postgraduate studies, or for all the eleven years until my wedding night. Such abstinence was the result not of any trauma or shame but rather of my being unable to make any sense of what I had done. I had enjoyed myself, or at least a part of my body had, until it had been fucked and sucked and slapped and pulled and pushed to the degree that it had stopped feeling anything and fallen cold upon my thigh. Even then Cosima was encouraging, as she slipped her hand beneath it and said, "If Yale's endowment matched yours, we wouldn't have to pay tuition," and I found her words arousing and my cock recalescent. But for what? This might be life; but it wasn't art. This might be living for the moment; but I, like every thinker, wanted to live for the fortnight, if not eternity. Let all the other randy, red-blooded American boys follow what they believed to be their biologic destiny, treating the *mons Veneris* like Mont Blanc and having sex as often as possible with as many part-ners as possible. And then let them swagger and jactate among their fellow barbarians. To me this was nonsense. I was simply— and now I could speak from experience—not interested.

As for Cosima, her value to me was not in her blandiloquy or even her skillful and ultimately good-humored initiation of me into what I then believed was the meaninglessness of sex. It was, instead, in her introducing me to the work of Friedrich Nietz-sche. By calling me an ascetic priest, Cosima had begun the process of getting me to have sex with her. By answering my questions about just where she had come up with the notion of the ascetic priest, she unwittingly opened the door for me into my entire future and closed the door for herself into my trousers.

I had always been a studious, inactive boy. But with my discovery of Nietzsche, I became a true ascetic. I wanted to be one of the "great, fruitful, inventive spirits" he wrote about in *On the Genealogy of Morals*. When he said that in such spirits you always encounter asceticism, that was for me.

I was in the perfect position to practice the three ascetic ideals: chastity, because I had now experienced, and found incongruous, its opposite and was perfectly content to embark upon "that melancholy sexual perversion known as continence"; humility, because I had been rendered humble by my father and was truly humble in my confrontation with the body of knowledge it was my ambition to unclothe; and poverty, which it was simple for me to practice because the wealth of my family had taught me to want nothing but what was abstract, like knowledge itself, and I was about to become, as George Steiner would years later describe the brilliant wife-murderer Louis Althusser, "inebriated with abstraction."

I even decided that I would follow Nietzsche to the extent of becoming a student of the uses and power of language, specifically a rhetorician, because Nietzsche's first job had been to teach rhetoric. I would master the *Einreden*, the power of rhetoric, what Mikkel Borch-Jacobsen calls "the whole domain of suggestion, of mimetico-affective contagion, of the magical power of words."

Words became my life, words in the search of truth, and it was through words that I would rise above the brutes or sink to the level of the demons. Nietzsche said in *Truth and Lie in an Extramoral Sense* that we possess nothing but the metaphors of things. Though he warned often enough of the terrible threat to one's sanity in seeking the truth, the truth is what I sought, even as I sat in the shade of the leaning tower of Wimsatt and was taught that dualism, conflict, the clash of desires, are the key to the truth in art as in life. Is that not what every intelligent young person is striving for, or should be, before the illusions of life on the outside of the mind take over? Is that not what every old person, slipping feet first into death, desires? To know. The truth.

The connection between my obsession with Nietzsche and what might seem my obsession with the use of safeties is not as tenuous as it may seem. I had been raised at a time when safeties were seen as a means more of birth control than of inhibiting disease. And if there was anything that frightened me from the time I learned from my mother how babies came to be, it was the idea that I might have a child. I must have known intuitively what I was to learn under the tutelage of my friend and seducer, Cosima, who that very same night of my seduction gave me that most popular book of Nietzsche among undergraduates, *Thus Spoke Zarathustra*. It was at dawn the next morning, when I was back in my dorm room, nursing my sore member and feeling quite at peace with myself for having experienced and disposed of sex in a single encounter, that among Nietzsche's "great fugues of thought" I came upon these words: "In your children you shall make up for being the children of your father; thus you shall redeem all that is past."

I knew then that having a child would be for me the most meaningful act of my life and perhaps the only real act in a life devoted not to action but to contemplation. Is it any wonder, then, that I became celibate and would no longer even consider depositing my seed into the reinforced reservoir of what today has become a virtual symbol of enlightened sexuality, the condom?

Safe sex? There is no such thing. No sex is safe. And the sex in marriage, even if both of you are virgins when you meet (hardly the case with Clara, thank goodness, though almost with me) and remain faithful all your lives, is the most dangerous sex of all. Sex in marriage is always threatening, in and of itself, to renounce its own powers in mockery of your commitment and to leave you in perpetual grief and mourning. The ravages of AIDS to the body cannot compare to the devastation to the mind wrought by the slow evaporation of passion. AIDS kills you; marriage, mercilessly, lets you live.

Clara and I do not use condoms. We have never used any form of birth control. We are not "trying to have a baby." We are simply mixing our lives, which is what marriage should be and is a vastly better definition of it than the "joining" of lives, which implies a mere hitching of people rather than a coalescing of their beings. Concinnity is our goal in life precisely as it must be for the rhetorician in his discourse, that logic and harmony out of whose enactment come tranquility and beauty.

Our sex itself is redemptive. And if a child issues forth from it, as I hope a child will, that child shall redeem not only all that is past but also all that is to come.

Though I know for certain that I have had no children and that Clara has had no children, I have no idea how many men she might have had a child with, except that there were many. I have more than once asked her to tell me in detail about her past, but she has demurred. "I wouldn't want you to get the wrong impression of me," she has answered on more than one occasion. And once I responded, "What you don't understand is that there could be no wrong impression of you for me. There is nothing you might have done that could turn me against you. And I want to know everything. Down to the last detail." But still she refused. "You'll just have to imagine it," she said, because she knows me so well as to know that I do imagine it. Vividly. "If you won't tell me, then I'll just have to read your diaries," I threatened. "Oh, please," she scoffed.

I have found myself longing to know everything about her. You cannot love someone until you love her whole life—every moment, every passion, every cry of pleasure or pain in the aphotic, inaccessible night of the past. The great injustice of love is that it arrives encumbered with unimaginable loss. I have never understood those people who say they would rather not know.

15

You might as well marry some piece of statuary in a graveyard, cold, dead, and silent, from whom the very abrasions of lust have faded. Or is that not what most husbands and wives become to one another, while still alive?

Not we. I shall not let that happen. If marriage is a gradual opening up of one mate to the other, then surely all the secrets of the past will be revealed.

I do not know what thrills me more: knowing that there are secrets or knowing that I must someday learn those secrets.

At the moment I am balanced between the two. My imagination feeds me equally well from Column A or Column B.

IT IS AN apt metaphor, for I am planning to order in Chinese food this very evening. I can even now picture myself lifting the chopsticks to my mouth, surrounding with my lips a dumpling or more likely some culinary general's chicken, sucking a sesame-pasted noodle through them like a child whose manners are in suspension because he thinks no one is looking at him.

However, the metaphor does break down in its specifics. In our neighborhood, where we live among the artists and their dealers and their austere watering holes, there are no surviving Cantonese or Mandarin restaurants where you can actually order from Column A or Column B, as we used to when I was a child and my parents would summon their driver and we would travel from Park Avenue to the wild West Side of Manhattan as if it were another civilization and sit down in a booth in what my father called a Chinks establishment and create a dinner for ourselves by ordering, literally, from Column A or Column B, "expense be damned," as my father would say with a smirk, the whole meal costing so little in fact that he always made it a point to leave a tip that was larger than the tab itself, though it perpetually annoyed him that even this extreme munificence never got him recognized the next time we would show up at the same restaurant on our culinary excursions to what he called Immigrant Alley or Junkies' Junction—Broadway in the Nineties—and he would excuse this discourtesy, which he would never experience from an East Side maître d', by telling me and my mother that Oriental people had destroyed their memories through opium, interbreeding, collectivization, and an unwillingness to open fully their tiny, belligerent slits of eyes.

But am I hungry?

Not yet.

Even when I get hungry, I want to get hungrier still. After all, I ceased being an ascetic priest when I married Clara. And if the most radical form of the ascetic ideal demands a desire even to stop desiring, a will to terminate willing, then I want to overthrow that ideal tonight. I want to let all my senses drift through the entire cavalcade of desire until I am stretched to the very edge of desperation, and only then to fulfill them. I want for myself what Steiner names that "particular effect of musical resolution—unreconciled energy inside repose." I want to become orectic without, as it were, becoming erect.

What could be less like marriage? Marriage replaces desperation, at least of one kind, with a fulfillment so regular that it threatens to become undeviating.

That is why I am grateful for this evening alone. I can let myself go, without having to go anywhere. I need not even leave this bed.

But I shall miss eating with Clara. We almost always have dinner together. It is not a ritual, our dinner, because there is nothing ceremonial about it. We might eat an elaborate dinner at home or a simple dinner out or an elaborate dinner out or a simple dinner at home. Regardless, it is at this time of day, when she has finished her work and I have finished mine, that we have come together, as darkness has slipped its hand into the glove of the day. It has been the time of our greatest sharing and consideration of one another, with the single exception of those later times, deeper in the night, upon this bed, on which, not in which, I lie.

I shall also miss talking with Clara. Discussion has always been an important part of our dining. Our whole marriage has been, I suppose, like Virginia and Leonard Woolf's honeymoon, when, as she described it, "We talked incessantly for seven weeks and became chronically nomadic and monogamic," though for Clara and me our wandering has been limited predominantly to the landscape of our bodies.

Whether we eat out or in, we talk to one another. Nothing (unless it was the image of separate beds) repelled me more about the idea of marriage than my fear of silence within it. I knew too well the lure of silence to the person alone and had given in to it myself quite dramatically. But to imagine silence within a partnership of woman and man was to imagine a living death.

Who among us, when young, has not had our vision of the future poisoned by seeing a man and a woman with the fabric at their knees touching beneath a restaurant table and not a word exchanged between them once the menu's lifted like a script from their desolate hands?

I have often thought that the real reason people have children is not to redeem all that is past but to give themselves something to talk about or, if they have forgotten completely how to talk to one another, at least someone to talk to, a child held captive by the power of the language of loss.

Clara and I have always talked to one another. When I have been able to take my eyes from her eyes, as I was speaking, or from the wet haze of her lips, when she was speaking, I have seen other couples, silent, watching us as we spoke. I could almost see their ears bending toward us like wintery plants toward the sun. Our intimacy, in the privacy of our conversation, which sometimes unfolds in a kind of rutting stichomythia, could fill a room. And I knew that those people looking at us talk and trying to hear our words were imagining our sex life. They could see us locked together in the dioecious discourse of the flesh.

And what did we talk about? The menu, naturally. What to eat. What to drink. And shall we share. The prospect of children. Music. Literature. Sex. I was always after something. I was always willing to be taught. There is, for example, nothing about her that is more mysterious to me than her orgasms. And while it may be true, as Steiner says, that the ineffable lies beyond the frontiers of the word, I have always encouraged her to tell me about them. I might inform her, in our ongoing discussion about the Bell family, from whom she seems to like to pretend she is descended now that I have told her about them, that Virginia Woolf's sister, Vanessa Bell, wrote to her husband, Clive Bell, that Virginia "gets no pleasure from the act." "Oh, how would they know that?" asks Clara, flying ingenuously into the scholar's web. "Because," I say, "Virginia herself wrote to a friend of hers: 'I find the climax immensely exaggerated.' And what about you, my dear?" I slyly suggest. Why am I so interested in this subject? Perhaps because it seems one thing about my wife that must remain forever mysterious, far more than the facts of her past that I might plumb merely through a reading of her diary, which I wholly expect to take place on my deathbed so I may go to my grave enlightened about the one human being I care to understand. But how ever might I enter that storm that breaks upon the fragile ambit of my being? I am there when it happens, of course, but that's like saying one is present at the birth of a star. No one can tell me about this but her. No one can translate this explosion of knowledge and transcendence of self.

In a good marriage, it is impossible to separate sex from conversation. Dicacity, as much as venery, marks our evenings. No topic for us is interdicted, though neither tells the other all we know. We share a healthy respect for the dangers of depletion and the potential vacuity of the future. Nothing must diminish the ardor with which we live with one another. Familiarity must breed not some great contempt but, however paradoxically, renewal. I do not want Emerson's complacent "friendship in possession." I want the passion of pursuit; which is not, I trust, too much to ask when the woman I love seems forever beyond my grasp. Nothing must silence the song that is our marriage.

Another apt metaphor, that, since music has become, apart from Clara and after the betrayal of language, my life. I have found that sex and music are the only surviving divertissements into which I can dive through the crust of self, in which I can drown, and from which I can emerge inviolate.

I have even, this past day, and to replace the conversation I would otherwise have had with Clara, planned the music that will carry me through this evening until her return. And I have programmed it within the ten-disc magazine of my compact-disc player to bring me to that very "edge of desperation" in the realm of sound that my hunger will bring me in the realm of food and the absence of my wife in the realm of desire. And just as the arrival of the Chinese delivery boy will rescue me from my first-world version of starvation, so will the arrival home of Clara rescue me from the disemboguement of mind that such music might bring and from the longing in my body that her absence will inspire.

Of course, technology being what it is in this benevolently convenient age of ours, I have at hand two devices that will protect me from going over the edge should I begin to lose control: a telephone to summon my food and a remote-control instrument to reprogram or stop my music. But there is nothing here with which I might touch my wife tonight. She is beyond my reach. In matters of love, we remain as primitive as the first human beings, whose primogenial words, according to Otto Jespersen, were sounds of courtship, "something between the nightly love-lyrics of puss upon the tiles and the melodious love-songs of the nightingale." So was language born. Is it any wonder we cry out in the darkness?

Just before Clara left this evening, I played Celtic guitar music. And when she was gone, I did something I had never done before: I danced with only the feel of her in my arms. Then I lay down here and used the remote to change the music. I have never been able to listen to it without her.

So now, alone, I am listening to Bach's *Inventions*. All the evening's early discs are for solo instruments, to reflect my solitude. I have chosen the recording on the clavichord, as distinguished from the harpsichord or piano, because it is the "smallest" of the instruments, the least intrusive, the most homey. It was the domestic keyboard of choice, and the most practical, at the time. I thought it fitting to lead off my music tonight because I am planning to have so domestic an evening for myself, so comfortable and cozy, and the kind of journey of self-discovery that only solitude and darkness and the absence of one's beloved can provide.

I believe in these contrasts. There is no desire without deprivation. There is no hunger without depletion. It is not simply a matter of the tempo of life, as it was in the high Renaissance, when a slow dance would be followed by a fast. It is as much a matter of texture, as it became in the Baroque. Musically, I see it as the difference between the *stylus phantasticus* and the *stylus canonicus*. Philosophically, it is the dreaminess of Apollo awakening into the rapture of Dionysius.

And I love the name *Inventions*. It suggests a certain improvisation, even chicanery, though Bach seems to have used it to mean something as simple as motif. He stole the name from some teaching pieces by the little-known Antonio Bonporti and wrote his own *Inventions* so his eldest and most beloved son, Wilhelm Friedemann, who was ten years old at the time, might have something interesting and instructive to play while learning the clavichord.

It is as if your father, to teach you to dance, provides you with instructions on how to leap from the floor and not come down until you so desire.

When I have thought of having a child, I have been either inspired or intimidated by the example of such magnificent didacticism. I have wondered what I would hope to pass on to him: my philomathic passions; my ability to be both of the world but not in it and in the world but not of it; my fidelity to ideas and to the flesh of one woman; my control over the chaos of life that might, by a stretch, be equated with the taming of chaos that Bach attained in his music, that transport "from the world of unrest to a world of peace," as Albert Schweitzer put it in writing about *The Well-Tempered Clavier*, that other, more taxing collection of teaching pieces that Bach himself described as being "for the use and practice of young musicians who want to learn and for the amusement of those who already know this study."

Amusement! His unaccustomed modesty is a weapon, and so can his music be unless you learn not to compete with its transcendence. If you listen to such music and say, "Why can't I do that?" you will hate yourself to the end of your days. It is not art but the failure to achieve it that drives one mad.

Know your limits. Will I have the courage to pass that on? It is surely the hardest of life's lessons.

Love your mother.

Love her not the way I do, for I am her husband, but love her just as well.

Love your father too and in so doing redeem all that is past.

But what good are rubrics? Wilhelm Friedemann, on whom Bach bestowed the purest of his paternal love and the most patient and gentle of his contrapuntal initiations, ended up a drunk and, worse, stopped believing in his gift.

Even Bach could not provide ease in the world for his child. Not for any of them. And he had twenty.

I have spent much time pondering what evidence there is of his prodigious sexual life. All those children aside, there is the serious trouble he got himself into with the authorities at Arnstadt when, as they wrote it up, "he caused the strange maiden to be invited into the organ loft and let her make music there."

I picture him, as I listen to his *Inventions*, passing from two-part to the increased difficulty of three, the Sinfonias, though never does he leap so far that he stops cradling the delicate sensibilities of his firstborn . . . I picture him bending this strange maiden over the bench of his Gottfried Silbermann or Arp Schnitger and lifting her skirts with one hand while with the other he bangs out something he'd learned on his recent pilgrimage to Buxtehude in Lübeck.* The strange maiden herself releases him from his britches and says, "That's quite some organ," and Bach responds, "Yes, it's a Silbermann," or, "Yes, it's a Schnitger," and they both enjoy the joke, and prolong it, as the strange maiden says, "Enter here, Silbermann," or, "You must have received a nasty blow, Schnitger, for you are all swollen," and Bach responds to the strange maiden, "It is time for you to sing, with the accompaniment of my organ," and as her fingers play along the length of him and grasp the thickness of him and finally force him headfirst through her silent, open lips, she begins to sing the only song that pullulating man never did set down.

Strange maiden. Since I first read of Bach's encounter with her in the organ loft in Arnstadt, I have become obsessed with her. She has become not simply whoever that adventuresome girl might have been back in 1706 and who is now dust's dust in some grave surely as unmarked as Bach's first, but every girl, any girl,

*Actually, it was Johann Friedrich Wender who built the organ in the Neukirche at Arnstadt, but John's little joke is more amusing in his employment of the sibilant names of those other great organ builders, Silbermann and Schnitger. JDL

who might lift her skirts and laugh and guide a strange lad into herself and then step off the page of history into oblivion.

It is marriage itself, and Clara as its embodiment, that has made a philogynist of me. When I walk with her in the street—for I am almost never out unless I'm out with her—I am assaulted by the beauty of the strange maidens I see at every turn. They seem etched into the very air even as they part it with the long blades of their legs. But then the air surrounds them, and they are gone, she is gone. Goodbye, I cry silently to her, goodbye into your life. She never hears me, and if she sees me, it is only inadvertently. I am part of the landscape of the city, another man in a tie bleak against the sky. I do reach for them, these women, but only with my eyes. It is not that they are necessarily unattainable, for who knows? Any one of them might yield, if spoken to, illaqueated in the lepid net of language. But then she would be a stranger no longer, and I would no longer long for her. A strange maiden's desirability resides precisely in her remaining indeterminate and unexplored.

A wife is as far from being a strange maiden as a woman can be. A wife is known, from the permutable textures of her hair right down to the camber of her toes.

I am as rare in my mammalian monogamy as the klipspringer, the siamang, the reedbuck, and the incongruously named dik-dik. I want no other woman than my wife. The others, the strangers, who vanish like death, only break my heart. My wife holds it together.

Those who came after Bach and sought to sanctify him, as they believed he sanctified the evil in the world with his masses and motets, proclaimed that the strange maiden whom he lofted by the organ in Arnstadt was his cousin Maria Barbara, soon to be his wife.

They sought to excuse his sins by uxoriating them. How little they knew of marriage, which withers without the exaltation of sin.

Bach's wife died when he was away from Cöthen, where they lived while he accomplished such little things as the *Brandenburg Concertos* and—how cruelly ironic—the *Wedding Cantata*, in whose opening adagio the oboe impregnates the soprano.

When he arrived home from his travels, he was told that Maria Barbara had died and been buried.

No goodbyes. No final embrace. No vision to carry forever of his wife vulnerable and inviting on her back with her hands on her breasts and her legs demurely open beneath her shroud and within her closed eyes the knowledge of all the untold secrets of her life, never now to be whispered to him through those dry, dampened lips.

I think of Clara dying without my being there and without my even knowing. I never worry about this during the day, when we are separated, she running her shop, I right here where I always am. But sometimes, at night, when she is out, I feel like Pergolesi's Orfeo, afraid of death only to the degree that I am separated from her. But we are almost always together at night. We love to sit and talk and drink our wine as this infinite room grows ever darker until finally we grow invisible to one another and our disembodied voices become entangled vapor trails in the illimitable sky. As long as we are talking, I know we are alive.

I get up from this bed and go to the north windows. The city spreads out before me the chaotic aftermath of a lavish dinner party, all tumbled glass and unfinished heaps of life. Where is Clara in all of this? Is she safe? Is she whole? Is she real? At least she had been wise enough not to carry her handbag in a city where you expect to see people wearing signs that say NO ILLU-SIONS—ALREADY STOLEN.

But what if she too were to die and be buried before I had knowledge of either? I would lie down upon her grave like Julia Duckworth upon her husband's and attempt to lift from it the veil of grass as I do the nightgown from her knees and thighs at night and claw my way through the dirt into the haven of her arms.

Unlike Bach, I would take no other wife for as long as Clara were to remain dead.

Bach lasted hardly a year before he relinquished a maiden's strangeness and married her.

She was twenty years old, and her name was Anna Magdalena. That is a wonderful name to be able to whisper over and over as you sink ever more deeply into its proprietress, even better than Maria Barbara, and we may be sure Bach whispered it many times, for Anna Magdalena bore him an even greater number of children than he had been left with by Maria Barbara.

But what is most enticing about Anna Magdalena, and why I sometimes whisper her name myself into this room when I am alone here in the day and listening to the music I now call forth with my innocent remote, is her being the inspiration for a sarabande that Bach wrote down in a little notebook.

Clara writes things down in little notebooks too. Not music. Private things. She records her life and fantasies in a handwriting that is such a salmagundi of slashes and dots and scars and the amputation of abbreviation that it is literally cryptographic and therefore leaves her life and mind indecipherable to anyone who might be so crude as to attempt to violate her diaries.

Only on the day of our first meeting was I privileged to see what sort of thing she records in those pages. Since that day, I have not even peeked, though I find it more difficult as time goes by and we consume one another within the fire of our marriage not to want to see her in those pages, to experience her mind and history apart from how we live our lives together.

The closer we become in our marriage, the more a stranger she seems to me and the more a stranger I seem to myself. It is as if our separate identities were being erased by the very thing that secures our identities. I am losing Clara even as she becomes more a part of myself. I am losing myself not simply as I become more a part of her but also as I lose her. When there is no difference between gain and loss, the result is not stability but chaos.

It is ascertainable even in our lovemaking now, which approaches masturbation in its familiarity and inspires aprosexia, as it were, in the very midst of sex, driving us to push one another away in order to be closer, to become strangers in order to remain confidants, to pretend we are not who we are as we claw at each other's skin and minds on that bed there.

I do not want to read Clara's diaries in order to know her better. Quite the opposite. I want to read them in order to know her less well, to be able to say, "My word, this is not the woman I know," and thereby to find myself wanting her even more than I do. After four years of marriage, I discover it is necessary to recreate the person I know best and love best. This cannot be done without her collaboration, however tacit. But I have promised not to read what she has written. And so, in order to strengthen our marriage and deepen my love for my wife, I must someday betray it and her.

I am not afraid to encounter Clara's past or even her most dissolute thoughts about the present. I am not possessive that way. What she did before we met can trouble me only in that I was not there to see it. Sometimes I wish we'd never met because I didn't meet her soon enough. Her past is beyond me. I mourn my absence from every moment of it. My fondest wish is transport back into the womb with her. As for what is possible, I simply want to see her. Apart from me. Out there. Being someone other than the self she has become with me.

She is, perhaps, that way most when she is on the floor out there beyond our bed, which is centered in the room but is not precisely in the cynosural position of Louis XI's *grand lit de justice*. It is, in fact, flush against the long north wall, so that our hair is tossed uptown while our toes tend toward Tribeca. We are thereby, it is true, deprived of a *ruelle*. But since we live here quite alone and entertain no one but ourselves, this is no sacrifice at all and provides my head its walled support for reading or the contemplation of my wife when she is writing in her diaries. I often lie here at night and watch her at it, always with her back to me, arched, her shoulders fanned, her neck curved. I imagine her eyes closed, the tip of her tongue protruding from between her slightly overbiting front teeth, the notebook fast upon her clenched, unyielding knees, and one of the many pencils she keeps lined up on the rickrack-pattern hooked rug scratching out words that no one but I can read.

The pencils no longer confound me. In fact, I grow ever more entranced by the very evanescence of their transfer of life from the mind to the page. Like the women in the street who dissolve into the air itself, what is at risk of disappearing becomes all the more desirable. Besides, as Jonathan Goldberg so pointedly explains in the very same essay in which he brilliantly remarks that for both Heidegger and Barthes (despite their differing sexual orientations) "the scene of writing is one that betrays phallic desire," the pencil and the penis are "etymologically cognate."

Clara has been decomposing pencils in her notebooks since the day she arrived in New York alone at sixteen, merely a year shy of the fifteen years that Bach waited before he resurrected from his own notebook, which was more literally a musicbook, that sarabande as the opening aria of the Goldberg Variations, which at this very moment Glenn Gould begins to play for me and I fall once more upon the bed.

The sarabande was originally a concupiscent sort of dance that, like many things in celebration of wanton carnality, was banned. It was described in the aptly titled *Treatise Against Public Enjoyment* by Father Juan de Mariana this way: "A dance and song, so lascivious in its words, so ugly in its movement, that it is enough to inflame even very modest people."

Inflame them to what? A desire to suppress the dance and song? Or a desire to join in? Or are those not the same? Suppression is inevitably inspired by an appetite for what it condemns.

So BAN THE SARABANDE went out the call back in the 1590s. But they could not keep a dance step down. By the time it got to Bach, it had gained in dignified beauty what it had been stripped of in licentiousness, rather like the idealization of an old marriage.

This particular sarabande is a theme that is not repeated in these Goldberg variations. In that, it is as unusual as a woman whose beauty is so great that you cannot bear to see her ever again. But then, on your deathbed, you summon her forth, as Bach does at the very end of the Goldbergs as an *aria da capo* immediately following the final variation, the quodlibet, one of whose melodies borrows from a pop song of the day, *Ich bin so lang nicht bei dir g'west* (which translates into something I hope I never have to sing to Clara: Long have I been away from you).

Glenn Gould is less the romantic than I about this sarabande. To him it is some sort of mindless flirt and masculine as well. He calls it "a singularly self-sufficient little air which seems to shun the patriarchal demeanour, to exhibit a bland unconcern about its issue, to remain totally uninquisitive as to its *raison d'être*." What a condemnation: to shun one's own children and never to question why one is here.

And lest anyone think I and Huxley are alone in finding music "palpitatingly sexual" and sex musical, it is Gould himself who says, "The aria melody evades intercourse with the rest of the work."

I take from that a definition of the good marriage: the married person evades intercourse with the rest of the world. Is it any wonder I rarely set foot from here unless accompanied by Clara?

Bach went blind toward the end of his life. I close my eyes and listen to these variations. I am not trying to use them to fall asleep, though they were commissioned to cure or at least make tolerable a count's insomnia. The count asked an eleven-year-old named Johann Goldberg, who worked for him and was also a student of Bach, if Bach wouldn't write something to help the count get through, one way or another, the night. Bach responded with these variations. The count responded with the biggest payday of Bach's life, henceforth and thenceforth. Many a night would the count summon his immortal harpsichordist, who would himself die very young: "Dear Goldberg, please come and play for me my variations."

I myself am doing a splendid job getting through this night. I am even more content in my solitude and excited by it than I had imagined I would be. And I do not want to sleep.

But I do close my eyes. I close them in order to be blind like Bach.

And then, I open them.

I open them, because ten days before Bach died, his eyesight miraculously returned.

I like to lie here and replicate that experience. All is darkness. And then, ten days before eternal darkness, sight is restored.

What do I want to see, in this brief time before the lights go out forever?

I want to see Clara.

I want to see Clara naked, unmasked, anew.

I do not know what Bach saw in his ten remaining days or what he wanted to see. Anna Magdalena, perhaps.

He certainly would not have wanted to see his grave. Not that there was anything to see, once he had been thrown in and endirted. Though you would have thought that however many of his twenty children had survived would have bought him a headstone, nothing marked the place of his burial. And nothing would until nearly a hundred and fifty years later when his grave was accidentally dug up to make room for the augmentation of the church in whose yard he had shrunk to the size of an oboe.

Do our children think they can sweep our dust even beyond the corners of their minds once we have ceased inventing life? Apparently so. These were the same Bach children who later allowed Anna Magdalena to be buried in a pauper's grave, far away from the husband who had immortalized her with a sensuous if not exactly lascivious sarabande.

If I am buried far from where Clara is buried, I will dig my way through the wet, wormy earth until I lie with her again, forever.

9 P.M.

The Goldbergs have put me to sleep. For a few minutes, then, though I am unconscious during them, I am Count Keyserlingk.

"Dear Goldberg," I whisper aloud to that young boy who has soothed me with such beauty, "please do not die so soon."

Nor you, Glenn Gould, most enviable of men, to have found ecstasy in art and art alone, and art on its loftiest mission in solitude, and peace, for goddamned once, in death.

That melancholy aside, I am full of happiness. Never, in fact, have I felt at such peace.

I have awakened into almost total darkness. The only illumination in this one huge room of ours comes from the minuscule coinedge of moon that is visible from where I lie through the west windows and from the lumpy counterpane of light that floats in the sky over this city every night, smothering the stars.

I cannot see my own toes. I doubt I'd be able to see my own erection, were I moved to generate it. But I am not. With Clara gone, this place is sexless. I am free of stimulation. I am at peace with my body. My body is my own.

How nice to have one's wife away, not to miss her but not to miss her.

I, former rhetorician—failed rhetorician, to be honest, or at least defeated rhetorician—I wonder if I've created a new figure of speech with that: not to miss her but not to miss her. I have never encountered its like, though some argument might be made that it is a kind of deviant chiasmus, balanced to a degree that would compare with the disconcerting experience of looking in a mirror and confronting your image unreversed.

But better than that, it is as great an example of the need to split an infinitive as there might be: not to miss her but to not miss her.

Still, not missing her, I find myself missing not missing her. It compares to the feeling of guilt over the absence of the feeling of guilt over something that should have produced a feeling of guilt in the first place.

Why do I not miss her?

I turn on my side in the darkness and take one of her pillows from next to mine and pull it into the middle of my body. "Clara," I say.

I am reminded of August Strindberg, with whose life I became familiar when I learned he and Nietzsche had exchanged correspondence (in four languages, two of them dead), though very few letters actually passed between them before Nietzsche slipped wholly into madness and ceased communicating altogether. Strindberg had experienced his own insanity, particularly after his third wife, Harriet Bosse, had left him. It was at that time he began to have hallucinations, visions, fantasies, which were to him, in a grand display of what Husserl would come to call transcendental subjectivity, their own reality. "If I see my pillow assume human shapes," wrote Strindberg, "those shapes are there, and if anyone says they are fashioned only by imagination, I reply: 'You say only?' What my inner eye sees means more to me."

I bend my neck and kiss the pillow. I kiss the pillow chastely. But it is, after all, only a pillow, though a special one, for Clara claims to have covered it herself with a piece of Log Cabin quilt that her grandmother had made and given to her in the irretrievable days before she was born into my life. It does not assume human shape, this pillow. It is not Clara herself. She has not left me. Though if she had, I am sure I would have gone mad too and have hugged the pillow to me and have discovered that it *is* Clara, as Strindberg found his wife Harriet back in his distraught arms.

But it does smell of her, the pillow. It smells of the different smells of her hair, of her neck, of her shoulders, of her back, of between her legs from when she flings it down there and, laughing, says, "Fuck me, Johnny."

"Oh, Clara," I say, remembering her, and I laugh first at the remembrance and then at the fact that I'm talking to a pillow.

It occurs to me that I never once talked aloud to myself in the year that I talked aloud to no one. It takes the absence of Clara to turn me into everyone's image of a lonely man.

It is interesting to me that I do not want her. It used to be that I could want her just from the smell of her, from any of the smells of her. And the smell needn't emanate directly from her skin or hair. I might smell her on a pillow, like this, or a chair, a plate, a towel, a brush, my undershorts or hers, and I would want her so much that I seemed to become nothing but desire, shrunk to an impenetrable density of need, like some black hole.

Desire. Not the fulfillment of desire. Desire alone. That longing so pure it decontaminates ambiguity.

When I do not desire her, it is as if she does not exist.

A wife, then, might be said to exist in direct proportion to the husband's desire for her. And vice versa, of course.

How, I wonder, do we stay alive to one another while the years erase us like a reproachful teacher buffing a blackboard?

As I ponder these perhaps unanswerable questions as if I had all the time in the world and find myself hoping that Clara will not come home too soon, I become aware that the CD changer has continued to provide a choice of music that perfectly accompanies my emotional needs.

It is still soloing, as it were, but it has left Glenn Gould's piano for Yo Yo Ma's cello and the Bach suites, for me perhaps the most anamnestic of music since I cannot hear them without being reminded of Clara and my wedding day.

As I am unable to lie here and not think of Clara, though she has, in a sense, ceased to exist for me, so the music seems unable to abandon Bach and his Anna Magdalena.

There is great mystery surrounding these suites for cello. While still living in Cöthen, after the death of Maria Barbara, Bach produced in 1720 a clean copy of his six sonatas for solo violin, perhaps the only music that tortures me even while its beauty makes me weep (no fool I, those pieces are not programmed for this special evening of listening enjoyment).

On the title page of that copy, Bach put the words "Libro primo." So if that is Book One, where is Book Two?

There is nothing labeled Libro secondo. And there cannot be a First if there is not a Second, which is to say, the First becomes a First and not merely an Only by virtue of their being a Second.

But here are these six suites for solo cello. Except there is no surviving original clean copy of them. There is nothing but a copy written out in the hand of Anna Magdalena. And while that copy has significant mistakes involving tempo markings and bowings and ornaments, it is still fortunate that Anna Magdalena's handwriting was not quite so sphingine as Clara's, or I would probably not be lying here this evening feeling the sound of this cello in my tranquil loins.

It is my theory that these cello suites were indeed the Libro secondo and thus that they were written soon after the completion of the violin sonatas in 1720 and thus further that they were composed in the heat of Bach's preparations for his 1721 wedding to Anna Magdalena, a prenuptial display of his affection, passion, his desire to lie with her and, to judge from the music itself, dance with her. So, even before they married, he gave her the original of the scores for her to copy them out. For a composer, it was like giving someone your diary to read.

Anna Magdalena was clearly receptive. Suffering from temporary dysgraphia, she could hardly write straight as she heard the cello in her mind. Perhaps she even felt like the cello, held firmly between the legs of her man, stroked by a bow that she knew to be, and to remain, hard, for in the early 1700s the flexible bow for cello was not yet used, which accounts for a certain lack of polyphony in these suites if not in the reaction of Anna Magdalena to them.

They were, in essence, a kind of wedding present to her, or so I have always theorized, which is why, aside from their tendency to make me feel like dancing, they were the music I chose to play at my wedding.

It was a simple wedding.

It was the most wonderful day of my life.

But it was not the most important day of my life. The most important day of my life was the day I found Clara. Had I not found her, I could not have married her. So the day I found her was the most important day of my life. More important even than the day I was born.

Had I not been born, I would simply not have lived.

Had I not found Clara, I would not have come to life.

ON THE DAY we met, barely four years ago, I was wandering the city, listening to music through my headphones, trying to escape the tyranny of language.

I was functional, at that time in my existence, only when I was moving. It was, in the words of Matthew Arnold, an "illiberal, dismal life." Today, I leave this room without her only to take back something secret for her. Then, I was always out in the street, always walking, like some tormented St. Jerome in Chalcis, trying to keep up with my thoughts and to escape my thoughts.

I was afraid that if I lay down, my thoughts would race ahead of me, a visible net of words that would spin from my mind and wrap round and round my head until I was bandaged from crown to Adam's apple, featureless, sightless, suffocated. Words can be a merciless enemy, and I tried to avoid them the way one would some deadly, unseen bacillus or a plane about to crash whose shadow swells upon the rutted surface of the earth.

In those days, once I returned home from my daily sciamachy with morphemes in the hope of embracing the gentler Morpheus, I even tried to sleep standing up, because I hoped thereby to induce in myself a habit of sleepwalking so I might keep moving. Thus, while others all over the city were lying in bed and pulling their blankets to their chins and pounding their pillows, I was finding a congenial corner in one of the many rooms of my apartment and leaning into it with my eyes closed and my hands prayerlike to protect my face from the insidious crack where walls meet.

I never did learn to sleepwalk, or if I did I managed to do it without ever waking up or stepping out a window, and I always returned to the corner to which I'd condemned myself the night before, where I'd awaken at first light to find myself on the floor with the top half of my body against one wall and the bottom half against the other wall and my posterior, suitably enough, in that crack, though my crack and the walls' crack, with what I thought was equal idoneity, made the sign of the cross.

It was a terrible way to sleep. It was a terrible way to wake.

But it was not, I thought, until I found Clara and learned how to live, such a terrible way to live.

I was rich from inheritance.

I was free from the necessity to work or even to educate myself.

I was able, from the moment I awakened on the floor to the moment I went to sleep where walls met, to search for myself without having to ask directions of another.

So there I was, walking aimlessly around the city with my portable tape player hooked into my belt, my cache of AA batteries in the pocket of my suit's trousers causing me to look as if I wore myself on the left instead of the right, and my fanny pack bulging with whatever tapes I had taken along that day for the eighteen to twenty hours I customarily filled my head with music to accompany or better yet obliterate my thoughts.

I don't remember what I was listening to when I found the notebook. I would remember had I known how significant a moment that was to be in my life. But I didn't know. And so the music that chaperoned the first touch of my flesh to something touched by Clara's flesh has escaped the catalogue of my existence. I have tried so incredibly hard to reconstruct that moment and hear what I had been hearing when I saw that little notebook hanging open over the curb, colorful binding up, the edge of the curbstone in the gutter of the book so that half of it faced the serenity of the sky and half the gurging traffic in the street. I wondered why I thought, "Look at that book asleep there," until I realized, as I stepped over to it and looked down upon it, that it was bent just like me when I lay asleep on the floor, split in half by the crack of the walls.

I leaned over and picked up the notebook. I could see and feel it was one of those common blank books sold in most bookstores and representing today's most popular and accessible literature. But its covers had been overlaid with a cloth material that was worn and faded and skinsoft like something that I recognized even then must be from an old quilt. It was glued or pasted, one piece on the front, one on the back, so the spine of the book was blank and black with its original imitation-cloth binding.

I stuck my thumb into the place where the book had fallen open over the curb. I was afraid that whatever might have been written there would have been erased by rain or the sodden slime that regularly accumulates along the edges of the city's streets.

But when I turned the book over to look, I found myself elated to see writing covering both pages that faced me.

I was shocked, however, first to see that the writing was in pencil, which to me was almost as evanescent as something written in chalk and that in fact had already begun to fade, though whether from its being in pencil lead or from its lying in the street I did not know.

And then I was shocked to see the writing itself.

I had never seen anything like it. It was chaotic and seemingly indecipherable. But I reminded myself that language was my game, had been my life, and that if this were a new language, I might as well be the first human being to learn it. So I thumbed off my music in what turned out to be a profoundly aposiopetic act—I broke into earsplitting silence, as it were—and began to read what was written there.

I don't know what stunned me more: to find that I was able to read it or to read what it said.

A man came into the shop and said he wanted to buy a quilt for his wife. "Do you want it for the bed or for hanging?" I asked. "For the bed," he replied. "Does the bed get much use?" I asked. "I don't see what business that is of yours," he replied. "I'm trying to determine fragility," I explained. "She is very fragile," he replied. "Of the quilt," I said and laughed. "We're not going to fuck on it if that's your concern," he said. "I'm sorry to hear that," I said. "My hanging quilts are for admiration. My crib quilts are for comfort. And my bed quilts are for fucking on." Now the man laughed. But nervously. "We've been married for 12 years," he said. "So." "It's dead," he said. "My quilts are alive," I said. "If you buy one you'll kill it." I wouldn't sell him a quilt. He left. I spent the rest of the day happy at the thought that I hadn't sacrificed one of my quilts to his unhappiness. I also imagined spreading out a Star of Bethlehem on the floor and having him fuck me while my hands held onto the points of the star and my heels rode his ass all the way to Jerusalem. When we were done, that's the quilt he bought. It saved his marriage. I watched him spread his wife out on it. They were beautiful together. I numb my fingers. Words fail me.

I stopped reading, not because of any effort it took to decipher such griffonage—I found it barely more difficult to read than something printed in the most relaxed Helvetica—but because my hands were shaking. I suppose my reaction was like that of someone to whom money is important and who finds some large sum of it lying on the sidewalk: he can't believe his good luck; he flushes; he trembles; he is afraid someone is watching him; he grasps his treasure to him; he is filled with an unfathomable desire for more.

One feeling he does not experience, however, is the wish to locate the true owner of what he has found. And of all the feelings I had with that notebook clutched to me, none was greater than my desire to return it to the woman who had written it. (I assumed it was a woman, though the handwriting was not particularly feminine, and there was nothing in what I had read that apodictically qualified its author as female.)

Who would write such a thing? I wondered. For whom? Was this Derrida's Mystic Pad, meant to isolate and consolidate the world? Who would run a business like that? Who would deal with inanimate objects as if they were alive and would be affected by where and with whom they lived? Who would laugh like that? I could hear her laughter in my head, where the music had been. Who would desire such a man given up as dead and record such a fantasy of sex and betrayal and forgiveness and reparation? Who would find the failure of words to come from the numbing of fingers on the pencil as mine had come from the numbing of my entire being?

How, I wondered, was I going to find her? I could go to every shop in the city that sold quilts, but even I knew how popular those vanishing old pieces of American history had become, so that would encompass almost every antique store, and they numbered in the hundreds, I was sure.

Then I opened the book again and looked at the first page. It was blank except for these words:

See. Be.
.Won Ton Disc

She might as well have written: If Found, Please Return To . . . I knew exactly where to find her. I nearly knew her name.

I remember laughing happily. The sound of it, even within the sounds of the horns in the street and the wheeze and plop of tires and the yapping of passing pedestrians, startled me. It had been so long since I'd heard from myself.

So I marched off to do my good deed. I listened to no music on the way. Instead, I rehearsed what I was going to say. I thought I'd better do that, since I was so out of practice.

Sure enough, right where I thought I'd find her, not at some Chinese restaurant (Won Ton) or a record store (Disc) but at 200 Columbus Avenue (i.e., one-tenth One Ton Discoverer of America), I came upon a small shop ingenuously named Call It Quilts, and after I had pressed the crime button and in my suit and tie was immediately buzzed in and walked up to the young woman who walked right up to me so that we met in the middle of the shop with quilts hanging all around us the way they do now here in this loft of ours, though it is too dark now to see them, I held the notebook behind my back, cleared my throat, and said, "Hello" (my final choice from the trinity completed by "How do you do?" and "Here").

It was the first word I'd spoken in over a year.

I do not know how to describe her. How I wish I could bring her forth the way Roger Fry does the adulterous Vanessa Bell in a letter I found in the Tate. "I can tell of your beauty," he informs her, and goes on with the most exquisite description of the queer silkiness of her palm and the waves of hair that ripple round her ears and the great planes of her torso and even the compelling shape of her armpits. I have never been able to see Clara in order to describe her, not to myself, and there is no one else to whom I would have had either the opportunity or inclination. When she is not before my eyes, and I try to see her, she explodes in my mind into a million pieces, and they do not coalesce until she walks through that door, as she will do soon enough though not too soon, I hope, for I am enjoying myself immensely alone here on the bed in the dark while the music from our wedding lustrates my being.

This indescribability of her, as if she were wholly ungraspable, has both perplexed and pleased me. I think, "She is your wife, you ought to be able to summon her image at will," and I think, "She is your wife, but she remains forever mysterious."

And so I live with her poised between guilt and beguilement and feel I may never actually see her until I see her in our children. But then, I wonder, will our children be like me and not want to see us in themselves or will they love us enough to be pleased that we inhabit them?

When I think of our daughter, who exists now only in the mirror of the future, then I believe I can begin to see Clara.

Sometimes I think she is not beautiful to anyone but me. I can hear my mother, who had died before I met Clara, saying, "She is an acquired taste, like licorice," which my mother pronounced like the alternate *ambergris*. Be that as it may, it was a taste that I, who admittedly had very little experience with women, acquired very quickly.

"May I help you?" she asked.

So unsure was I that I could render language concrete, as if sound itself might be considered lithoid and words little stones tumbling from the tongue, I cleared my throat again. I spoke. I recognized my voice and felt reunited with myself.

"I would like to buy a quilt for my wife," I said.

"Do you want it for the bed or for hanging?" Her voice was exactly as I'd heard it in the notebook, provocatively world-weary, ironic.

"For the bed."

"Does the bed get much use?"

"Oh, yes." I found myself excited to be departing from her script. "Why do you ask?"

"I'm trying to determine fragility."

"I'm very fragile," I whispered, a secret between us.

"I can tell," she said, surprising me completely.

I took a deep breath and, still keeping my hands behind me with the notebook in them, stood up straight and stiffened my body. "How can you tell?"

"I can tell," she said certainly.

"I'm very strong." I wanted to show her my hands.

"Fragile things aren't weak. They're delicate. The best old quilts are some of the strongest things ever made by hand. Their fabric is supple like skin. Their stitching holds forever. But over time they've become fragile. Their delicacy is their strength. It's

43

their beauty. They don't want to be lived on anymore. Or touched. Just admired."

"That sounds wonderful."

"How much do you want to spend?" she asked.

"It doesn't matter."

"Quilts have become very expensive. Especially in New York. People in New York know nothing. They'll pay anything for the right quilt."

"It doesn't matter," I said again.

"What do you suppose your wife would like?"

"A Star of Bethlehem."

She smiled for the first time. Her eyes were the color of the skin of a plum. I remember now how I noticed that then. It was not a color I had ever seen in anyone's face, not that I had really looked up all that often from my books or out from my mind into the faces of other people. But even I knew how unusual a color it was to find in the eyes of another. (I have since learned that it is a fairly common sort of dark purple used by the Amish in their quilts, combining blue and a kind of carmine red that plays off so subtly against their favored blacks, very much like the two cellos in the Schubert quintet, to which I will be listening soon if this blissful evening proceeds according to plan.)

"I don't have a Star of Bethlehem," she responded. "The only star quilt I have is a Broken Star. It's hanging over there." She pointed toward a quilt on the wall (a quilt she says remains there to this very moment, for she refuses to sell it in honor of our meeting that day). It looked like some sort of geometric optical illusion. Its pattern was shaped from diamonds, squares, and tri-angles with one red-and-black eight-pointed star in the middle surrounded by a wholly beige star, also with eight points, and that was encircled by wedges of red and black that resembled some vast circular star with an uncountable number of points.

"It's also known as a Carpenter's Wheel," she said.

"It's very beautiful."

"Do you think she'll like it?"

"Who?"

"Your wife."

"No."

Anger flashed in her eyes. They deepened almost to black. She looked ready to defend her quilt to the death.

"We just don't like the same things," I explained.

"How long have you been married?"

"Twelve years."

"You must have been married very young."

"Yes."

"Think of all you've missed."

I did. I stood there thinking of all I had missed, but I could think of nothing. To miss something implies a desire for it. I had never desired anything I didn't have or couldn't get, and I desired very little. My books. My CDs and tapes. I had never wanted a woman. Or a wife. Or a child. I was still an ascetic priest and before even having them had given up most things. Speech was the only thing I'd lost, along with my faith in language, and now I had speech back and was actually talking to someone and enjoying it immensely, though I seemed to be easing into the reality of conversation by carrying on a fiction.

"I haven't missed anything," I told her.

She shook her head. "Done it all?"

"To the contrary," I explained. "I haven't really done anything."

Her hand moved toward me. I thought she was going to touch me and prepared to swing one of my arms around in front of me when she held her own hand back. "You haven't done anything? Really? That's so refreshing. Everyone who comes in here does everything. Lawyers, doctors, brokers, architects, contractors, decorators, designers, writers, painters—they're always just back from skiing or South America or skiing *in* South America and they're getting divorced and married and they all have interviews and book contracts and their children are auditioning and they're using their cellular phones to call a Town Car and they think if they buy a quilt and put it on their bed or their wall that everything is going to slow down for them. Have you ever noticed how people drive themselves crazy to be sure that every minute of the day is filled and then want to spend their money on things they think are going to make them contemplative."

Her question had turned into a statement. Even the movement of her voice bespoke conviction. And she disdained her customers. What better formula for success in New York than that.

"People want to be at peace," I answered.

"People say they want to be at peace. So do countries."

"You're a cynic!" I blurted out before I realized I didn't have the least idea how to speak to a woman.

"I hope so," she said and laughed for the first time. It was the laugh I had heard when I read of it in her notebook, full of delight and utterly without weight. It was the ultimate cynic's laugh, for it displayed only joy at knowledge of the truth.

"I have a confession to make," I said. "I didn't come here to buy a quilt."

"I know that."

"You do?"

"You came here to bring me flowers."

"I did?"

"Why else would you be standing there looking ridiculous with your hands behind your back?"

I felt stricken. If I could have made flowers sprout out of that notebook, and that were to squander the one supernatural feat I had been granted in my life, I would have done it.

"I'm sorry. I don't have flowers for you."

"I'm relieved to hear that." Her hand moved toward me again as if to receive whatever it was I might be holding behind my back.

"I like more permanent things, like quilts and paintings. And if you did have flowers, I'd have to wonder just who you are and why you're bringing flowers to someone you've never met before." She signaled with her hand for me to show her what I was hiding.

I fought hard within myself to avoid informing her that permanence is absolute and brought the notebook out into the space between us. "I found this in the street. I believe it may belong to you."

She didn't seem surprised to see it. For a moment I thought it wasn't hers after all and was confused over my attraction to this woman to whom I would then have been led by the false trail of someone else's confession and fantasy. But if it weren't hers, how could she have followed the script? Why would she have said, "I am trying to determine fragility"?

"Let me see it." She didn't grab for it. She made me put it into her hand. It was our first touch, shared through the binding and pages of that blank book.

She opened it up and read something to herself. I watched her eyes move back and forth over the page. Her distraction offered me my first opportunity to stare at her. I could not take my eyes from her eyes. I longed to know what part of herself she was encountering on that page. I tried to read those mangled words as they were reflected in her irises, in vain.

When she came to the bottom of the right-hand page, she was tempted to turn over the leaf and read on, but then she seemed to remember I was there and looked up. She had on her lips the half-smile of someone who is being entertained by images passing through her own mind. "Is it yours?" I asked.

"It's my diary," she said matter-of-factly. "Did you read it?"

"No."

"Did you try to read it?"

"No."

"Did you look at it?"

"Only to try to find out whose it might be."

"And?" She raised her face to mine. I loved where her head sat in relation to my own. As I have said, we are the perfect height for one another. Even then, I could feel what it would feel like to have her head on my chest and the claret highlights of her hair sanguinating my face and the smell of her hair, which I inhaled then for the first time, purifying me.

"I couldn't read a word of it."

She smiled like a lawyer. "See, you did try to read it. You're not as innocent as you look. What kind of person could pick up something like this off the street and not try to read it? You did try to read it. But you couldn't, could you? Or could you?" She seemed disappointed, and this confused me, but I remained afraid to tell her I could read it.

"It's my handwriting," she went on. "Nobody can read my handwriting. Nobody. I kept failing in school because of my handwriting. They said I was dysgraphic. It freaked my parents. They thought I was brain damaged. They talked about having me institutionalized. I used that as an opportunity to leave home at a very early age. I'd always wanted to leave home. It was the best decision I ever made. I never went back to school again either." She gazed into my face as if to see whether I understood the implication of what she was saying—that she had been a free person for a long time and had experienced life in a way that she could not have done had she lived at home and gone to school—and shrugged her shoulders in a worldly way. "But why am I telling you all this?"

I didn't want her to question why she was talking to me. I wanted her to tell me everything about herself as if I had become that diary she was holding open in her hands. So I ignored her question and asked, "Did you always write like that?"

"Always."

"Then you aren't brain damaged. Dysgraphia is evidence of brain damage only when it appears in someone whose writing has theretofore been normal."

Her laughter mocked me. "'Theretofore'! You sound like an old fart. You even dress like an old fart." Her eyes roamed over my body. "But you don't exactly look like an old fart. What are you, anyway? What brings you out walking the streets and finding women's diaries in the late afternoon?"

"I'm a young fart." What a stupid thing to say. But I had no idea how to talk to someone like her.

"But how do you know about dysgraphia? Are you a speech therapist?"

"I used to be a rhetorician."

"Oh, there's a practical occupation!" There was glee in her sarcasm. "I've been waiting all my life to meet a rhetorician. And just what do you do as a rhetorician—or what did you do before you quit?"

"A rhetorician is someone who studies the power of language."

"To do what?"

"To do whatever language does. Explain the world. Display the truth. Define beauty. Influence others. Teach and persuade them."

"Seduce?"

"Oh, most definitely."

"Somehow I don't see you as much of a seducer."

"I'm not."

"I am. So does that make me a rhetorician too?"

I didn't know how to respond to her claim or boast or confession that she was a seducer, which itself was seductive, so I said, "Yes, that does make you a rhetorician. And that really is a coincidence, because it's not a very crowded field."

"I'll bet it isn't. 'What do you want to be when you grow up,

Johnny?'" she said in the gruff voice of a demanding father. "'Oh, a rhetorician, Dad,'" she replied in the puling voice of a lad who'd wear his trousers suspendered just under his nipples.

"Another coincidence," I remarked.

"What?" she said, as if it were nothing. "Your father didn't approve?"

"Actually, he did approve. He said what he always said: that I don't belong here. He told me he thought I'd found the perfect profession for myself."

"As a rhetorician?" she said disbelievingly. "You have a father who wanted you to be a rhetorician? How refreshing."

"I didn't say he wanted me to be a rhetorician. I said he thought it was the perfect thing for me to be. He used to tell people that his son was a born diaskeuast. Can you imagine the effect that had on me?"

"Frankly, no." Her eyes registered . . . what? Contempt? Admiration? How to tell the difference when you have so rarely looked into a woman's face?

"It was devastating," I confessed.

"I'll bet." She was smiling. But was it with me or against me? "It's a wonder he didn't have you put in a zoo."

"I beg your pardon."

"With all the other diaskeuasts," she explained.

"A zoo?"

"Exactly."

I didn't know what she was talking about. "Are you sure you understand?"

"May I be honest?"

"Oh, please."

"I don't have a goddamn clue."

"Do you know what a diaskeuast is?"

"Oh, sure." She opened her arms to encompass the entire shop. I wanted to run into them. "I get them in here all the time. Some of my best customers. I call them diascuties."

"Diascuties?" It was either a brilliant agnominative response or a defensive logodaedaly of the first order.

"That's right. And if they're cute enough, I have sex with them."

"Holy Christ!" I didn't know what else to say. "Holy Christ almighty!"

"So tell me," she said.

"Yes?" What was she going to ask me? Would I be able to confess to her that I wasn't a diaskeuast after all? And if I did, would I, then, never possess her?

"What's a diaskeuast?"

"You really don't know?"

"I really don't know," she said with disarming frankness.

I was surprised, as I always am, when a word, any word, is not known to someone else. I have assumed that those of us who are meant to communicate therefore share the same body of sound and meaning. But, then, I had also believed that words were the most benevolent of man's gifts to himself and had come to learn that they were also the most discrepant (a word whose ugly sound and even look are mirrored in its meaning when it's used to signify, as I do here, discordance). It was I, after all, who had stopped speaking altogether. It was fortunate she could understand anything I was saying. And she had, in *diascutie*, concocted a lovely logodaedaly after all. Imagine my delight, meeting a woman who creates her own whimsical neologism.

"The literal meaning of *diaskeuast*," I explained, feeling very much as I had when I was a graduate student trying to inspire freshmen to abandon their Frisbees for forensics (at which I lasted only a week when my own frustration caused me to decline swiftly into gibbering glossolalia), "is someone who interprets things. Which in a way is true of me. But it's come to mean something else. An editor, specifically. Someone who revises things, repairs them. But I don't do that. That's not what I do. I don't touch anything. I leave everything just as I found it. That, to me, is the least destructive way to live. I like to let everything wash over me, and as it does, I absorb whatever I may come to love. And then it's mine forever."

She tilted back her head and looked at me over the bottom rims of her purple irises. It was a most unsettling and welcome scrutiny. "That sounds like the most wonderful life."

If she believed that, perhaps she could make it that. Perhaps she could transform not my life (for one's life is one's inner life, and that is immutable) but my belief in its value and thereby in myself.

"My father described my life as utterly worthless and me as abjectly murcid—his word, not mine. I would have preferred he call me merely languid, such an expressive word, so utterly stretchable into its own very meaning. He said that when I die, I should have a headstone that will be completely blank, not even my name, to signify that I've done absolutely nothing with my life. My father believes that the world is divided into active people and passive people, and passive people are without meaning. He was fond of quoting Wittgenstein quoting Goethe: 'In the beginning was the *deed*.' But for me, in the beginning, as I am sure will be the case in the end, is the word. I turned out to be a passive person. I ceased to have any meaning to him."

"What does *he* do?" The disdain in her voice was endearing.

"He's a lawyer. A judge. Criminal court. He's not unknown. You may have read about him. His nickname is Too Good. That's not a reference to his virtue, though he is a virtuous man. He received it when he was a young judge on his first murder case and the killer came before him for sentencing, and he said, 'Execution's too good for this miscreant.' Then he pronounced his sentence: 'Make him invisible.' That's all he said. He got up and left the bench. Nobody knew what he meant until they got a written copy of the sentence. 'Make him invisible' meant he was giving him life without parole. That's what he's given every convicted murderer if they haven't worked out a plea bargain with the prosecutor. My father doesn't believe in plea bargaining. And he doesn't believe in parole. He was always quoting Judge Torres: 'Your parole officer ain't been born yet.' He believes in evil. He believes in putting evil people away forever. That's what he means by making them invisible. He just erases them. He's an outspoken conservative, but he confuses people because of his adamant opposition to the death penalty. He thinks the death penalty is lenient. He believes there is no worse punishment in creation than to be locked up in a room with nothing but your thoughts. I don't agree with him. Sometimes I dream of being locked up forever in a room."

I can remember going walking with my father, before he'd given up on me. There was no part of the city we didn't visit together. He'd make me look at bums and prostitutes and drug addicts and what he called sharpies in their big cars and parents who were slapping their offspring and raging black people and jaundiced gamblers in Chinatown and strutting rodomantades on Wall Street. "Epictetus is wrong," he would say to me. "People are evil. They are vulgar and hideous. And they breed. So generation follows generation poisoned with hatred and self-interest. No one is not guilty. If it were up to me, I'd wipe them all out and start again. Paradise would be an empty world except for you and me." Then he would buy me a hot dog from a vendor who would inevitably wither under my father's scrupulous gaze.

She stepped closer to me. I thought it was because she was feeling sorry for me. I told her I was sorry.

"No." She moved her hand toward me but did not touch me. "I like it. I told you: I'm sick of people who are always moving around and think they want to find a place to rest but don't really because they can't bear to stop and look at what they really are. They look at the back of a quilt and admire the intricate stitching because they can't imagine anyone could sit so long to do that. They buy a quilt and ruin it by looking at it with their restless eyes. I detest them." She stepped back from me, still without touching me. "So what would you do in that room of yours?"

"Listen to music."

"Is that why you're wearing those headphones around your neck?"

"Yes."

"What about your career as a rhetorician? Did you work for one of the top firms?"

Her little joke was really quite witty, the idea of firms of rhetoricians competing with one another for business throughout a city where the formal beauty of language has been sacrificed to the polyglot elisions of the hearing deaf.

"Language failed me," I explained and wondered if she would recognize the echo from her own notebook.

"Sometimes words fail me," she said, absolutely echoing herself and watching me intently as if to see if I had heard the echo and thus could read her writing. She was devious and direct at the same time, which I found enticingly confusing. "Words fail me," she added, "after I've had sex."

"Words fail me before I've had sex," I responded and knew even before she'd burst out laughing that I'd made perhaps the first spontaneous joke in my life and not at all the sort that I and my fellow students of language, all of us having had to be dragged kicking and screaming into the eighteenth century, used to make in college and that generally involved intentional catachresis, which is of course the misuse of words themselves.

"You're a funny man. You talk funny. You think funny. You dress funny. You have a funny haircut and funny glasses and funny shoes. But you do have a beautiful face. Do you know that? You have the most beautiful face I've ever seen."

"My mother used to tell me that."

She put her hand to her mouth and turned around and walked away from me. I had not seen her from behind or noticed what she was wearing. She was dressed in many overlapping layers of colorful clothes: perhaps three shirts whose sleeves were of different lengths, a tiny purple skirt, green tights, droopy gold socks over the bottom of the tights, and short, black boots. She was like a quilt herself, harmonious, inviting, distinct.

I had never understood the importance of the rear view. In my wandering through the streets I had turned not to watch women but to watch other men turn to watch women and had wondered why they'd turned and if there was any bond between us or was I not, with my peculiarities, a man like other men?

The significant things were in the front, after all—the voice, the eyes, the sex. But as this woman stood now with her back to me, I realized that validation was somehow effectuated in the backside. It was the final place for desire to stamp its approval.

Hers was held within that tiny skirt a round and perfect planet. I could only imagine it halved, atop those thin, green limbs.

Under her influence, like some new emotion to which I had been dead all my life, fantasy was feeding my blood.

She turned around. Her hand was still at her mouth as if to hold in her words. "So are you gay?"

No one had ever asked me that before. I was surprised no one had ever asked me that before. I was highly educated. I was something of an aesthete, within the confines of my continued asceticism. And, yes, I was fair of face and hard of build. Perhaps, they would say, he's not a heterosexual, but he's certainly a heteroclite. I would have assumed that I would be assumed by some to be a homosexual, so superficially is judgment rendered in this sophistical culture of ours. But as was said by the sign my father kept at the very edge of the desk in his chambers, right in the nose of those who sat facing him across that huge span, ASSUME NOTHING.

I had sometimes thought I would have liked to be gay. At least it would have been to have been something. But I could not do it. I could not even imagine it. It seems no easier to become homosexual if you are not than it must be to become heterosexual if you are not.

In answer to her question I scoffed and pretended to be offended. "Just because you like my looks you think—"

"Looks have nothing to do with it. The world is full of ugly gay men and straight men so pretty you want to ask them who does their lashes. What I want to know is do you fuck women?"

The bluntness and vulgarity of her question confounded me enough to make my answer stupidly equivocal: "In a manner of speaking."

" 'In a manner of speaking'!" she mocked. "Give me a break."

"I told you. I'm married. I—"

She looked toward the ceiling as if she expected to see hovering there the spaceship that had brought me here from my planet, Naïveté. "Almost all my male customers are gay, and half of them are married. So tell me: do you or don't you—"

"Women," I said. "Only women. Yes. But it's been awhile."

She finally walked back to me. "How long?"

I had no idea how long. I had, at that time, no memory of sex whatsoever. I might have been a virgin, for all I knew.

So I didn't know what to answer. But I sensed from the way she was looking at me, hungry for my innocence despite the bravado of her own talk, that I would not embarrass myself by claiming the truth. "I can't remember."

"Maybe you really are married." A wicked glee danced in her eyes.

"Maybe you really are a cynic," I responded. "It's nothing to be ashamed of. Camus said that cynicism is the temptation shared by all forms of intelligence."

"But you aren't."

"Intelligent?"

"Married," she said impatiently. "You're not married."

I didn't know how she knew, but I confessed quite happily, "No, I'm not married," for I had been worried about how I would tell her that in fact I had no wife.

"I'm glad . . ."

What relief her words brought to me, what hope.

". . . because now I won't have to sell you my Broken Star."

If she was going to play with me, I was going to play with her. "Are you afraid that if I buy it I'll kill it?" I quoted her notebook.

I couldn't catch her. Did she know? Did she know I could read it, or did she think it was just another coincidence that my words came close to her words?

"You lied to me," she said. "You don't have to tell me the truth. But don't lie to me. Understand?"

The truth. What did she know of the truth? I had spent my whole conscious life trying to understand the truth. There was so much I could tell her. "Nietzsche said that the truth—"

"Do you lie in bed too?"

I knew what that meant. I knew what she was seeing: the two of us in bed and her heels riding my ass all the way to Jerusalem. How could I lie to her? How could I find her not beautiful or desirable?

"The only thing I do in bed is listen to music." That was certainly the truth. I slept against a crack between walls.

"Did you ever play it?" she asked.

I knew what she meant, but to see how she would respond I said, "I play my tapes every hour I'm awake."

"Did you ever play it *actively*?" she said pointedly, and I was glad she seemed to know me well enough already to know just what to ask.

What harm in telling her? I had no idea whether I would ever see her again. I was waiting for a customer to walk in and render my companionship redundant or for her to decide even while we were by ourselves that I was too strange or weak or inexperienced. She might as well understand that from my point of view I had become, in my search for the truth and through considerable pain and confusion, one of Nietzsche's free spirits, one of his new philosophers, an investigator of myself "to the point of cruelty," as he said, a night owl in broad daylight, pedantic, incapable of being born into either the incomprehensible or the irrational. And what I called the world would be, Husserlianly, created only by me—my image, my reason, my will, my love would thus be realized.

"When I was a little boy, my father bought me a violin. It was a great extravagance, like most of what he did. He was a very generous man. He believed that a person could be overwhelmed into performance. So he bought me a violin made by Carlo Bergonzi toward the end of the eighteenth century, though its fittings were modern. And a bow that was even older. He then hired me a very fine teacher, from Juilliard. I studied the violin for seven years. That's a short time in the life of a violinist but a long time in the life of a boy. Sometimes I loved that instrument and hated to play it, and sometimes I hated that instrument and loved to play it. During that whole time, I was waiting for when I would be ready to play Bach's sonatas and partitas for solo violin. There was no music I loved more. I would listen to them for hours on LPs. The more I listened, the more I came to love them. Even when my teacher said I was ready for them, I refused to study them. But then one day I gave in, or gave up, and bought the score. I wasn't so foolish as to think I might be able to play the chaconne, at least without embarrassing myself and my teacher and my father and the already long-suffering ghost of Carlo Bergonzi. But what I wanted from that same suite was the sarabande. That was my dance. That was my favorite. But I could not play it. Its great ornamentation and its high polyphony eluded me. I had never loved a piece of music more or come to hate a piece of music more. One day as I sat before it I became para-lyzed, or at least my arms and hands did. I screamed for my mother, but it was my father who came into my room and took my violin and bow from me. I've not played since."

She reached across to me and put her hand on my wrist and moved her fingers up beneath the sleeves of my suit jacket and shirt, where they rubbed the sensitive skin on the underside of my arm. "Where are they now?"

"In a closet. At home. In my apartment."

"I'd like to see it."

"The violin?"

"Your apartment."

I looked down at her hand on my arm.

"Say something," she said.

I was so overwhelmed by her directness in saying she wanted to come to my home and by her touching me that I could think of nothing to say that was my own. I watched the back of her hand move further up my sleeve and said, "You have uninhibited fingers."

Her breathing quickened at my words. One of her fingers pressed into my skin as if I were a violin myself. "You have no idea."

"I was quoting Nietzsche," I confessed. "One of the attributes of free spirits is what he called uninhibited fingers for the unfathomable."

"I'm a free spirit," she said.

I could imagine she was. "He was talking about people who sacrifice everything in their search for the truth. He called them the new philosophers."

"I didn't think he was referring to girls who went around swinging their underpants over their heads."

She was the first person I had ever wanted to hold in my arms. I wished I knew how. It is such a long and dangerous journey out of emptiness.

"Stop laughing," she said, "and take me home."

10 P.M.

I press the pillow once more to my face, smelling her though being careful not to speak to her, before I throw it back against the headboard and reach in the darkness for the console on Clara's side of the bed. There I find the rheostats that control the entire rectangular track of lighting along all four walls of the loft.

I push one slowly up. The far wall emerges in the light breathing with color.

I am enveloped by quilts. Clara has hung them all with great care, stretching each one over a wooden frame so its weight will be distributed evenly. The quilts in her shop, on the other hand, are hung by Velcro or are folded in piles, though once a month, wearing latex gloves, Clara refolds each one.

She has taught me to love quilts and their creation as I have taught her to love music and its creation, beyond her own fancying of Led Zeppelin and Steppenwolf and Madonna. And as I feel my human connection most to those who have died and left their music behind, so Clara feels joined to those women who pieced or appliquéd scraps of fabric into entire designs of great beauty and durable life. She has read to me of, and imagined aloud for me, the great quilting bees of the two centuries before ours, and we have imagined together the life of a young woman beginning the traditional thirteen quilts in the days of her maidenhood—twelve for quotidian use and the thirteenth her bridal quilt—and then the bee itself, which could not be held until she had betrothed herself to her beloved, when she would be joined by her friends and they would back and interline and finish her bridal quilt, and through their very gathering announce to the world that she is to be married.

I have joined the life of my country through these quilts around me and ended what I realized was a lifelong exile in the culture of Europe. As I lie here on the Double Wedding Ring that covers our bed and was Clara's wedding gift to me, I am the true, evolved American man, beyond action, beyond provincialism, beyond greed, ambition, destructiveness, and the illusion of omnipotence.

Surrounding me are a Stair-Steps Illusion quilt from Kentucky, a Friendship quilt from Ohio, a Mennonite Light and Dark from Pennsylvania, a Sunshine and Shadow also from Pennsylvania, a Beloved Flag from Hawaii, over near the kitchen a Broken Dishes quilt from Indiana (which Clara gave to me on our first wedding anniversary and to honor the fact that we had broken no dishes, had no fights, as if it were conceivable to me even to raise my voice at her), a Stairway to Heaven (one of Clara's favorite songs) quilt from Ohio, and next to that Jacob's Ladder, also from Ohio, a Maze or Labyrinth from Kentucky that puts me in mind of Pope's "Love in these labyrinths his slaves detains" (far better a line than those he wrote so poor Pergolesi's *Stabat Mater* could be sung in English), and above, toward our immensely high ceiling, Birds in the Sky from Massachusetts, a Log Cabin Streak of Lightning from New York, and another anniversary present, a Star of Bethlehem from Maine on whose points I sometimes picture Clara's hands as I lie on my back on this bed with my penis in her mouth and the straight furrow of her ass at the tips of my fingers.

Clara has always placed her quilts strategically (and separate from the Madonnas I have given her as gifts) and with the sense of humor that I had never imagined could accompany sexual mystery. She keeps threatening to find a quilt called Trip Around the World to hang like a flag from the ceiling above our bed, and already, on the wall behind the bed, there is an Amish Puss in the Corner, and there, directly across from our bed, is a Swastika from Missouri, perfect evidence of the corruption of beauty in the *mêlée* of history.

She has also joked to me that someday she is going to buy me a Contained Crazy if I don't get out more.

But I don't want to get out more. I prefer my life here in the loft, which has become my version of Wittgenstein's eternal hut, though he, lover of men, chose always to live in the utter solitude I had believed to be my own destiny B.C., as I might denote my life Before Clara. I remain, however, some kind of underground man, even if in my case I am buried in the sky. (Though I must confess that when I still dared read fiction I was infinitely more impressed with that other madman's voice that could say, "It was I killed the old pawnbroker woman and her sister Lizaveta with an axe and robbed them.") And with these quilts all around me, and the little antique rugs and samplers Clara has put here and there, I feel I am in the very midst of America, right in its fist, as it were, as I so often find myself in Clara's fist and I see myself as she sees me and learn to love myself as she loves me in that great generous blessing of self-acceptance that marriage, finally, sweetly, kindly brings.

As I have said, this loft is one great room. We designed it ourselves and deliberately created no place for either of us to hide. The only private spaces are the two bathrooms, hers of Italian tile and with a bidet, mine of stone and with a sauna, and the two giant closets.

Those closets are nearly as large as other people's studio apartments, and while neither of us has had occasion to hide in our closet, we do keep all our things in them, for when you live in one big room and are as menseful as we two and want that room to be as orderly as we want ours, you must have a place to put all the incredible number of things one accumulates on this earth, from clothes and papers to weapons and toys.

I have never been in Clara's closet, and she has never been in mine. (Only Elspeth, our maid, who comes but once a week, like all good maids on Thursday, 10:00 A.M., has been in both.) We agreed, when we created this large public space of ours, that each of our closets would be off limits to the other. In the beginning of our marriage, we locked our closets. But I have not locked mine in months (years, now that I think of it), and to judge from the way she will open her closet door after a long day at work and throw in her clothes before coming to me with a smile and a greeting to get her hug and glass of wine, I don't believe she locks hers either.

My clothes are in my closet. (I haven't many, and they are as conservative as I, Clara's attempt to Armani-ize and brief me notwithstanding; I have always been the first to admit that it is my mind that is dandified, not my corporeality.)

So are my books.

And whatever we have in the way of security for life in a city as renowned for its violence as its vertu. This is the place, after all—this pinnacle of civilization, this hub of finance and the arts, this seat of learning and lotophagy—where women are thrown off roofs in some sort of post–forced-coital *tristesse*, where tourists invite the knife by their very blondness, where the automobile siren is the Queen of the Night's nightly aria, where beggars are our village idiots, and where democracy will, probably in the nick of time, yield to what Arnold called "the refinement of an aristocracy, precious and educative to a raw nation," or else to the "thou shalt" of the herd. In the meantime, and for all the good they may do us should the hordes of victims of the failure of family planning reach our loft, I have a sword Clara bought me at a flea market, a bayonet from an army-surplus store, a baseball bat my father once gave me in the mistaken belief that the wand makes the magician, and something called a 2-Pound Camp Wonder that combines a hatchet blade, hammer, nail-puller, and pry bar, which Clara and I ordered from *The Sportsman's Guide* early in our marriage when, like many couples, bestirred by a bucolic urge and goaded by the apparently inescapable urban image of making love in a sleeping bag, we said we should try camping, though we came to our senses before we'd bought a tent, a tarpaulin, or even the sleeping bag itself. All this is laughable, of course, both in its fire power and its necessity. Or thus I feel it, so ubietously content am I, contained securely in my marriage and my home, which I leave so rarely, my little piece of safe and colorfully quilted (I am tempted to say, as I lie in bed, buntinged) America. We are immune here to the ravages of the dissolution of law in this city, this country, and to the violence of domestic breakdown when love has died and in its place comes, like some aberrant antonym, rage.

Because I have accumulated fewer things than has Clara, I have volunteered my closet for our financial records, including canceled checks and tax returns. It also holds: a copy of my thesis (I never was able to confront the oral part of the exam); my bust of Nietzsche, which I thought rather audacious, even modish, for my undergraduate lodgings first in Vanderbilt and then in Jonathan Edwards, though now I realize that it probably would have kept the girls away if I hadn't succeeded in doing that without its help; "The Final Resource of French Atheists" as well as the other erotica with which Clara has tried to enlighten me;

and my old violin, which I have kept despite its painful associations and the large sum of money for which I could undoubtedly sell it because it reminds me of that first day in Clara's shop when she said, "I'd like to see it," and I said, "The violin?" and she responded, "Your apartment," and that is what led me to have the courage to invite her home with me that evening and to be with her every evening, every night, since then, which is why it is so comforting to have this night to myself, as I listen to the music that played at our wedding and find myself beginning to grow hungry and wondering if Clara is growing hungry or whether she has eaten by now and where she might be eating and with whom.

I was very careful not to ask her anything about her evening when she told me this morning she had a dinner date for tonight. I simply said, "That's nice," and told her I would miss her.

In anticipation of her absence, I found as the day went on that I desired her less, as if my body had been in preparation for this evening and my mind had known enough to start early on its journey toward the kind of self-discovery that can be made only in separation from thoughts of, and desire for, the beloved. I am willing myself to learn the truth about myself. I want to make "all being thinkable," as Nietzsche said. He called that the will to truth and said it fills one with lust.

I am still waiting for the lust. But I'm in no hurry.

So that when Clara came home from work, I found I could not wait until she'd leave again for dinner, so interested had I become in what I would discover in her absence tonight.

Without emotion, I watched her dress. She replaced one set of layers with another. I have never met anyone who dresses like Clara, with such cepaceous perfection. It is as if she is making a quilt of herself, fabrics and colors overlapping one another, textures and revelations. She usually wears tights, whether with or without a skirt, and I find her shapely legs, with their thin ankles, muscular calves, and girlish thighs, even more sensual wrapped in bright, opaque colors than naked. If the tights are worn simply as leggings, she will often offset the startling sight of her high, arcuated behind with a clashing pair of drooping socks, though sometimes she'll also wear socks over the bottom of her tights when she wears a long shirt atop them, sometimes one of my shirts, which I gather has always been a woman's stratagem to make a man desire her (though I can't imagine that its opposite— a man wearing a piece of his woman's clothing—would have the same effect on her).

Tonight, just those few hours ago, she put on no tights what-soever, which surprised me, and a dress, black, a color she rarely wears. It didn't occur to me then that she might be dressing this way to try to assure me that wherever she was going and what-ever she would be doing, she was invading her evening in her most demure apparel. And it probably didn't occur to her that she was all the more desirable for the somberness of her outfit, like a beautiful woman at a funeral.

"You look beautiful."

"Thank you," she said distractedly, for she was bent over her handbag and pawing through it.

"You're not planning to take that out, I hope."

"Of course not."

She emerged from her handbag with what looked like house keys, some cash, a blank check, and a credit card, which she put into the pockets of her dress. Clara seems to be the rare woman who can be separated from her make-up and comb for long periods of time and not feel as if calamity might strike. She does little enough to her face to change it: some eyeliner to amplify the warmth of her gaze and occasionally a dusting of some sort of fleshly powder when the effects of our lovemaking are still visible on her artless skin. Her hair scarcely needs its comb. She keeps it short (I doubt very much she is out getting a haircut tonight), it always seems to fall with its own perfect taste over enough of her ears to allow her earrings their mysterious dangle, and I never love it more than when we sit at an outdoor cafe for dinner early on a summer evening and I watch as her hair takes more light from the carmine spill of the sun than does the glass of chilly Chénas in her hand, unless it's when I see it swept between my fingers when her head is in my hands and her eyes are in my eyes.

"Are you going to cook?" she asked.

"You know I can't eat my own cooking when you're not here to tell me that Jacques Pépin won't be sending out a death squad."

"Order in?"

"Yes."

"What? Burmese? Rwandan? Yemeni?"

"Chinese."

She seemed surprised. "Slumming?"

I'd given her her exit line.

She walked toward me for what I knew was a goodbye kiss. "I was going to tell you not to wait up," she said. "But if you're going to be slumming . . ."

As she reached for me I reached for the remote control of the CD changer and punched up the Celtic guitar pieces. The exquisite opening harmonics of "L'Hertiere De Keroulaz" shivered through the loft.

She stopped to listen. I knew she would. As she had enveloped me within her quilts, I had done the same to her within my music. We have both learned to acknowledge and appreciate a beauty we had not known before. These intangible new passions are perhaps the greatest gifts we have given one another. Marriage, despite the promulgations of the diamond, gold, and automobile industries, can be measured by no better bestowal. When you close the world around you, you open up the world to one another.

"Dance with me."

"I can't. I'll be late. But I will when I get home."

She put herself into my arms. I held her lightly, formally, as if we were dancing. Then she was gone.

As you can feel a hat on your head after you've removed it, I could feel her in my arms. I held her until even this discarnate memory of her body had floated away into the air around me. Then I changed the music and, good housecock that I am, lay down on the bed, waiting for Clara.

We dance often, Clara and I, always at home, alone, slowly, close, to the dances I so love in Bach—for example, the cello suites' allemandes and bourrées and gigues and the sarabande from the fourth that we played at our wedding—and to slow jazz tunes by Miles Davis and John Coltrane and even the normally screaky Ornette Coleman and sometimes to Clara's music, "Stairway to Heaven," perhaps, before the allégro di bravúra, music with words, and she will hold me with both arms locked around my waist and turn up her head so her lips are at my throat and sing to me in a whisper as we dance here alone in our life, "There's a sign on the wall, but she wants to make sure, because sometimes words have two meanings . . ."

We dance because we love the touch of hand on hand, hand on back, cheek on cheek, the whispering, the innocence of it as prelude to the deeper innocence of the jabber and scream and penetration of unembellished sex.

We dance to tease ourselves into a desire even greater than that we experienced from looking at one another, particularly as the weeks and months and years went by and the surprise of finding someone else at home, even someone ripe and naked, faded, and with it faded also that lust for her or him who was before you, new and unknown.

Nietzsche wrote about becoming who you are and knowing who you are through an abandonment of "all faith and every wish for certainty," so that you would walk forever on what he called insubstantial ropes and dance near the abyss, and only then would you be free.

We dance because what is marriage if not a dance on the abyss?

I AM GETTING hungrier. It is a good feeling, a kind of emptiness to match the emptiness of my home and arms. I am slowly becoming one piece. I am slowly becoming longingness.

But I am not so desperately hungry as to want to order my Chinese food. I am not yet on that edge.

So I activate the remote control and match my own welcome melancholy, which is an emotion I had sought out and loved all my life and have found virtually impossible to locate within the happiness and present-tenseness of my marriage, with Schubert's Quintet in C.

This was one of Schubert's last pieces. As was the case with each of his symphonies, he never got to hear this quintet played, at least not in the corporeal world. But he must have heard it inside his head, just as I would hear language inside my head in the midst of my long period of silence. Schubert would simply lie down in bed, where, like me, he would do most of his work, and write out whole pieces of music in his virtually illegible hand, the way Clara can sit down and bend over her notebook and write out whatever it is she writes out, for the music already existed within him, like an actual event rather than a fantasy spun out of nothing.

Even as Schubert lay dying in bed, the music kept pouring forth if not out; he shrieked right until his final moments that he had new melodies in his head. What an enviable annihilation. I can remember visiting his grave in the Währingerstrasse Cemetery in Vienna and putting my head to the ground in case those tunes might be heard still floating around in his skull. Needless to say, I heard nothing but the sounds of the grass growing richly on the fertilization provided by the rifacimento of the flesh beneath it.

The epitaph on his tomb speaks of "yet far fairer hopes," for he was only thirty-one when he died.

I am hardly older than that now. And I know that if I were to die tonight, I, like Schubert, would have left behind my greatest work, for I have achieved inner peace in an existence that sets each man to war with himself.

As for Schubert, no matter what melodies he may have been hearing in his head on his deathbed, this piece to which I am now listening is his greatest and would not likely have been surpassed by him. He knew that, no matter what he shrieked. He is speaking a new language here. He tells us he is going to write in sunny C major and then sets out moving from one key to another nearly from one bar to the next through shifting harmonies and a perplexing tonality that probably would have gotten him shot, or at least ostracized, if the manuscript of this work hadn't sat around unnoticed, undiscovered, unknown for twenty-five years after Schubert's syphilis carried him off. And even then it bothered people. (The music, not the venereal disease.)

As Nietzsche said, all true music is a swan song, though he himself in his misguided desire to be an artist fell into the trap of writing romance (he called his compositions names like "Sweet Mystery" and "A Brook Flows By," and a piece he composed for Cosima Wagner's thirty-third birthday he entitled "Echoes of New Year's Eve, with Processional Song, Peasant Dance, and the Pealing of Bells"), and romance is what appeals to those human beings born without a mind and therefore condemned forever not to know they have no mind. Hans von Bülow, the canonical Cosima's first husband, whose name is synonymous with sexual humiliation, proved himself a more astute judge of music than of women. It was not out of jealousy but mere good taste that he told Nietzsche, in perhaps the greatest critical one-liner ever uttered, "Your composition is more terrible than you think."

Schubert's quintet was indeed the death knell of the Classical era, even as it adhered to the classical form. But its confessions of feeling, its language, is Romantic, in its ambivalence, its suffering and joy, and its constant speculation on both.

Is it any wonder that I so love this piece and that it so disturbs me? I know who I am. I know what I was. The same thing has happened to me—not that happened to Schubert, for I am alive, but that happens in this music.

I have found myself, my voice, and my life in my love for my wife. And I am able to talk about it now, naked, openly, truthfully, when before I met her I could talk of nothing but of what I knew. Never of what I felt.

I am the new man.

I am the very hungry new man.

As PART OF my Classical self, I very rarely miss a meal, particularly dinner when Clara and I are together and, whether home or out, we let the meal go on endlessly as we talk and then, after she has written in her diary and I have lain on this bed watching her write in her diary, we come to bed together, always together, never one and then the other. And if bed is, as Huxley says, the poor man's opera, though we are scarcely poor, we have not wanted for fioritura in the rendering of our love.

But on our first night together, the night of the day we met, as I stepped into my Romantic era, I ate no dinner, I kept to no pattern, I perished. I gave up my life for a new one.

PROBABLY THE ONLY person more astonished than I that I should be walking into my apartment building on Park Avenue with a woman was the evening doorman. He had never seen me with a woman. The apartment had been in my mother's family, and when she left it to me in her will, I told the people renting it that their lease would not be renewed and moved in when they vacated. That had been some five years before. No woman

71

had visited me, aside from Elspeth, who cleaned for me then as now.

But what astonished the doorman even more than the presence of a woman at my side was my speaking to him. For reasons that I could hardly have explained, unless I'd written him a letter, I had stopped speaking to him about a year before. He must have been perplexed, for I had always been friendly in my greetings, and I wouldn't be surprised if he didn't at first feel I had singled him out in my silence, until he must inevitably have discussed with the other doormen and with the superintendent as well what he took to be my rudeness, at which point all of them would have realized from their common experience with me that I had simply stopped speaking. I am sure there was such a meeting, for I noticed, much to my relief, so uncivil had I come to think they must find me, that they all stopped greeting me at precisely the same time. From then on, they might open the door for me as I left on and returned from my daily walk into the city or hand me a package they had signed for and kept secure in the parcels closet, but they never said a word, not even when I tipped them. These doormen were, after all, with Elspeth, my only consistent human contact during that period of my silence, and I found it comforting that we be equal in the exchange of language and therefore that the burden of speech be lifted from us all. (Elspeth, for her part, went right on talking to me as she dusted and polished, with her usual lack of concern that I even be in the same room, to say nothing of her seeming obliviousness to my utter lack of response to everything she said.)

But how, then, it must have shocked the evening doorman, whose eyes had already opened wide beneath his quasi-military hat at the sight of my jaunty companion in her rambunctious clothes, when I said, as we passed by him through the door he held open, "Thank you, Frank."

He actually let go of the door, which would have slammed into my shoulder had I not put out my hand to stop it.

"Good evening, Mr. Chambers," he finally found himself able to say, though by that time I had caught up to my new friend and was walking through the chalcedony lobby toward the elevator.

"I'm terribly sorry," he called after me, and only the spreading open of the elevator doors, which struck me for the first time as something vaguely sexual, kept me from turning around and asking Frank what he was sorry for: nearly slamming the door on me; having the clean simplicity of our silence come to an end; or seeing me with a woman for the first time and believing like most men that there has been no dictator yet born who can subjugate a man the way a woman can?

The elevator operator wore white gloves. I was tempted to hold out my right hand to him and let him congratulate me on my reentry into the world. But I settled for a mere "Hello, Eddie" and was amazed to find that he held out his hand to me and seemed about to wrap his other hand around my shoulder until he realized that the elevator would have ground to a stop should he remove that hand from its semicircular brass controls.

"Nice to see you again, Mr. Chambers." Eddie shook my hand as if I had been gone for a year instead of merely silent.

I could feel his eyes on my companion's bottom as we stood together on the landing while I turned one key and then another in the locks on the door to the apartment, of which there was one per floor. Only after I had closed that door behind us did I hear through it the clangor of the metal gate being pushed shut and then the coming together of the elevator doors themselves. I thought of Eddie rushing down to the lobby and leaving the elevator while it was still bouncing as he limped to Frank to describe the lascivious pleasure he had taken from his *oeillade* and to ask Frank if the dead man had spoken to him too and did he think that woman might have been the one who brought him to life with her fabulous backside and the light in her plummy eyes.

73

"Have you been away?" she asked as she began to walk into the apartment and I followed, as if it were her place and not mine.

Did the apartment look so uninhabited, I wondered, that it appeared I didn't stay there or perhaps even live there?

"No," I answered, "I haven't been away, not for a while. I used to go abroad at every opportunity, but lately I've been staying here in the city. Why do you ask?"

She walked through the front parlor and the music room and into the library and headed toward the formal dining room, where not a morsel of food had been eaten since the renting family had departed. I followed her within this maze of my life. "Because the elevator man said it was nice to see you again. That's what people usually say to someone who's been away. But you haven't been away. Maybe he's been away."

"Who?" I wondered if she thought I was made up of more than one person. The very idea made me feel desirable, and it was all I could do to keep from sprinting so I might catch up with her and put my arms around her from behind and press her to me and feel the roundness of her buttocks at that place on my upper right thigh where my testicles slept, we being the perfect height for one another.

"The elevator man," she explained.

"Oh." I stopped for a moment, but she walked right on. "No, he hasn't been away either." Now I hurried my steps just to be able to see her as she went through the kitchen and then the pantry and opened the door to the laundry and tried the locked door to the wine room, which would have been too cold for her despite her three little shirts, and found the door at the rear of the kitchen that led to the back of the apartment. "He didn't really mean it was nice to see me again. He sees me every night when I come home. If I get home by eleven, that is. If I get home after eleven, then it's Juan who sees me. Juan is the night elevator man. What Eddie meant was it was nice to hear me again. I had stopped talking for a while. I hinted at that in your shop when I said that language had failed me. I stopped talking for over a year, actually. Today's the first day I've said anything for over a year."

I thought that might make her halt her self-guided tour of my home, but she just kept on going. "I'd like you to tell me about it. I assume the bedroom's back here?" she asked.

She went on down the long corridor that led to the bedrooms and various bathrooms and the maids' quarters and whatever else might be back there in some room I hadn't slept in and so perhaps had never bothered to open.

"All the bedrooms are," I answered.

"I meant yours."

"I sleep in different rooms," I confessed.

"No wonder," she said with utter lack of condemnation as she opened one bedroom door after another. "I don't know how anyone can live like this. All these rooms. All these walls. Everything cut off from everything else. Did you know there didn't used to be bedrooms? People slept right in the middle of the house. In the great hall. They didn't go off into private chambers. They didn't try to hide. They even entertained there. Their guests would walk around the bed in what was called a *ruelle*. But what about you? Don't you have a room where you usually sleep? Don't you keep your clothes somewhere?"

She had finally stopped and had turned to look at me. She was lost. She needed help. The apartment had defeated her as it had undoubtedly defeated me.

"Not really. There are closets everywhere. I hang my suits in one room and keep my shirts in a linen closet outside one of the bathrooms. They smell so clean when I take them from there and put them on. I really don't have a room of my own here. I didn't grow up here. I inherited this place from my mother."

"Then this can be your room," she said as she opened the door to one of the bedrooms and looked in.

I followed her into my new room. It was a room in the cracks of whose walls I had sometimes tried to sleep. Like most of the rooms in the apartment, it was furnished with antiques, mostly American like the Federal cherrywood chest of drawers made by Triphem Gorham in Connecticut at the turn of the eighteenth century and the simple Chippendale maple blanket chest made in Rhode Island about a quarter-century earlier, though the bed was a Charles X mahogany *lit en bateau*, chunky and substantial but not, thank goodness, a four-poster like the beds in some of the other bedrooms, with their pleated canopies and pencil posts or fluted columns and not at all suited to the night of love I could feel crawling up through my thickening blood as she pushed the claw-footed brass doorstop against the door to hold it open and went to the bed and pushed off her short black boots and lay back against the square white pillows and I prepared to follow her because I didn't know where else to go when she pointed to the Irish fools chair opposite the foot of the bed and said, "Sit there, I want us to be able to see each other," and I sat there utterly in her thrall.

I looked at her. She looked at me. I was happy to be exiled to this chair against the wall, for I was afraid of my desires, or at least of my being able to fulfill them in some way that would fulfill hers also, and at the same time I wanted to leap across that space between us and bury her beneath me until she might try to claw her way out into the peach light that melted into the room through the frosted globe held aloft on the tiny muscular hand of the naked male figure of the spelter lamp on the table beside the bed.

I knew she sensed both my fear and my desire. I was grateful to her for this more than anything, more even than for being there with me in the first place: for recognizing my ambivalence.

"Somebody sure mixed the woods in this place," she said.

I was amused at the thought of my mother so painstakingly collecting all these valuable pieces, only to have the first girl I'd ever brought home point out so casually how they were inharmonious. I felt that I had somehow been put together in the same way, with my unearned muscles and my careful woolens and my guarded spectacles on my pretty face and my vetust mind.

"So talk to me," she said. "I love to hear you talk. I loved your story about the violin. Tell me about how you stopped talking."

"One day I just stopped."

"Just like that," she said skeptically.

"That's how it seemed. One day I was reading about the death of rhetoric and how it coincided with modernization, with rationalization replacing religion, and when I saw the word *axes*, the plural of *axis* and a word I'd been reading in book after book because it's the kind of word that language people love, I read it as *axes*, the plural of *axe*. And no matter how many times I read that word over and over and over again, all I could hear was *axes, axes, axes* in place of *axes, axes, axes*."

"So is that when you stopped talking?"

I nodded.

"Say something."

"Yes."

"So you were chopping off your head to spite your mind."

It was an image so clear, and so clearly accurate, that I found myself bending forward as if there were literally a blade at my neck.

"You might say that."

"I'm glad you didn't."

"Didn't what?"

"Chop off your head."

"I, as well."

"You do have such a beautiful face."

I touched my face.

"But you're not gay."

It was only half a question now. But it disturbed me. "Why do you keep asking me that?"

"Because I was in love with a gay man."

"How can that be?"

"How can it not be? It was. He was the most beautiful man I've ever seen."

"Who was he?"

"My boss."

"What happened to him? Did he die?"

"He left me."

"How can that be?"

"Thank you for asking. I destroyed his life."

Please destroy mine, I wanted to say. I will never leave you. "Do you want me to be gay?" I asked.

"All men are gay."

"Well, I'm not."

She smiled as if the whole thing had been a big joke. "But you do admit that it was a homonym that made you stop talking, that gave you—"

"No," I interrupted.

"—your epiphany," she went right on. Then she held up her hand to stop me from contradicting her again. "Sorry. Bad pun. But that is the right word otherwise, isn't it? *Epiphany*? I always wanted to have an epiphany myself. Not the religious kind. Religions are repressive. They crush women like *this*." She crossed her arms over her chest and flattened her hands upon her breasts. "A revelation," she went on. "Where everything comes together and you feel you know the truth about things. That's never happened to me. On the other hand, I do have the most incredible orgasms. Maybe some people are given epiphanies and other people are given orgasms. Can you imagine what it would be like if you had to choose for yourself? It would be like *Sophie's Choice*, except instead of choosing which child of yours was going to live and which one was going to die, you had to choose between two ways of knowing the truth. Epiphany or orgasm. Which would you choose?"

"Epiphany."

"Figured." She smiled and wiggled against the bed, under her hands, which she had kept on her breasts but were now cupped gently over them, as if to protect them from religious persecution.

I found myself reverting to pedantry as I looked at her long, thin fingers unable quite to cover her breasts beneath her shirts and whatever undergarment she might be wearing.

"It wasn't a homonym," I explained.

"*Axes* and *axes* isn't a homonym!" She sat up and opened her eyes wide in mock horror. "Hundreds of tax dollars wasted on my education!" She took her hands from her breasts and, with them still crossed, reached down and grasped the bottoms of all three shirts and pulled them up over her head. I noticed first how this disheveled her short, auburn hair, which fell across her face over one eye and made her look like a child taunting me with a naughty smile. Then I let myself look down and saw she had been wearing no undergarment at all. From across the room I could feel her breasts burn the skin of my palms. "So if it isn't a homonym, what is it?"

"A homograph."

She looked at me doubtfully.

"Homographs," I went on, "are words that are spelled the same but are pronounced differently and mean different things. Homonyms are words that are spelled the same and are pronounced the same and mean different things. And then there are homophones. Homophones are—"

"Homophones?"

"Homophones are—"

"Homophones! Give me an example."

"*Freeze* and *frieze*," I said. "*Autarchy* and *autarky*."

"Oh, that's a big help."

"Homophones," I elucidated, "are words that are spelled differently but are pronounced the same and mean different things."

I knew that what I was saying was correct, but I felt that I didn't know what I was talking about. I was defining language at the same time that language was once again losing its meaning for me. But I wasn't frightened this time. I wasn't alone this time. I was with a strange, unfathomable woman who was stripping her body naked as she seemed to expect me to do with my mind.

"Tell me what happened," she said as she lifted her hips from the bed and pulled her tiny skirt up around her waist and hooked her thumbs under her green tights and pulled them down and raised her legs in the air so the tights would leave her feet, which they did, taking with them the gold socks, which clung to the tights and hung over the bed's footboard like a ballerina's slippers in the fourth position *croisée*. "Tell me about how you were undone by your . . . homograph, right?"

"Homograph," I repeated, wondering what it meant. "I read *axes* and heard *axes*. Everything just fell apart at that moment. I had spent years studying rhetoric. It was all so orderly—my life, my studies. Apollonian, if you will. I loved rhetoric for its order. I read Aristotle and Quintilian and Cicero and Longinus. I learned to love all the rules that governed the way words are used to try to arrive at the truth. *Inventio* and *dispositio* and *elocutio* and *memoria*. Even *actio*. I used to go around chanting them in my head like a song. It must sound stuffy and dry and foolish, perhaps even sciolistic . . . excuse me, superficial . . . but it is really about the power and beauty of language, and language, aside from bodily functions and the termination of bodily functions, which is to say death, is the only thing shared by all human beings. And language was the only way I knew to understand the truth and to try to express the truth. And the truth is all I ever wanted. What is truth? Nietzsche asked. I asked. What does it mean that we ask what it means? I went looking for the metaphors of things. I dived into language, I went far beyond rhetoric. I studied linguistics and psycholinguistics, semantics and graphology. I analyzed conversational implicatures with Grician exactitude. I examined the great medieval trivium, which added dialectic and grammar to rhetoric. *Philosophus grammaticam invenit*—it's the philosopher who discovers grammar. I thought I was a philosopher because I thought I was in the process of uncovering the truth. But the truth itself came under attack, or at least the means to get to the truth. Rhetoric was attacked and destroyed. Kant attacked it. The Romantics attacked it. People in our own time, Roland Barthes and Paul Ricoeur and Tzvetan Todorov, they attacked it. Even my beloved Nietzsche. Wittgenstein moved from the worship of language to the belief that it actually bewitches our intelligence. I realize now that I believed they were attacking me, my life, my meaning. One day I was in a bookstore up on Broadway near Columbia and bought a book, and when the clerk gave me my change, I counted it, as I had always done, because that's what rich people do. And I saw that one of the coins had been rubbed completely smooth. There was no writing on it, no picture. I slammed it down on the counter and screamed at the clerk and accused him of trying to cheat me. 'This is worthless,' I said, 'worthless!' I don't think I had ever screamed before in my life. I was lucky—"

"You screamed for your mother," she said.

"No, I didn't. I didn't scream for my mother. How would you know? You weren't there."

Unperturbed by my contradicting her, she explained, "You screamed for your mother when you couldn't play the chaconne on your violin."

"The sarabande," I answered. "It was the sarabande I couldn't play. But yes, I did—I screamed for my mother."

She smiled at me, not smugly but sympathetically, though she seemed already to have a greater hold than I upon the facts of my life. "You were saying," she prompted, gratifyingly eager for me to continue.

"I was saying I was lucky I didn't get arrested. For screaming, I mean. I actually pictured myself getting hauled before my father in court and hearing him say, 'Make him invisible.' The clerk looked at me strangely and shook his head and unlocked the cash drawer and took out another quarter and put it down on the counter next to the blank one. I could see he didn't even want to put it into my hand. So I left it there. I left both of them there. That's what rich people also do. I walked back here to this apartment trying to put the whole strange incident out of my mind by concentrating on what I was going to read when I got home. But all I could think of was that coin, the emptiness of it, the evidence of time passing and reducing it to a kind of unseen dust, the illusion of its value. And suddenly I knew where that coin had come from. I remembered that very image in a book by Nietzsche called *Truth and Lie in an Extra-moral Sense.* Nietzsche said that language had lost its sensual power and compared it to coins that had lost their image and were worthless. They were an illusion. Language was an illusion. Truth was an illusion. It was that day that *axes* became *axes*. So I did what seemed to be the most natural thing in the world. I stopped talking."

"Until today."

"Until today."

"I'm flattered." She passed the tip of each middle finger quickly over the end of her tongue like an old person preparing to turn the page of a book and brought each middle finger, now wet, down upon the aureole of each nipple and moved the fingers round and round each nipple, which rose quickly. I had never seen anyone do that. She looked down at them and said, "Oh."

"You should be," I said.

"I should be what?"

"Flattered."

"I thought you meant aroused."

"Are you?"

"I'm getting there." She smiled at me in such a way that seemed to be begging my patience. "So just how rich are you?" she asked.

"Rich enough."

"For what?"

"I don't need a job."

"I'm not offering you one." She laughed. "I'm glad you have money."

I suppose it might have occurred to me that she might think that I might think that she had come with me tonight because I represented some sort of catch because of my wealth. But I had never considered myself a target for women in search of money. I had never thought of myself as wealthy, only as someone who need never be concerned with earning money. I had never measured myself in terms either of how much money I had or of how little—nothing, really, except continue on, which I suppose is all most people ever do—I had had to do to acquire that money. This absence of a feeling of triumph or guilt over money was another way in which I felt I deviated from the American norm. Jacob Needleman said that only in this culture in all the history of mankind have people longed for money beyond anything else. Not I. I was not quaestuarial. I did not want money. I merely had it.

"Why are you glad?" I asked.

"Because I have money too. I own my business. I work very hard at it. Long hours. Alone. I don't have any help unless I'm out of town, and when I'm out of town I'm out of town on business, and sometimes I just close the shop rather than hire someone to look after it. I love my quilts. Each one is different. I work hard at finding them and I work even harder at selling them, because I won't sell them to just anyone."

I thought of what I'd read in her notebook. I saw her in her imagination spread out on the Star of Bethlehem and now, in what almost seemed like my imagination, spread out on my bed.

"I didn't have to work hard for my money." I was not ashamed to admit this.

"Where did you get it?"

"My mother left it to me. I'm an only child. My father told her to. He didn't want it. He cares more for prestige than money — so he has the perfect profession as a judge. He made her do it. He told me it relieved him of the guilt he felt that I was never going to do anything to support myself. I studied language not to be able to do something with it. I wasn't going to teach; I'm not even an academic, because I've never belonged to an academy. I wasn't going to write books. I wasn't going to spew incisive epic-rises in *The New York Review of Books*. I wasn't going to amuse people at dinner parties with my scholarship. I simply wanted to be able to live with words. I wanted to be a hero. Every boy wants to be a hero, I expect. And I thought I was a hero. I really did. The real hero in this country is the person who does nothing, the propaganda of fecund utilitarianism to the contrary. The person who sits and thinks. Who lies in bed and thinks. Evil is manifest in action, and action is easy. Passivity is hard. Action takes you out of yourself. Passivity takes you into yourself. And where would most people rather be? Outside or inside themselves? Of course my father never understood this. He never understood that there is no more courageous, dangerous activity, as it were, than to face the blank wall of existence with nothing to hand but questions. He used to tell me that there is no room for intellectuals and thinkers, not in America. 'You don't do anything,' he would say. 'You won't produce anything. You set no example for anyone else. God help you if you ever become a father.' He made no secret of the fact that it was he who told my mother to leave me her money. He told me that before and then during the reading of her will. And that was the last thing he ever told me. He hasn't spoken to me since."

She sat up in bed, holding her breasts but no longer moving her fingers upon them. "Have you tried to talk to him?"

"I left messages. It was years ago. Now I talk to him only in my mind."

"What do you say?"

"I tell him I'm still looking."

"For what?"

"Nothing."

"What about the truth?"

"I found it."

"What is it then?"

"Nothing. It's that coin. It's nothing."

"So why are you still looking?"

"Because once you know it's nothing, it becomes everything. 'All I know is that I know nothing'—Socrates. So you keep looking. You can never get enough."

"Of nothing?"

"Of everything."

"It's like sex," she said.

"I wouldn't know," I admitted.

"I'll teach you." She swung her legs over the side of the bed. "I need a hard surface. The floor."

She put her feet down on the rug and started slowly to pull down her underpants.

"Did you see *Truth or Dare?*" she asked.

I watched as her fingers stayed under the elastic and peeled those simple white pants off her body.

"You probably think I don't know what you're talking about," I said.

"I didn't ask if you'd heard of it," she said with a testiness that made me blink. "I asked if you'd seen it."

"No, I haven't."

"You made me think of it when you mentioned *Truth and Lie*. And music. Are you a Madonna fan?"

"Of course."

"I'm not talking about the Madonna dal Collo Lungo."

I laughed. She'd caught me.

"Don't lie to me," she said. "I told you before: you don't have to tell me the truth, but don't lie to me."

She stood on one leg and lifted the other to remove her underpants from that foot. She stood before me completely naked now except for the white pants in her hand. I envied the shadows that hovered on her skin. I felt I had never seen anyone or anything so beautiful. I felt I had never seen nakedness itself before and not simply because I had no memory of when I had seen it. Her breasts were full, particularly in contrast to her thin, taut arms, their nipples still tight from her having massaged around them. Her pubic hair, positively musteline in its softness, had been pressed down by her clothes and opened only slightly where the lips of her vagina were soft parentheses swollen around that place to which I felt I was being sentenced for life.

"I won't lie to you," I said, compelled to stand up now and come to her. "And certainly not in bed."

"Sit down," she said and motioned with one hand for me to do so while the other rose into the air with her underpants still upon it.

I sat back down as she said, "I lied to *you*. I said I was a free spirit but I didn't go around swinging my underpants over my head. And I do!"

And she did. With a giggle, she twirled her underpants over her head on one finger round and round until finally they flew off her hand and landed right at my feet.

"Lucky shot," she said, giggling some more as she sank slowly before me to the floor onto the inscription cartouche at the edge

86

of the dark Bakhtiari rug upon which I had once tried, unsuccessfully, to sleep.

And there she sat, legs crossed and spread, both hands beneath her buttocks, as she said, "So tell me what it's like not to talk for a year."

I tried to remember what it had been like. Here, I'd broken the fast of language—or, more accurately, of talking aloud—for a mere few hours, and it was as if I had never abstained in the first place. The joys and confusions of communicating with another person had come rushing back through my throat and over my skin. I felt I wanted to talk forever to this colorful, young, malicious woman, as Nietzsche might describe her, full of thorns and secret spices.

She was sitting there on the edge of the rug, almost at my feet, upon her hands, looking up at me with impatience, the way one does at a door that is supposed to open and stays shut.

"There really isn't much to tell about," I said quickly.

"There has to be. Everybody talks. Most people talk all the time. They talk. They move. They say things. They do things. And they still end up dead. But you didn't say anything for a whole year. You did what other people only dream about. And you don't *do* anything, not the way most people do things. You're like somebody with the secret of life who doesn't even know he has it. I've never met anybody like you. I want you to talk to me about everything."

"About not talking as well?"

"I want to know what it's like."

"It's not as profound as you might imagine. It's more inconvenient than anything else."

"Go on," she said.

"Aren't you cold sitting down there?"

"Thank you for asking. I'll get back on the bed soon."

"But why are you on the floor?"

"I told you. I need a hard surface."

"Do you have a back problem?"

"Hardly." She smiled and looked down at herself. "I'm so supple I can kiss my own toes. Without bending my knees."

"So why are you sitting like that? On your hands? Are they cold? My violin teacher used to make me sit on my hands in the winter to warm them up before I played my lessons for him."

"I'm numbing my fingers."

I thought of her notebook and wondered if she was still trying to find out if I could read her writing. I remembered how, back in her shop, I had wanted to *be* that diary so she would tell me everything about herself, as she now seemed to want me to tell her everything about myself. Could it be that we would have no secrets from one another?

"Why?" I asked.

"Why what? Why am I on the floor? Why do I have my clothes off? Why am I sitting on my hands? Why am I doing this with a stranger?"

"Why are you numbing your fingers?"

"Watch." She rose to her feet. "Watch me. I'll show you."

She lay down on the bed again and drew up her knees and put her left hand under her left buttock and her right hand between her legs.

"Tell me about not talking," she said as she spread the lips of her vagina with the index and middle fingers of her right hand and then let those same fingers settle in between. "You were saying it was inconvenient."

"Well, you can't really take cabs very easily or order food over the phone at all. And of course you don't have to talk on the phone at all. That becomes quite a relief, though at the beginning I found the ringing of my phone to be a terrible distraction and even a mockery of my silence. But by the time I began to get used to the ringing of a phone that I knew I was not going to answer, the phone pretty much stopped ringing altogether. I must confess that sometimes when the phone did ring, I would pick it up. I would never say anything, just listen. The sound other people make when they talk becomes purer when you don't talk yourself, though no one talks very long to silence on the other end of a phone line. You do become a bit of a dolt when you're out among people and you eschew the common courtesies, the 'pleases' and the 'thanks yous' and the 'excuse mes' that are inevitably part of social interaction, not to mention how disdainful you must seem to a waiter when you merely point out on the menu what you would like to eat. But I have not been very social anyway during this time. Whatever friends I had have through their own silence disinvited me from their homes. And I had had friends. Quite a few. I had visited them. I had dined with them. I had gone to concerts with them. I had discussed the world with them. I never had managed to get a television, or even to watch one, but I had listened to the radio sometimes and had read the newspaper every day and for years had lived in what I had thought was the world and had gotten along quite nicely, thank you, for a scholarly celibate. But one day it all went blank. Words failed me. I could understand nothing, but I couldn't even describe what I failed to understand. So I stopped talking. I moved, as it were, *au-dessus de la mêlée*, pardon my French. But even in my silence and my withdrawal, I believe I have offended as few people as possible. And I set out to offend no one. In fact, I never set out to be silent in the first place. It's the kind of thing that just grows on you, or in you. You don't talk to anyone for a day or two, and then you don't talk to anyone for a day or two more, and pretty soon, even before you're really aware that there is a new pattern in your life, it's become a kind of habit. You need not talk to anyone. You become addicted to something you don't do rather than to something you do, until the thing you don't do becomes the thing you do. And then the thing you are. I became silence. It was not a matter of Wittgenstein's 'What we cannot speak about we must pass over in silence.' It was wholly secular. It seemed the most natural thing in the world—not to talk. And the most comfortable. There were times when I thought that no one really wants to talk, no one. It takes such an effort, and the pitfalls are so great—using the wrong word, saying the wrong thing, giving the wrong impression, because words are nothing but impressions, are they, and always, always, suffering ambiguity, which grows greater with each word spoken. Of course, you do go on talking, even in the midst of silence. You talk to yourself. Not aloud, at least in my case, thank goodness. It's not words you've given up or language, even if it was language you were trying to escape in the first place. It's just sound. The sound of words, of talking. You can never escape from the language of your thoughts. I could see my thoughts. I could see words spinning silently from my mind and was afraid I would get all wrapped up in them and disappear and die. So I wandered around during every waking minute and tried to sleep in the corners of these rooms and tried to kill the language in my mind with music. So I listen to music. I don't play it. I don't write about it. I don't teach it. I don't make a living at it. I just listen to it. I try to let it lead me to feel myself in the midst of its sound, the way I once did with language. I believed I would never talk again. And listen to me now."

I laughed. I thought she might laugh too. But she didn't, and I wasn't even sure she had heard a word I'd said. Her eyes were locked into mine, and mine were locked onto her fingers, first of one hand and then, when she would put that first hand back under her bottom, of the other hand, moving back and forth, and then quickly, fleetingly, up and down, upon herself.

When I stopped talking, I became aware of her breathing, which intensified and then subsided according to how she moved her fingers, and as I listened more intently I could hear the liquid click of the juice she was drawing out of her body and the small, almost breathless words she was saying.

"There. There. Right there. Pardon *my* French. There. Do it. Oh."

I stood up. Was she making fun of me? I didn't care. My penis had grown hard and caused the front of my trousers to stand out.

"Sit down!" she whispered. "Just watch me. Watch me. I'm going to come. Watch me come. Sit down. Watch me."

I obeyed. With both hands now working almost frenziedly she raised her buttocks from the mattress and her head too and stuck her tongue out and seemed desperately to be trying to lick her breasts, though no matter how supple she might be, and how gracefully long, I noticed, her neck might be, and how much she might be able to push her breasts together and raise them by moving her shoulders toward one another with her arms pushed against her sides, her tongue could reach no farther than the tops of her breasts and the beginning of her cleavage, where drops of her saliva collected and glowed faintly in the soft peach light.

But she didn't seem to mind. She was smiling now beatifically as she said, "Oh there, oh there, oh there. I'm there. Oh please. Help me. Help me. Help me."

I didn't get up this time. I knew enough to know she wasn't talking to me.

All her words were lost in the great scream of pleasure that burst from her throat and the mist of joy that lacquered her purple eyes and the thrashing of her body and rippling of her legs and the cadenzaed movement of her fingers fast upon her glistening pudendum.

I thought she might fly from the bed and wanted nothing more than to be able to catch her and hold her in my arms and feel her shudders through my bones and let my body damp her shivering.

But slowly, by herself, she began to come to rest, until finally she turned her hands palms-up upon her thighs and let her head fall back upon the pillows so she was staring straight up at the ceiling. She smiled contentedly and purred softly and then slowly brought her chin down until she was able to look at me again.

I waited for her to say something. But she just lay there, looking at me. And I remembered what she had said about words failing her, words failing her after she had had sex, and I had to admit that this unusual way of having sex was certainly having sex nonetheless.

So I let her lie there quietly and watched the rise and fall of the bifurcated muscles beneath the tight skin of her chest and waited for her to become ready to say something. It was enough for me just to sense her in all her muliebrity, the roundness of her parts, the fullness of her satisfaction, the sound of the air passing her full lips, the talcumed smell of her genitals, which I noticed was new to me in the absence of the odor of the rubber or latex or whatever it was in which I had so fastidiously invaginated myself on the one occasion I had been with a woman. The one other occasion.

Finally, she spoke, her voice hoarse at first.

"That was wonderful. Not an epiphany maybe, but wonderful. Thank you."

I must have looked at her questioningly.

"For watching," she explained. "It was better with you watching. I hope you didn't mind."

I shook my head. "Will you tell me now why you numbed your fingers."

She sat up and looked at me with kind forbearance. "You still don't know?"

Now I was forced to shake my head in ignorance..

"What happens when something's numb?" she asked.

"You stop feeling."

She clapped her hands gaily and said, "Exactly! You stop feeling. So when you numb your fingers, and you touch yourself, down here, I mean, when I make myself come, it's the best of both worlds."

"Both what worlds? What both worlds?" I didn't know how to say it.

"Both worlds." Impatiently she raised her hands and held them apart, cupped as if each contained a small globe. "The world of other people"—she shook one hand—"and the world of yourself"—and now she shook the other hand.

As my gaze went from one hand to the other, she brought them together over her body and let the fingers of one intertwine with the fingers of the other. I felt she had explained the universe.

"Would you like to try it?"

I peered over the corner of the mattress at her beautiful vagina, sumptuously wet and swollen, veiled now with tiny ringlets of her pubic hair.

She caught me staring between her legs and said, "Not me, silly. Yourself."

"Oh, I couldn't possibly . . ." I stood up like a man who's been summoned from a room and doesn't know why.

"Take off your clothes and sit down on the floor the way I did. On your hands. And when you can't feel anything in them, come up here on the bed. Go ahead—do it. And start with those ridiculous shoes."

For a moment, I wished I had been summoned from the room. I think I looked around for someone who might rescue me. "Really?"

"Really."

I walked to the open door to remove the stop and was about to kick it away with one of my ridiculous shoes when she said, "Leave it open. It's more exciting when you think someone is watching."

My hand was on the door. "Please. I'm too private. I don't want to pretend anyone is watching."

I could see her try not to laugh. I could see, and hear, her fail. But at least it was a kindly laugh at my finical young-fartness. "You won't have to pretend. I'll be watching. So let me pretend someone's watching me watching you. Now leave the door open and come back here. Get undressed. Stand there where I can see you."

She pointed toward the edge of the beautiful old rug where she had sat before me on her hands. I followed her finger.

"The shoes," she said.

To steady myself, I held onto the stern of the bed and removed one shoe, one sock, then the other shoe and the other sock.

"Jacket . . . Tie . . . Shirt . . ."

The buttons in my fingers were like huge coins with which I was clumsily trying to do tricks to impress my audience.

"Undershirt. I didn't know men still wore undershirts. None of the men I——"

"They probably don't." I pulled the white, sleeveless shirt up over my head as I always did by grasping its hem.

"Very sexy. You look like a Calvin Klein ad. I never thought you'd have muscles like that. Do you work out?"

"No."

"I can't believe it. Where did you get that build?"

"Inherited."

"Like the money."

"Like the money," I acknowledged. "I'm a paradigm of bestowal." I chuckled at realizing how true that was.

"I'm happy to see you loosening up. Now the pants."

I was glad that my belt was fastened, as always, in the last of its five holes. I had never before taken pleasure in this sign of my body's unchanging shape. It was the first manifestation of vanity, at least in the physical realm, I had ever noticed in myself.

The buttons of the pants came undone more smoothly than had those of my shirt.

"The fly."

The fly.

"I love that sound," she said. "Someone should make a recording of nothing but flies being unzipped. I'll bet it would sell better than waterfalls and thunderstorms and whale songs. Better than white noise, even."

"Does it bring back memories?"

My question seemed to startle her. It certainly startled me. If this was sexual bantering—and I was not sure it was—it was my very first experience with that particular kind of verbal interchange.

"A flood," she answered finally.

I pictured it, a flood of men, literally a cascade of naked male bodies tumbling in clear waves upon this beautiful small woman sitting naked in this pinkish-yellow light and she opening her legs for each of them as he flew into her and then was washed away.

"Where do I fit in?" I asked, naïvely unaware of my play on words but then proud of it when she answered, "Who says you're going to get in?" She pointed at my crotch and waved her finger up and down. "Underpants. Or whatever you call those things."

"Boxers."

"And I see they're putting up a good fight."

It was true. An erection—mine, apparently, which I supposed I'd had so long it had come to feel natural—kept my undershorts pinned against my waist. I found that instead of pulling these pants down, as I normally did without a thought, I had to lift them by their elastic up and over the head of my penis, which stared up at me as I stared down at it.

"Look at you."

It was then I realized, with some embarrassment, that that was precisely what I had been doing.

"I've never imagined a cock like that. Put your hand on it."

It was her hand I wanted on it, but I didn't know how to ask for that. I did notice, however, that I was bending lordotically so that my loins would be pushed toward her, like something Clara would one day give me out of James Gillray's "Presentation of the Mahometan Credentials." Just touch me, I wanted to say. I believe I would have given my life just to have her touch me.

She seemed to miss nothing. "Put *your* hand on it."

I put my hand on it.

"Around it, you idiot."

I moved it from my fingertips into my palm.

We were like two children, I suppose, though such games had never been part of my childhood, exploring one another's body with such innocence that we did not even permit ourselves to touch on the other what was crying out to be touched.

I bent at the knees and sank to the floor and placed my hands beneath me and sat on them. My penis remained unabatedly erect so that I must have looked to her like the sort of ancient Mochica pitcher of which she would later bestow upon me a reproduction, whose container was the seated body of a man and the spout his upright member.

As I sat there waiting to lose all feeling in my hands, and she sat above me on the mattress with her legs now crossed, she said, "So tell me more. Tell me why all of a sudden you started to talk to me when you hadn't talked to anyone for a year or whatever. It couldn't be because you knew you were going to end up naked with me here watching each other have sex with ourselves." On the one hand, I found the notion that I might actually have anticipated this so outlandish that I smirked, and on the other hand I found her words for what we were doing here so intricately confusing and at the same time glaringly direct that I gasped.

"What's so funny?" she asked, though she had already joined in the levity with at least an indulgent smile.

"It's just that I'm not in the habit of meeting women and having them take me home with them, or having me take them home with me, or having them take me home to my home with them, which I guess is what happened here." Then I couldn't help asking. "Are you?"

"I'm used to everything," she answered, hiding nothing, which I was beginning to realize, putting aside the mystery of her diary, was the way she was and was the way she was going to be, and if I wanted to be with her, as if it were a thing already accomplished, as if it were what my future held, then I would have to get used to it, her directness, as I would have to get used to the idea that she had indeed been flooded by an endless stream of men, while I had lived, to express it epizeuxistically, as we ascetic rhetoricians would say, a dry, dry life.

"I want to know everything" I said, convinced at that moment, as at this moment, that it was, and is, so.

"That's what you think," she replied, which I found made me want to know her and her secrets all the more. And I certainly knew, though she didn't know I knew, which was perhaps my only advantage over her, where to find them.

"I talked to you because I found your diary," I said.

"Did you read it?"

"You asked me that earlier."

"If you couldn't read it, how did you know where to find me?"

"From the quilting you put on the cover of the book. I tracked you down."

"So why didn't you just hand the thing to me? Why did you talk to me?"

"Because of your handwriting."

"You thought I was brain damaged after all." She put her hand on her head and moved it into her hair. I watched as it went through her fingers like some soft, uncut grass I had seen stirring one night in the wind beyond the Festspielhaus in Salzburg and have never forgotten because of the K. 573 played there that night. "Is that how you like your women?"

"I don't have any women," I confessed, unafraid of being as direct with her as she was being with me and convinced that she would find me all the more interesting for my being as artricial as a newborn soul, which of course proved me sublimely mantic. "When I saw your handwriting, I thought it was like my not talking. A form of silence. And at the same time so mangled that it shows a healthy disrespect for the word. Just like me. And nobody could hear what I was saying. We're both imprisoned in the freedom of our privacy."

"So you really don't think I'm dysgraphic."

"I know enough about chirography to know you're not dysgraphic," I announced like a surgeon.

She shook her head. "Thank God your cock's as long as some of the words you use."

As I fought the urge to cover myself and kept my pinned-and-needled hands beneath me, I said, "You write in a kind of shorthand. A private shorthand. That's what almost all shorthand is—a private form of written speech. It goes back to the Greeks—Xenophon used shorthand to transcribe the memoirs of Socrates. And later the Romans—Tiro devised his own system so he could take down the speeches of Cicero. That's how I learned about it, because one can't study rhetoric without studying Cicero, without reading *De Oratore*. And then, there was a time, in the Middle Ages, when shorthand disappeared, because it was believed to be a code used by witches."

"That explains it!"

"You admit it's a code?"

"Of course it's a code. That's why I didn't care when I lost that book. I knew no one would be able to read it. Except of course I do want someone to be able to read it. I decided I would marry the first man who could read it. He would be the only one to know all my secrets."

Did she know I could read it? Was she playing with me? I

remembered how, back in her shop, she had seemed disappointed that I couldn't read it. This was beyond me, this playing with knowledge between man and woman. What are we supposed to know of one another? And what are we supposed to want our beloved to know?

I knew I was going to marry her, or to try. I had known it even before she mentioned her little fairy-tale method of choosing her husband. But did she know she was going to marry me? Did she know I had cracked her code?

"Cinderella," I said.

"My foot," she quipped and moved one leg off the bed and brought it toward my penis and held her cyprian toes so close to the skin that I could feel their warmth.

"How are your hands?"

My hands were no longer mine.

She withdrew her foot and waved me toward her. "Come up here now."

I obeyed and noticed how careful she was not to allow us to touch. Still seated, she moved to the other side of the bed and spread out her hands to indicate that I lie where she had herself lain.

My hands might as well have been someone else's, particularly when I followed her eyes and grasped my penis in one hand and then did as she motioned with her head and began to stroke myself. When I closed my own eyes I could imagine it was her hand upon me, and I did. For the first of what would become countless times, I imagined my Clara in the act of love.

"That's so beautiful," she whispered. "Thank you for letting me watch."

"I've never done this before," I managed to mutter.

"Done what?"

I didn't know what to call it. "This."

"What?"

"I've never masturbated," I said.

"Neither have I."

As the feeling returned to the hand on myself, I brought my other hand out from under my buttock.

"Open your eyes," she said. "Look at me."

I looked into her eyes looking at my hand and tried even to see the reflection of myself in them.

"Your veins are like the veins in your hand," she said. "And look, I see little drops of come. Wet yourself with it. Go ahead. Pretend you're inside me. I'm still so wet. Go ahead. Do it."

I had never heard talk like this before. It was so simple and direct but also seemed removed from reality. I could not imagine what it would sound like in the world. But where I was now, it was angelic.

I found the semen coating the crown of my penis and rubbed it around on my palm and brought my still senseless hand back down onto the shaft and grasped myself as I had never had occasion to before and moved my hand heavenward and hellward until just as the feeling began to return to my hand and I became aware of the swelling and even greater tightening of the organ within it, my head seemed to burst. She said, "Now, darling. Now, darling." My life flew out of me with the dehiscence of my seed and flew into me through my eyes on her eyes. Seemingly endless white ribbons streamed out of me to adorn her lips and chin and neck and then seeped slowly down the shadow between her breasts, snaky sweet ylem on gravity's paradisiacal course.

I could hear my cries of pleasure merge with her delighted yelps. We fell silent together, filling the room only with the sound of our breath.

I wanted to touch her, hold her, but when I reached for her, she motioned my hand away and said, "Not yet." Then, when she seemed confident I wouldn't grab her, she leaned toward me and asked, "What's your name? Aside from Chambers, I mean. I'm not going to call you Mr. Chambers, like the elevator operator, though you are a kind of mister, aren't you? Mr. Chambers here in his chambers, his many chambers, but I can't call you Mr. Chambers now that I've seen your cock and you've come into my face. So tell me, what's your name?"

She was right. How could she not know my name? Is this what comes from the habit of long silence? I speak, yet I remain a stranger. And so is she.

But I was thrilled by her having said, "I'm not going to call you Mr. Chambers," because that meant she was planning to call me something, that we would talk again, meet again presumably, that she had some reason to believe she would address me again. Of such small tokens, I was learning, is love sustained and fear put to rest.

The only woman I had ever loved, or believed I could come to love if love could not be born from one such afternoon and evening as this, was not going to dump me.

"You know my name," I answered. "You said it earlier in your shop. That's one of those coincidences I mentioned to you there."

She put her finger childishly on her wanton lower lip. "I don't remember."

"Johnny, is what you said. No one's ever called me that. I'm hardly a Johnny. But it's close enough. My name is John."

She shook her head and tried unsuccessfully to stifle a laugh and bent forward and put her hand on my shoulder. It was a conciliatory rather than romantic gesture. "I'm sorry. I wasn't being psychic. I'm not a witch, really. It's just another code, I suppose. I call all men Johnny. As a group, I mean. Men I don't know. The way some men call other men Jim or something, or the way men used to call all women Sister. So it was just a coincidence. Believe it or not, I've never actually known a man named John before. Or Johnny, even. And that's what I'm going to call you: Johnny. My Johnny."

I was stricken. "But that's what you call everybody."

"Not anymore, you fool." She bent and kissed me lightly on the lips. I could feel the breath leave her nostrils so I breathed through my own to capture it.

"I hope you don't kiss like that all the time," she said.

I didn't laugh until I saw the merriment in her eyes. If I had ever been teased before, except by my father and by boys at school who had resented my wealth and the wall of words behind which I lived, I hadn't known it. It turned out to be a peculiarly flattering kind of attention, at least coming from a woman with whom I was so treacherously smitten.

But Johnny? I was not a Johnny. No one had called me that in my life. Even my mother in lifting me from the bath and wrapping a towel around me and singing Gluck as she put me into bed (*"Chiamo il mio ben cosi, quando si mostra il di . . . ,"* a veritable Pauline Viardot) had not called me Johnny. I was a John. A common slug of a name, uneventful, unelongated, destined, I had thought, gratefully, to be eternally without hypocoristication. Johnny? I? I would not have believed that I could be reborn, become a child with a pet name and learn to beam and scream with the fun and pleasure of love, of marriage.

"Don't you want to know my name?" she asked.

"I've wanted to know your name ever since I met you."

"Then why didn't you ask?"

"I was afraid."

"To know me?"

"To lose you."

"And you thought that if you knew my name . . ." She stopped not because she seemed puzzled but because she wanted me to say it.

"Then you might be real."

"I am real." She put the back of her hand gently on my ear. "I wouldn't have told you anyway. I don't tell anyone my name until I trust him. I'm ready to tell it to you now."

"Let me guess."

She shook her head. "You'll never guess. It's a funny name. It makes people laugh. I used to hate it so much that I never forgave my parents for giving it to me. I ran away—all the way from California to New York. I was sixteen years old. It was almost exactly ten years ago. I'm probably the only person who ever ran away from home because of her name."

"I know your initials," I said.

Playfully, she looked down at her naked body and investigated it the way one might for moles or insect bites. "I hope you don't think I'm the sort of person who wears monograms."

"C. B."

I'd finally said something that shocked her. My year of silence, my confession of sexual innocence, my father's condemnation— none of those seemed to push her off the axis of her beguiling upper-handedness. But she seemed genuinely surprised, almost violated yet pleased to be violated, at my having said her initials.

"How do you *know*?" She had taken me by the shoulders and was shaking me. Her breasts bobbed unnervingly near my mouth.

Though I knew it was dangerous, I couldn't resist telling her. "Your initials are right in the front of that notebook I returned to you. As words. *See. Be.*"

She released me. Tears came to her eyes, even as they wrinkled in a big smile. "You fucker! You cracked my code! Now I'm going to have to marry you. So what," she challenged, "is my name?"

"I don't have the slightest idea," I said, which caused both of us to burst into laughter.

"Guess," she insisted.

"To tell you the truth, I don't like guessing games, especially onomastic guessing games."

"I know what that means," she said coyly. "And you should be ashamed of yourself."

"It only sounds like masturbation," I explained.

"It isn't masturbation when someone's watching. So what's my name?"

"Constance," I hazarded.

"Not in a million years." She held out her hand. I took it. "How do you do," she said. "My name is Clara. Clara Bell. I was named"—she let go of my hand and threw herself, at long last, into my arms—"after a fucking clown!"

"Clara," I said for the first time and felt my lips and tongue embrace her name.

WE DID NOT make love that night. We did not make love until our wedding night. This was at Clara's insistence. She wanted, she said, to purify herself. I told her, in my lame effort at premarital seduction, that she was a virgin to me.

What we did do that night, and have done every night since, is sleep in one another's arms.

I had come up off the floor and out of the cracks in the walls.

I was reunited, through her, with myself.

11 P.M.

I am lying in bed, waiting for Clara.

I am positively esurient. My senses are all atumble. I taste the music and hear the quilts blazing on the walls and see Clara on my skin. So does hunger rearrange one, to say nothing of how it loosens the mind in the way it devours thoughts.

I get up from the bed and then am nearly tossed back onto it by what the Shostakovich cello sonata does to my feet. It sounds like a piece of this fractured city that's been torn out and cast up to this peaceful halidom, bullets shot at the pavement to make you dance.

Its anarchy is perfect for me now. I am free of everything but desire. And there are those who believe that this was the last piece Shostakovich himself wrote as a free artist, before his music was condemned as "fidgeting, screaming, neurasthenic, and messy" because it was created to no political purpose. And to this I say, it would have been political had he never written it down but merely heard it in his head. The least of politics are its public manifestations; the most political acts are those most private. It's not the public hanging that's political; it's the hangman's dreams.

I dodge the music like some unbound wraith before a firing squad and prance half the length of the loft to the kitchen and pull down the box of take-out menus and decide to order from Take A Wok rather than Oriental (how un-PC) Palace or Auntie Ha Ha's, not because the food is better but because I like the name (its playfulness puts me in mind of Call It Quilts, though it lacks the underlying religious provocation of Clara like Parmenides giving God the name of It).

I shall order no dumpling or noodle or military-brass chicken despite the earlier image of my ingesting them, for that was an image born not out of hunger but out of an oily vision of the food itself. Now I want nutrition and purification and beauty, so I choose vegetables only, to obtain that perfect green of the spinach and of the broccoli that snaps in the bite and the purple of the eggplant that were it not quite so dark would match the color of my beloved's eyes and why not throw in a few black mushrooms that can be rolled on the tip of the tongue like her pinguid clitoris that in its swelling resembles more, now that I think of it, a palmaryly perfect pearl onion.

I am forced to repeat my order several times and to suffer its being repeated back to me several times, each time incorrectly, so that when I am finally told, "Okay got it, mister, okay," it is I who must ask to have it repeated yet again and it is wrong again and I resign myself to the very real possibility that I will find a carton of sautéed string beans in place of my spinach. I dread the arrival of the delivery man, who will be even more oscitant than this man at the take-out phone.

"Okay thirty minutes, mister, okay," he says and hangs up as if I might question his ability to tell time as well.

How am I going to survive thirty minutes without food?

But wait.

I realize I am no longer hungry.

What is it about Chinese food, I wonder, that in the ordering of it quells the hunger for it?

On that night of the day we met, as I have said, we ate no dinner. I slept in a bed for the first time in over a year and in the arms of a woman (as a grown man, I mean) for the first time in my life.

When I awakened in the morning, I was struck by how little hungry I was, which only added to my sense of the unreality of the whole encounter. Had this really happened? And if it had, had it happened to me? But then, I wondered, what after all do people do behind all those windows out there? They do, I realized, exactly, in one variation or another, what we had done. Wake up and smell the linga, John!

When Clara finally opened her eyes, I said to her, "You were sarmassational!"

"God am I hungry," she replied.

So was I.

We ordered breakfast to be delivered, for I had no food in the apartment.

She hated the place. I put it on the market the same day.

I confessed I didn't know anything about the clown after whom she claimed to have been named.

"You've never heard of Howdy Doody?"

"I'm sorry," I said, "but I fail to see the humor in someone greeting a bowel movement."

Perhaps I was being too literal. Once she had stopped laughing, she told me all about Howdy and Clarabell.

I told her about the Bloomsbury Bells.

I showed her my violin.

She showed me each and every quilt in her shop and began to educate me about them.

Clara is visual, visual and tactile, the ideal combination for someone in her business. She seems to believe with Wittgensteinian instinct that there are things that cannot be put into words, that make themselves manifest, and this belief renders her mystical. *See Be*—the perfect motto for her, coded initialing aside. She is positively eidetic, able to see something forever in her mind if she has seen it once, whereas I cannot see even her, though I am unable to take my eyes off her when she is with me and I see myself so much more clearly through her seeing me (I tell her that I call this Clarafication and that I cannot imagine her with any other name).

She told me about Madonna.

I asked her birth date.

"November 22, 1963. Why?"

I was taken aback. "That's the day—"

"Kennedy was shot," she said impatiently.

"I wasn't going to say that," I said, for John Kennedy's death had hardly been an occasion for mourning in my family, which I remembered though I had been but three years old at the time. "I was going to say that it was the day Aldous Huxley died."

She told me about the Doors.

From then on, for each of her birthdays and on inconsequential occasions as well, I have bought her as fine a print as I could find of a Madonna. I started, naturally, with Il Parmigianino's Madonna dal Collo Lungo and followed that with Botticelli's and Cimabue's Madonna with St. Francis and the seductive van Hemmessen and Lochner's Madonna in the Rose Garden and da Vinci's Madonna of the Rocks and Raphael's Virgin of the Fish. For her thirtieth birthday in two months I shall give her another Raphael, his Madonna del Cardellino (as well as a 1929 first edition of the Hogarth Press *A Room of One's Own*), unless by then we know we have a child on the way, in which case I will give her a Madonna with Child, probably Fra Filippo Lippi's, which I've decided, under the tutelage of my all-seeing wife, is the most magnificent of all.

She played popular music for me.

I played classical music for her.

We learned about jazz with each other.

The only thing we didn't do was make love.

True to her word, she wanted to wait.

I might have thought this was a ploy to get me to marry her sooner, but I didn't think that, because I could not make myself believe she might want to marry me in the first place.

"What do you see in me?" I finally worked up the courage to ask her.

"Someone who can read me," she said.

"Innocence," she said.

"The father of my children," she said.

"The love of my life."

At our wedding, which was the simplest possible thing at City Hall, I got the clerk to let me turn on Clara's boombox to play Yo Yo Ma's recording of the sarabande from the fourth cello suite, and with that as our hymeneal, I told the assorted throng of strangers awaiting their turn to do what we were doing that when I met Clara Bell I felt what Henry James Senior had felt when first he met the woman, Mary Walsh, whom he was to marry. He reported, to Emerson: "The flesh said It is for me, and the spirit said It is for me."

No one there seemed to know what I was talking about.

WE CAME HOME to this loft of ours, which we'd bought and designed together and had furnished in anticipation of that day, that night, and we drank champagne and talked for a while until finally Clara said, "Fuck me, Johnny," and we consummated our marriage upon this bed.

I sit on its edge and recover from the desperation of hunger only to have it replaced, blessedly, by the desperation of lust. At last, I am approaching that pinnacle of desire that I have suffered so much, in being separated from Clara, to attain. Nietzsche called us the bravest of animals and those most accustomed to suffering and knew that we not only don't repudiate suffering, we *desire* (his italics) it, so long as we're shown the meaning of this suffering.

I try to picture her now, not in my usual hopeless attempt to see her but to see what she is doing. I cast her out from my mind in order to bring her into my flesh. I create of her a stranger.

Where can she be? With whom?

She is not with another man, which is to say she is not *with* another man, though the chances are good that she's with a man, for most of her dates and meetings in the evening are with men: her hairdresser is a man; her internist is a man; her gynecologist is a man; her accountant is a man; her aerobics instructor is a man; those people who truck in with quilts from America are men (and not one of them homosexual, according to Clara); her masseur is, obviously, a man.

I have in the past enjoyed the image of Clara having a massage. Then I can see her, not her face, really, which is half-obscured by the table on which she lies, but the rest of her, naked, only a small towel over her buttocks, while a man moves his hands across her skin and presses them down upon her, hard enough so that the outside edges of her breasts become visible upon the surface of the table. When his hands have reached that marvelous little concave small of her back, where the solid strength of her supple spine meets with charming incongruity her two darling dimples, his little finger slips under the white towel. Her buttocks flutter beneath the towel. As he moves that finger and then the next and next and next down the crack between them, her whole ass rises, magnetized. The towel slips off and falls slowly from the table to the floor. I am so happy to see my wife's beautiful ass I could weep. My cock quops with delight.

It is not that I want my wife to be with another man. I merely want to see her with another man. It is she who has taught me to see things—paintings, quilts, my crescive cock in her mouth that she eats like a croissant, delicately and edaciously at the same time.

It is Clara who has opened my eyes. She has shown me that the only way to see her is to see her not merely as someone apart from myself but someone apart from herself.

To have her, truly, I must give her up.

So I do. I give her up to my imagination and in that way get to keep her, real and for real.

What is more exciting, after all, for a man: to imagine having sex with another woman or to imagine his wife having sex with another man?

The former erases her, casts her out; the latter recreates her.

I have never dreamed I was making love to another woman when I was making love to Clara.

But sometimes I dream that I am someone else making love to Clara.

Someone from her diaries, her past, a forgotten lover from among the multitude of her lovers, given life anew by me and in turn giving life to me and through me to Clara, for I've found that I can bring myself to an absolute frenzy of desire by using a succedaneous cock on her and watching her use it. My frenzy is contagious. Clara is delivered to bliss. "Sometimes I don't even know who you are," she says. She looks at me through lust-puffed eyes as if she has never seen me before.

I say nothing but her name: "Clara." I say it again and again. How powerful a sound it is, this name of hers, fresh off the lips of a stranger. No other word quite so arouses her, no vulgar sex word, no description of what's happening between us, no tease or praise or demand. I say her name as if I had just come upon her, as if I were saying it for the first time, as if it were flesh itself. She pulls my head down to hers, my lips to her ear, and hears the whisper of her name until she cries out mine in her climax.

111

And thus I have her, truly, by having given up myself.

To imagine your beloved is someone else insults her, diminishes her, and removes her from you and you from her. Even that old hypocrite St. Jerome was wise enough to recognize that the husband who is lost in immoderate love is exalted in sin when he screws his wife so passionately that he would have done it with like abandon even were she a stranger. (It is he who also said, "The wise man should love his wife with judgment, not with passion." So how, then, is a man to love his wife?)

Is it not the greatest of all relationships, this accidental bond, this lifelong pledge, this pleasure, this plicate gathering of limbs and breath in the hasp of sex and the trust of sleep? We come together as strangers, aliens, and are folded, crushed, into a single, resurrected blood. Out of thin air, with someone who did not exist until we met, we make family. This is the will to life. This is the death of death.

Is it any wonder that I wonder where she can be? With whom?

I am right where I want to be. At home. Waiting for her. Beginning to ache.

I leave the bed and go to her handbag, from which she'd taken money and keys. It is lying just where she had left it on the floor by a small bird-cage tea table we'd bought on a quilt-hunting trip to western New York. The inside of the bag is comfortably cluttered, but I have no trouble finding what I am looking for. It is her Week-at-a-Glance datebook, which, I must confess, I do not consider sacrosanct like her diary, though into which, I must further confess, I have not peeked before except on those occasions when she's shouted to me from bathroom or closet to check her schedule.

She has torn off the corners at the bottom of the pages so that, when the thumb encounters the first untorn page, the book opens exactly to this week. This evidence of Clara's precision makes me miss her all the more. Has there ever been someone so wanton and unrestrained who is also so punctilious? It is my duty to know her and my desire that she remain, finally, unknowable. It is like wanting to get to the bottom of something that has no bottom.

I'm amused to find myself thinking of Clara's bottom. There is probably no happier sign of her influence upon me than that my mind should concoct a play on words to lead me from my admittedly endless, frequently metaphoric, rumination on her meaning in my life to visions of her tight yet bouncy ass. I, who have seen so few asses in my time, and most of those in advertisements in her magazines, cannot imagine there is any that compares to hers. How, I wonder, could anyone be so captivated by those perky globules of fat that, putting aside their cushional and excremental functions, would seem to serve no purpose except, perhaps, to amuse? But what a world they are, unto themselves, soft and hard, big and small, manifest and inscrutable. And what they do with light! Simply by lying prone there on the bed, still and naked on a late-summer day like this one, as day fades to night, she teaches me to see how shadow is God's paint and the picture never done. The golden fuzz is brushed aside, the texture rendered eggshell pure but for a moment, when the consequence of darkness proves the subtlety of lust. I am drawn to touch, a sculptor, even I with these crude hands, but while she yields, she also bounces back. There is nothing I, or anyone far more divine, could do to fashion something more comfortably enticing. But it is wholly for admiration, not penetration. I shall not have to perform the ten days' bread-and-water penance decreed a thousand years ago by Bishop Burchard of Worms for having one's wife "*retro canino*." She will reach around to finger me like a flute along the narrow of her ass. Yet once she arches up and aims me, it's toward the moister, softer, more modestly cucullated hole. Thus we get to do the dance while wearing looser shoes. And what a sight it is, to hold her bottom in my hands and gaze up along the river of her spine and see her shoulders twitch and neck slither and head grind the pillows. Her hair's her face and thus expressionless, though still it says so much. Its very anonymity arouses me, and so primitive too it seems, fucoid in its swing and even in its reddish-olive coloring. Also different are the sounds she makes, more guttural, deeper, fundamental, mimicking this assward view of life and urgent in their calling to this unseen man behind her, whoever she might imagine him to be. I box her behind in my hands and push and pull her up and down, or is it back and forth, upon myself, and the view I have is unparalleled, panoptic, all of her and all of me until I disappear and she groans, "More."

But instead of her before me it's her Week-at-a-Glance. I still can't bear to look. And so I think instead of the absurdity of this, week-at-a-glance, and remember how on the day we met she pronounced my otiant life refreshing in contrast to all those others for whom time is best compressed and her beloved quilts some talismans of contemplation. I could probably get rich, I think— or richer, for the small need I have of money even in this most lucripetous of cities—by issuing Life-at-a-Glance, the perfect little datebook for the active man and woman to remind them how fugacious are their unreflective lives. How strange, I realize, that I then should have ended up a sensualist, knee-deep, and deeper still, ball-deep at least, brain-deep, yes, in what only the uninitiated think is fleeting. Marriage is eternal, and so must be its pleasures, all.

I start at the beginning of the week and see, in her mangled handwriting, which only I can read, some things I know and some I don't: she's eaten lunch out twice; she's reminded herself to have her teeth cleaned; she's leg-pressed some fifty times-plus more than what I weigh, which makes me smile; her period is late; her estimated tax is due today; she means to buy some lobster, perhaps to celebrate the end of summer, some six days from now, and I think I must then chill an old Climens, the full 750 ml, thereby to guarantee enough to take with us to bed, for nothing sweetens up a kiss like that unless it is vin santo; she's had to have, unseasonably, her air conditioning serviced; she's sold four quilts and bought two more; and now, tonight, right now, she's . . .

Nowhere, it would seem.

It's blank.

There's nothing there.

An empty space where there's an empty space.

It's as if my wife has stepped off the page and disappeared, like some character in a book who's killed off without warning.

Or perhaps she never left.

"Clara," I say, but this time not to a pillow. "Clara," I repeat.

If she's here, she doesn't answer.

I look at her Week-at-a-Glance again. But I've made no mistake. There is nothing written down for this evening. No name, no place, no time, no words.

It's blank. And what a strange and empty kind of silence this is. I would much prefer some man's name there and news she'll raise her skirt and rend her little pants to him, to this. I may be fool, but I have never worried losing her to someone else. Perhaps I have too little experience in these things. Perhaps I should assume the passion of a marriage cannot be contained and women dash like squirrels through the world in search of nuts to rest their chins upon.

Besides, I thrive on images of her in ecstasy. One's wife, particularly one so ophelimitous, deserves the universal cock. And every husband worthy of the word will serve it up.

But Clara be untrue?

The question has no meaning. No matter what she does, she's true, for I accept her as she is. What else is marriage but such approbation? It has no greater truth.

But if she's nowhere, then she can't exist.

I wonder if I've dreamt her. Might I still be a man alone who doesn't speak except within his head and even there says nothing true?

What if I don't exist myself? It feels I don't. Is this what it means when people say, "Without you I am nothing"?

But if I don't exist, then why this emptiness? Since when can nullity be palpable?

Or is this blankness yet another of her codes? Has she left me? Is she hiding? Has the Earth itself dissolved and I float here in the whiteness of this piece of page?

I close and drop the datebook on the bed and listen to my voice: "Clara."

Nothing.

"Clara."

The same.

I go in search of her.

FIRST HER BATHROOM, where I don't really expect to find her—or, in fact, any evidence of her whereabouts—but which I've always wanted an excuse to visit. I've not set foot within this necessary, as they call it up north from whence hails our Star of Bethlehem, since I stood here with our architect and contractor and watched a muscular young man titivate these tiles by chafing microscopic specks of grout with sandpaper so smooth it might as well be chamois. I've never run from images of life's necessities as they might be required of, or practiced by, my wife. Defecation, for all its fetid honks, is both sensual and cleansing, and Clara is not so verecund that she won't sit there with this door open and her elbows on her knees and address me standing at the door concerning this or that while in its midst. I hope that someday I shall stand at her feet in a delivery room and watch her open like a rose and, my bride and grume, spill forth the juice and blood of love and life. I have no fear of, or even distaste for, these bodily matters. Clara has taught me to accept the flesh. To do so is to find the way to heal the mind. There is no other. We are so beautifully constructed. Accept the flesh. Accept your limits. Love your mother.

Right now I must accept the fact that Clara's gone. Or at least not here in her bathroom.

I even pull aside the curtain of her bathtub, hesitantly, because I cannot help but see behind it what most I fear: her body drowned or bludgeoned, naked in her death. I have never understood why we flood ourselves with images of destruction. I am not a superstitious man. I don't believe I ward off fearful things by imagining them first. And yet I greet with considerable relief her bathtub empty, so much so that I sit down upon its lip and open each and every container she has lined up on its inner rim, shampoos, conditioner, bath salts, an uncorked, hand-blown, never-opened bottle of La Baignoire Graminaceous Foam Bath I had ordered for her by mail two years ago, and, in a box, lozenges that smell as if she's given them her scent.

Missing her intensely, I put each thing back precisely as I found it, rise, and look down into her bidet. I try to see my reflection in the slightly moist porcelain, yet I see nothing but a hair, a lonely, curly, lovely, precious little hair, fallen from my darling and, like me, most sad to be apart from her. I nearly pick it up, but then I think, You're identifying with a pubic hair. I laugh and try to blow the thing away, but it sticks, it waits, like me.

I've been told that people love to look in other people's medicine cabinets. It's like looking through their skin, behind their masks, an expiscatory search beneath the surface of their lives for what can only be their weaknesses, their maladies, addictions, their suffering. And of course there might be pills to steal, those that slow you down or bring you sleep the most popularly pilfered, according to Clara, who continues to maintain, in her indirect justification of this lentitudinous life her husband leads, that what the sedulous truly seek is rest, is peace, is tranquil contemplation of the truth.

There are no such pills here. There are no grand discoveries to make of some disease or pain that she would hide from me. Only some expired Tylenol, generic calcium carbonate whose use I'm sure she keeps from me because it's occasioned solely by my cooking, and Midol for her menstrual cramps, a recent malady and one whose intensity, though brief, is quite severe and which I try to soothe from her by rubbing gently on her stomach while we listen to Julian Bream play Silvius Leopold Weiss and talk of anything but the pleasures of pareunia.

I am about to close the cabinet when I see a strange container that's shaped rather like a toilet seat. Its color reminds me most of the soft peach light from my mother's spelter lamp that bathed a nameless girl and me that night four years ago when first she taught me how to see her love herself and me to love myself and let her watch.

I open it and find a ring of empty, wizened plastic bubbles surrounding a dial imprinted with the days of the week. I count the days and find that each comes thrice. Twenty-one days. Three weeks.

A Duane Reade, of all the provincial purveyors, prescription slip pasted to the inside top prescribes one tablet daily. The drug is, as is required, named: Ortho-Novum.

The *ortho* I know best is *orthography*, which is usually used to refer to proper spelling but whose antonym is *cacography*, a splendid word whose first meaning has not to do with spelling but bad handwriting. I would have thought, then, that Clara, to cure her own case of this malodorous *Kraut und Rüben*, might in fact be taking Caco-Novum. But no, it's Ortho-Novum, which, according to the description provided on a flimsy slip of paper by the Ortho Pharmaceutical Corporation, consists of norethindrone and ethinyl estradiol.

I should know from the "estra" what I'm dealing with here. But I read on and learn that these are contraceptives, which, the Ortho Pharmaceutical Corporation informs me, have a failure rate of less than 1 percent.

I wonder whose they are until I read Clara's name above her gynecologist's, Dr. Leslie, on the prescription slip pasted to the cover of this ghastly device.

They are hers. Or were. All twenty-one of them, three weeks' worth, leaving seven days in which to bleed without meaning and thus complete the lunar month that so attaches women to the heavens.

The instructions from the Ortho Pharmaceutical Corporation confirm this: "After you have taken your last tablet, wait for seven days. During these seven days your period should begin."

Clara is obviously clocking these matters. She notes within her Week-at-a-Glance that her period is late. But her periods don't last seven days. I should know. During them we limit sex to mouths and fingers, though less for the sake of fastidiousness than variety. And sometimes, when she is bleeding or, as happened on one occasion, when she was diagnosed by her gynecologist to have an infection and was kind enough to put aside her shyness to so inform me, we abstain altogether—taking a breather, as this might so aptly be called. Can she possibly expect to bleed with the very dawning of the day after she's pushed the final pill from out the back of this peculiar pink contraption? Punctilious indeed.

What to make of this? She takes them not to have a child, or should I say, falsely chiastic once again, to not have a child.

But is it mine she doesn't want or someone else's? Better the latter. I'd rather the squelching of a child of mine be inadvertent than purposeful, even if this means she is untrue.

But I have recently determined that Clara cannot be untrue.

So what is happening here?

I don't know where my wife is.

And now I don't know if I know my wife.

I feel her gone. At the same time, I feel her leaving me, not merely in the usual way a wife leaves a husband but *leaving me*, emptying out from me, as if I had contained her but now she leaks away.

Is this what marriage is, the containment of the other, the inhabiting of one another's being, and when one leaves, the other one's as vacant as an empty house?

But this is what I wanted! To see her. Apart from me. Out there, naked and unmasked.

I know just where to look.

THE DOOR TO her closet is not locked. I reach for the knob the way one does after tredding on carpets in winter. But I feel no shock. Only excitement. I am not supposed to be here. This is forbidden.

I am in. Today's clothes lie on the floor at the portal. I see that the underpants she put on to go out were fresh.

Where to begin? My wife's closet is like her little house, a place her life resides no matter where she's gone. I stand here at its entrance and suffer what we rhetoricians call aporia. As language first and foremost seeks the truth, or should, no matter how disquieting the truth may be, I do the same.

It's her diaries I'm after, but I don't know where they are, and now I feel she's written on each and every object in this place.

It smells of her in here, her skin, her hair, the sweet breeze of her breath. I love her clothes and touch them where they hang. I shut my eyes and feel her in them and miss her terribly.

Her shoes, like mine, show little wear. But I go nowhere, and she is gone all day, my emissary to the world. So is she made of air? Or do the earth and pavement cradle her and not exact their normal toll? And might time do the same? Will I not get to see her old and shrunk and white and frail? I want her aged, in time. I want to see her close enough to see her change, and changed, I even want, as perhaps did Louis Althusser his own beloved wife, to see her dead, to know that part of her, to have her all, though I would also like to die before her, so I won't die of missing her. So I won't feel the way I'm feeling now.

I would dig my way through the wet, wormy earth to lie with her again.

But I want her on that bed out there. I want her back. And she has left me. I am here in her closet with her clothes within my arms and my lips upon the bottoms of her shoes as if to glue her to my face.

I look through everything and find no diary. My fingers spider through her drawers. My hands raise dusty mist in the dark corners where they come upon the green, etched bottle that she's seemed to've saved from our first blessed night together in this place. My eyes leap from box to box and smart from mothball gas. This is archeology in pursuit of my own lost civilized self.

And now, once I've dug in everything and overturned each shard of Clara's broken life, I see, in absolute plain sight, piled across a table near the entrance to her closet, some scraps of quilt and each one covering a notebook.

I would like to think they've crept themselves from out some kame to mock my excavations, but I realize they were sitting here all the while, in plain sight, unhidden, to be near at hand for Clara to put down her days at night and waiting there for me as well to read upon a night like this when I was left alone, when I was left, when I had nothing left.

I chuckle at the mockery of it—you dig until you bleed to ascertain the meaning of your life and then find out the truth is written on the back of your hand.

There are so many of these little books, each one quilted, no seeming order to their jumble. I touch one for the first time since

121

the day I found one in the gutter and remember handing it to her and feeling her touch me through it. The memory of it now arouses me even more than the actuality of it then. Each time I touch her, no matter how many times, my desire to touch her yet again grows stronger. Love accumulates even as it is expressed and spent. As if that weren't paradox enough, it also tells me this: we have reached perfection together on the very night she has disappeared off the page of our common life.

I pick up one of the thin books. It's covered with a piece of a quilt called Cross in the Square. I look into it. Her unthirlable hand opens to me once again. The pricks of her twisted letters scratch my eyes. I jump into the middle of her life, wherever that might be, for nothing here is dated, she merely lies across the pages, and start to read.

I go through periods when there's a piece of my body missing. It's not a limb or an organ. It's something that doesn't exist but that I need back. Orgasms rip me apart. They put me back together. But I don't want to have them alone. I need someone to watch me.

Tonight there were 2 of them.

Ron I've been with before.

Ron talked me into this. He said, "I want my friend to see you."

"See me what?"

I knew what he meant. But Ron didn't know how to say it. Men are not good with words.

"I told him you

The door chimes. I throw down the book. It falls among its sisters, closed. I turn off the lights in her closet. Then I turn them on again. I've lost my place! Which book is it? A hundred scraps of quilt stare up at me.

She's at the door. And yet I'd rather read her words than hear her voice. I want my silence back.

The door chimes.

Why is she ringing her own bell?

I want to stay inside her closet. I want to read her books more than I've ever wanted to read any book. But I also want to see her one more time. I can't remember what she looks like.

The door chimes.

I leave the lights on in her closet but slam it shut and run all the way across the apartment. My legs feel heavy. My shoes are all wrong. Not just for running. They have always been wrong. Women have laughed at them. I run across the apartment and think of nothing else. If I think of Clara, I think of death. I think, My shoes are running to her.

The door chimes.

I pull it open. It swings out of my hand and past me and crashes violently against the wall.

Standing before me is a man. He is one of those pathetic young Orientals in a grayish-white shirt that's buttoned to the neck over his scrawny bones and shiny black pants that are too long and sneakers made by his slavish countrymen back home for wages that have subverted the American shoe industry. His eyes are dull behind surprisingly large glasses that sit halfway down his small nose, which lacks the bone-structured character to hold them up. Those eyes seem not even to have registered the violent slamming open of the door. He is passive and silent, a recent immigrant who speaks no English and whose lone skill is an ability to move his legs round and round on his bicycle pedals.

In his hands is a brown bag with a bill and menu stapled to the top. He holds it out to me. When I take it our hands touch. His feels greasy. I fear the food has leaked and will get all over my own hands and tie and our granite countertop. I lift the bag up over my eyes and see no grease. I wonder if the grease ever leaves his skin. I wonder if he ever washes.

I take the bag to the kitchen and place it in the smaller of our sinks. I look over at him unnecessarily: he has not moved. He knows at least not to step over the threshold. His eyes stare straight ahead, dull, showing no interest whatsoever in this magnificent space that's been opened up to him. I would like to push his glasses back up where they belong. But I appreciate his docility. And I deplore it. How can anyone bear to live with a mind so dead in a body as disposable as the cartons in which he delivers his food and which he will spend his life delivering until one day his greasy hands slip off his handlebars and he and his bike fall beneath the wheels of a bus?

I almost thank him for appearing when he has. My own life seems now at least slightly more reclaimable than his could ever be.

He waits. I look at the bill. I walk back to my closet and enter and find my eelskin wallet. I remove a fifty. This will provide him a huge tip, but I know that if I ask for change he will stare at me uncomprehendingly, not out of greed but out of ignorance of the very currency with which he is so foolish as to try to support himself in this country. But I am always munificent in this situation and never suffer over it as did my father because I never expect to see this man again and would not care to be recognized by him if I do.

I emerge from the closet. He waits where he waits. I walk toward him determined not to touch his hand again when I give him the money. I picture my fingers trailing grease through Clara's diaries.

As I pass him the money, I notice a different look in his eyes. Even through the tiny slits I can see they have come alive. He is looking over the rims of his glasses and beyond me into the loft. His nostrils have flared slightly against his glasses. There is the beginning of a smile on his plump lips.

I wonder if he thinks he can come back here one day to rob me when I am out. I want to tell him I am never out. I don't need to go anywhere. I have the perfect life. She comes home to me each evening. We talk. We eat. We talk. We fuck. We sleep the holy, guiltless, ataraxic sleep of marriage.

He takes the money almost reluctantly. Our hands don't touch. I look up for some acknowledgment, not of my largesse but of our simply standing here together in the doorway carrying out this most primitive of transactions. I notice his ears. They move up slightly even as I look at them, and as they move up they seem to open. I realize he is concentrating on something. It is the contracting of the muscles of his face that has caused his ears to levitate. Is he listening for someone else in the apartment? If he thinks I am alone will he kill me?

I am alone.

My wife has gone out for the evening—or should I say for the evering?

Kill me if you like.

He smiles a discreet, knowing smile. His lips thin out and open up and display perfect, brilliantly white teeth.

He says something. It is foreign. I hear the word and fail to hear the word.

I must look puzzled.

He says it again.

"Shostakovich."

"What?"

"Shostakovich. The F-sharp minor." His voice surprises me. It is soft, yes, but aggressive, arrogant. And by no inflection does it betray his tramontanity.

I listen to the music. I wonder if my own ears move. I realize I have heard nothing since I opened Clara's Week-at-a-Glance. It appalls me to think there was music playing and I heard not a note. I wasn't even aware of when the Shostakovich cello sonata ended and this string quartet began.

"How do you know?" I wonder if somehow he'd run into the apartment while I was in my closet and read the name off the jewel box.

"I know the piece." He measures the words out slowly.

"I meant," I say testily, "how do you know the piece?"

He looks at me blankly, with that Oriental calm. "I play it."

"Which recording do you have?" I ask reflexively. It is a relief to find myself with something to chitchat about, particularly in the secure realm of musical small talk.

"The Manhattan," he replies. "But I meant I *play* it."

"Play it?"

"What's the matter with you, man? Am I not making myself clear? I *play* it. I'm a musician."

"You're a musician?"

"No, I'm a Chinese delivery boy."

"I thought you said—"

"I am a musician. I study music. I am *also*"—he is speaking slowly, as if talking to a child—"a person who delivers food."

"Why?"

"Why what?"

"Why do you deliver food?"

"Because people like you are too lazy to go out and get it."

"I never go out," I confess.

"I wouldn't either."

"You wouldn't?"

"Not if I could afford to stay home and listen to Shostakovich."

"Is that why you deliver food? For the money?"

"No," he answers. "I do it to meet interesting people."

I take that as a compliment. "Thank you."

"But I never do," he says.

I must look hurt, because he explains, "I was being sarcastic."

"I see."

He looks at the fifty, still in his greasy fingers. "You want change?"

What an interesting question. I think, yes, I want my wife back.

"For this." He waves the bill.

"No."

He looks suspiciously at the money before he slides it into the pocket of his shapeless pants.

"The food was late," he says, as if trying to fathom the perversity of my improvidence. "Hang told you it would take half an hour. 'Okay thirty minutes, mister, okay.' Right?"

His imitation of the man on the phone is perfect. Finally, he sounds Chinese. His own voice, without accent, sounds out loud the way I sound to myself within.

I don't care for mimicry, or otherwise I might well laugh at how he does this Hang. But I do say, "Right."

"It never takes thirty minutes. It takes thirty minutes to get the food out of the kitchen, forget onto the bikes and through the fucking streets. 'Thirty minutes mister, okay.' He doesn't know what thirty minutes is. Hang has no sand in his hourglass, if you know what I mean."

"No need to apologize," I say.

"I wasn't." He turns and walks out my door.

I follow him and actually put one foot outside the apartment before I say, "What do you play?"

As soon as I say it, I pull my foot back in. I realize how frightened I am to step into the life I led before I met Clara.

He turns back to face me. I can see behind him the pale button of a light that indicates he's pressed it to summon the elevator.

"Music," he answers.

"I meant, what instrument?"

"Violin."

"I used to play the violin." I remember Clara saying, "I'd like to see it," but meaning my apartment.

"No shit," he says, as if the world were full of violinists.

The elevator arrives. Its door opens. He steps in.

"I still have my violin," I call after him. "I'd like to show it to you."

He is in the elevator now and facing directly toward me. He has to hold the door open with his hand, or it will close automatically.

"I see enough violins," he says.

"It's a Carlo Bergonzi," I entice.

"Oh, really?"

"Do you know Bergonzi?"

"Didn't Al Pacino play him?"

"I'm afraid I don't know . . ."

"Al Pacino," he repeats.

"Is he a violinist?"

"You don't know who Al Pacino is?"

"No, I don't. Do you know who Carlo Bergonzi is?"

"Never heard of him."

"You don't know Carlo Bergonzi!"

He shakes his head. "I don't care who made your violin. Mine was a gift to my school from a benefactor in Connecticut. I love the way it sounds. I don't know who made it."

"But it's not a Bergonzi?" I ask.

"I wouldn't know."

"I'd like to give you my Bergonzi."

Instead of running out of the elevator and right back into the loft to claim his prize, he looks as if all he wants is to escape.

He shakes his head at me again.

"It's worth hundreds of thousands of dollars," I say. For all I know, it's worth millions.

"Right."

"You don't believe me, do you?"

"About what?"

"About anything. About my violin. That I even have one. That I ever played it. That it's a Carlo Bergonzi. That I want to give it to you."

"Why should I believe you?"

"Because I tell the truth."

"People don't give away violins." He still doesn't believe me.

"And that man from Connecticut?" I say like a lawyer trying mightily to prove a point.

"It was a woman," he says wearily. "And that was a tax thing."

"The last thing I'm worried about is the IRS," I tell him. "They think I'm a diaskeuast, for God's sake. I don't want a deduction. I don't want a receipt for value. I just want to give you the violin. What are you afraid of?"

"Nothing," he answers. But he doesn't leave the elevator.

I realize what I must look like to him. So much larger than he, my eyes undoubtedly filled with a desperation he cannot understand, my huge hands gripping the door frame.

"I'm not going to rob you," I say. "I have more money than I can ever spend. And neither am I going to make you eat the food you brought."

He is amused by that. I am so pleased he is amused by that.

He leaves the elevator. "Where's the violin?"

"Please come in," I say.

The elevator door shimmies closed behind him. As I lock us in my apartment, I say, "There is one condition."

He looks at me with his eyes so tight they are hardly eyes at all. "What're you, negotiating?"

"You have to play it for me first," I tell him.

He turns back to the door.

"What's the matter?" I ask.

"I have enough auditions in my life."

"Think of it as practice."

I get a smile from him. "You sound like my teacher."

"Who's your teacher?"

"What difference does it make?"

Beneath his antagonism, I sense a certain modesty or arrogance, which I realize can be indistinguishable.

"No difference," I answer placatingly. "I just wondered if I might be familiar with him."

"Her," he says pointedly.

"A woman," I say idiotically.

"Yes, of course a woman." As if further to prove his point, he names her: "Dorothy DeLay."

"Oh, you're at Juilliard."

"Yes, I'm at Juilliard," he says indifferently, wholly unimpressed with the fact that I might have heard of his teacher and know where she teaches. I suppose that when you live in the world of music, just as when you live in the world of language, you cannot imagine that what you know isn't known universally. Why not expect that the humblest laborer at his jackhammer would whistle the *Dumky* and know Dorothy DeLay? Why should we have to live in a world where more people know the wind-chill factor than the *Winterreise*?

"She is supposed to be the best," I say to flatter him so he will stay, though my flattery isn't excessive, for she is said to be a brilliant teacher.

"She's a better teacher than I am a violinist."

"And if you become a better violinist than she is a teacher . . . ?"

"That'll only mean that she's become a better teacher."

"Well put," I say and wonder if such pithy profundities are passed on within the Oriental gene pool, though this boy hardly seems Chinese beyond his appearance.

"Thank you," he says and comes toward me in the middle of

the room. Here he is a musician, and it's praise of his ability to speak that captures his attention.

"Where are you from?" I ask. "If you don't mind my saying so, you really don't sound Chinese."

"I'm from Queens, and I really would appreciate it if you would pronounce it right."

"*Queens?*"

He laughs. His laugh is deep. I would have expected a giggle from so slight a boy. "Not *Queens*. *Chinese*. It doesn't rhyme with *release or geese* the way you said it. It rhymes with *ease* or *cheese* or *freeze*. Chinese."

"Ease or cheese or freeze," I repeat. And then, to befuddle him in order to cover my own embarrassment at my apparent mispronunciation, I ask, "Is that *freeze* or *frieze?*"

"Is that what or what?"

"Is that *freeze* or *frieze?*"

"Yeah, it's freeze or frieze. Or freeze and frieze. Or just plain freeze. Or just plain frieze. Like I'm just plain Chinese."

"From Queens," I say.

"From Queens," he reiterates.

"They're homophones," I tell him.

"They're what?"

"Homophones."

"What're homophones?"

"*Freeze* and *frieze*, naturally."

"What are homophones? I assume we're not talking Nynex here."

Now I laugh. "No, we're not talking Nynex, though what an interesting name that would be for a new language. The language spoken over the phone. I don't use the phone much myself, but I'm sure it has, in certain subtle ways, a language all its own, a rhetoric, a rhythm, an etiquette."

I think of Clara and that implicit sexual play on *homophone* she concocted—my mind is playing word games of its own—that night of the day we met and only moments before she raised her legs and removed her tights and socks.

"What's the matter?" he asks me.

"Why?"

"Your lips were moving and you weren't saying anything."

I clap my hand to my mouth. "Really?"

"It was peculiar, man." He puts his delicate hand to his own mouth to try to quell his amusement.

"Homophones," I explain, "are words that are spelled differently but are pronounced the same and mean different things. *Freeze* and *frieze*, for example."

What greater antidote against laughter than pedagogy? Now he just nods his head in a pretense of interest.

How am I going to keep him here? I'm in no hurry to get the violin for him. Then he'll just take it and leave. I can't even force him to play it for me.

"Sit down." I lead the way to the sprawling leather couches in the middle of the loft, but I don't know if he follows. He steps so lightly in his homely sneakers. He makes no sound. I cannot feel him through the floor.

But when I turn, he's there, and when I sit, he sits. I am filled with great comfort. Across from me, he nearly disappears into the supple skin. He is becoming a part of the room.

"How did you get to Queens?" I ask, hoping that autobiography will long-wind him.

"Subway."

"That's not what I meant," I reply sharply.

"I know."

He is playing with me. I don't care. Just to have him here. I have never known this loneliness before. It's so much worse to be left alone than simply to be alone.

We sit in silence. As long as he doesn't leave. We look at each other. Or I look at him. I cannot tell what he looks at or sees. His eyes are withdrawn like a snake's.

"I'm third generation." His voice itself seems part of the silence we have created. I am soothed by it. "American. My grandparents came over here from Taiwan. On both sides. Years ago. My father's family is from Taipei. My mother's parents came from Taichung. Do you know anything about Taichung?"

"Nothing." I am grateful.

"It's up among the lakes. The Sun-Moon region. They told me it is the most beautiful place on earth. More beautiful than the Vale of Kashmir. More beautiful than Queens." He laughs. "That's all I heard about when I was little and they were still alive. Sun-Moon. That's what they called me. Sun-Moon. And that became Sonny."

"What is that in Chinese?" I take care to pronounce it correctly.

"English," he says contemptuously. "That's what they called me in English."

"It's a good name," I compliment him. "Night and day."

"Day and night," he corrects me.

"What's your real name?" I ask.

"One Gone Jew."

I must look surprised. "What did you expect, Henry Ding-Dong?"

I shake my head. "Will you spell your name for me."

"W-u-n G-o-n J-e-w. Jew is a common Chinese name. And yet few Chinese are Jewish."

"I don't imagine so," I respond.

"It's a *joke*." He's not laughing now. He seems angry with me. I still don't get his joke, and I ask him, "Are you Jewish?"

Now he laughs, deeply, almost uncontrollably. I wait for him to stop. At first his laughter hurts me. But then I realize he thinks I've made a joke and clearly a brilliant one at that.

133

"Buddhist," he says when he can speak again. He actually bows his head slightly when he says the word, in a rather enviable gesture of humility.

"I don't know much about it," I say, "except that George Steiner wrote about the Buddhist belief that the soul becomes purified through silence. He named that book *Language and Silence*, so I gravitated to it like a seed to an egg. It was very comforting to me to read that at the time I did. What do you believe?"

He looks up at me over his glasses. "Believe," he asks, "or believe in?"

"There's no difference."

His eyes narrow. "If I had to believe in the things I believe, I'd die. It's the difference between faith and resignation."

I am unconvinced by his philosophizing, but I don't want to argue with him, out of fear that he will stop talking. So I concede: "What do you believe *in* then?"

"Salvation." He seems to like the idea of it. He smiles contentedly. "In this life. Not in the next. Not like you Christians." I listen for some echo of contempt, but all I hear is the dullness of fact.

"What saves you?" I try to guess. Music. Sex. No longer for me knowledge of anything that comes in through the mind. Rather the breathing of one's beloved in the sable warmth of sleep.

"Enlightenment," he answers. "Through the spirit. We say the body is like froth. A mirage. Accept that, and you'll never see the king of death."

"I was dead once."

"Really," he replies. I can't tell if it's a question.

"Are you married?" I ask.

Nothing seems to surprise this man. It's as if his mind is working like my own, has attached itself to my own. He shakes his head. He smiles. "I'm pure," he answers.

I don't understand this. I shake my head.

He leans toward me. "We believe that the suffering in life is caused by desire, and the only way to end your suffering is through self-purification."

"Oh," I say, "ascesis."

Now it's he who's puzzled. "What?"

"Ascesis. That's what I've practiced my whole life. Someone once even called me an ascetic priest. Saint Johnny of Ascesis."

He nods now. He understands what I'm talking about. "In the Dhammapada it says that if you hold a blade of grass wrong, it cuts your hand, and if you practice asceticism wrong, you go to hell."

"That's where I am now."

I expect him to mock such hyperbole, but he is somber when he says, "I can tell. You seem so . . . so . . ." For the first time, he falters in his speech. He can't find the word he's looking for. His face grows foreign.

"Weak?" I say.

"Fragile."

He gets up. I'm afraid he is going to leave. But he goes not toward the door; he comes toward me.

He sits down with me on the couch. He takes my hand. His is dry, almost cold.

"What's the matter?" he asks.

It is such a touching question. It seems the perfect formulation of words.

"My wife is gone."

He pushes his glasses atop his tiny nose and gazes at me through them. It must be how he reads.

"Marriage." He looks to either side of me as if to imagine her there. But he cannot see her any more than can I. We are alone together here. "She left you?"

Not in the way he means. "No."

"Oh. Gone." He looks stricken, almost ashamed. I am learning to read through the indecipherability of his face. "She's dead?"

I have no words to answer that. I shake my head.

"Another man?"

I laugh.

He drops my hand. He thinks I'm laughing at him, his naïveté or cynicism or whatever it might be that would cause him to suspect one's wife would be with another man, when all I was laughing at was the redundancy of it.

"I deliver things," he says emphatically.

"I'm afraid I don't . . ." But then I realize what he means. I picture him in his business, riding up on his bike, carting his greasy food up stairs, let in, paid, and every once in a while, rarely, perhaps, but sometimes, surely, told he's wanted, told in one way or another, a word, a wink, a gesture, a raising of a skirt and a spreading of legs. I know this goes on in the world. I know it exists somewhere else outside my head. I can see him with Clara, entering her from above, his silver buttocks swimming through the air, her hands alight like sconces on his shoulder blades as she smiles at me from where her head nestles in his neck and calls out to both of us, "Fuck me, Johnny."

Wun Gon Jew says, "The Hindus say that the fiend of lust takes advantage of solitude."

"You don't have to explain," I answer. "I'm not as naïve as I may look. I knew what you were referring to. When you say you deliver things, you mean you come upon women who want you to fuck them." I swell proudly over my use of such Paphian language.

"Men."

"What?"

"Men," he repeats. "It's usually men."

"They want you to fuck their wives?"

He looks at me as if I can hardly be the man who only moments before was grieving over the absence of his wife. He is shocked. He has seen into my mind and misunderstood completely what I have been picturing there.

"They want to fuck me."

"The wives?"

"The *men*." His impatience is manifest, but it is balanced between humor and exasperation.

Life is far worse than I have thought it. His life. Even mine. I had pictured him some ruptuary, nameless, faceless, speechless, come to me with food, and he turns out to know a thing or two, to be able to say, "Shostakovich," and to take my hand when I am suffering.

Now it is I who takes his hand.

"Please," he says.

"Please what?"

"Please let go."

I do. "Sonny, I'm sorry."

He stands up. He says nothing, yet I know he is leaving. But he is not sure how to make his exit. I remember from my days in the world how hard it was to make exits. Meeting was awkward enough, but how to separate bodies or gazes or even voices on the phone once contact had been made remained a mystery to me. It was probably one of the reasons I went into retreat. I have never learned how to suffer with grace the shock of departure.

"I'll get your violin now."

That stops him. He seems either to have forgotten about it or not to have believed me in the first place.

I go into my closet. I know where to find the violin because I know where to find anything at all in my closet. But it takes me some time, for the violin is not so much hidden as buried away. Its associations are, to say the least, painful.

I worry that he won't be there when I emerge. I worry that he will have left and taken with him absolutely nothing.

But when I come out into the vast room holding the violin in its case with one hand and the bow in its sheath with the other, he is still there, though he's moved and in fact is moving still, walking along the far wall and looking up at it with his chin in his hand and his glasses down at the end of his nose like someone in an art gallery.

He becomes aware of my presence and turns around and says, "These quilts are beautiful. My grandmothers were seamstresses. They worked machines in the sweatshops. But they would have loved this stitching. It's so unbelievably intricate. It's like looking at a score for the first time. I wish they could have seen these things. They went to their graves saying that nothing beautiful had ever been made by American fingers."

I put down the violin case and bow on one of the Seymour brothers' Federal worktables and am drawn to where he stands, though whether by him or by the quilts themselves I cannot say. We stand together silently beneath them. We are directly before the Sunshine and Shadow quilt that Clara bought on a trip we took to Pennsylvania. I look into the spread of its irradiating diamonds of light and color until I become dizzy and have to close my eyes. This has never happened to me before. I grasp his arm and speak.

"This is all Clara's. All this beauty. She has the most amazing eye." I keep my own eyes closed. "Everything about me is internal—words, sounds, images of things I can't even manage to see. I'm a self-indulgent impressionist. That's what Santayana called Nietzsche. That's what he called himself. In a letter to a Mrs. Toy. T-o-y. Perhaps she was Chinese. Clara is not like me. There's a reality to her. Her body is the only thing I've ever been able to hold onto on this earth. Even that violin I couldn't . . . She has the most remarkable physical presence. That's what I'm trying to say. I wish she would just come home. I wish she would just walk through that door over there and you could meet her and we could listen to music together. Shostakovich. Steppenwolf. I don't care."

As I'm talking, I realize I probably sound like a lunatic going on about my wife and expect to feel Wun Gon Jew pulling out of my grasp to run toward the door toward which I am pointing. But he doesn't move at all, except to quiver in my hand, and when I open my eyes I find him trying to suppress laughter.

"Steppenwolf?"

"Not the Hesse," I explain. "The—"

Now Wun Gon Jew pulls away from me, not to run but to execute delicate little dance steps next to me in his horrid sneakers, and as he dances, he sings: "Why don't you come with me, little girl, on a magic carpet ride."

"That's it!" I shout.

He stops dancing. He stops singing. He does laugh now.

"She *loves* that song."

"Maybe she is real," he says.

"Maybe she is," I agree.

"Do you have a photo of her?"

"No."

"You don't have a photo of your own wife?"

I am getting irritated. "I told you no. I don't believe in photography."

I have never owned a photograph in my life. I don't like what they do to people. You see too much in them, the past, the future, a dozen faces frozen into one. This is stasis that shuts off life like a stopcock. Among my mother's effects were photographs of me. I looked into my pretty, pudgy baby face and saw a bit of her and some of him and gagged, literally. I threw them all away.

"It's not music," he agrees.

"No, it's not."

"So what does she look like, this wife of yours?"

I try to see her, but, as always, I fail. I can feel her in me, but I can't picture her.

"I don't know," I confess.

"Does she look like that?"

This startles me. I look toward the door, thinking she's come quietly home and he's seen her. But the door stands closed, bleak against the night.

I look back at him and see him pointing, not toward the door but toward the eastern part of the northern wall, where some Madonnas hang.

He walks toward them. I follow him. We stand beneath these holy mothers and look at them together. His eyes are up, and yet his head is bowed. His glasses touch his upper lip.

He's found her image. Not in one but shared among several: the condescending serenity of Raphael's Virgin of the Fish; the comforting intelligence of Botticelli's Madonna who closes her eyes so that the urchinlike John the Baptist can engage ours; and most of all van Hemmessen's sensual, pouting, permed seducer, whose lids are heavy with expended bliss, whose brows are so delicate a snake might have licked them into place, who rests her splendid face upon the caressing fingers of her beloved son.

"I see her," I say, in a way that I hope adequately expresses my gratitude.

"Who did that one?" He points.

"Botticelli."

"Look at that boy."

"John the Baptist."

"Rough trade." He reaches up and runs his fingers over the pronounced angles of the boy's suffering face. He does look like a child who has been, or will be, beaten. "I wonder if anyone has ever changed religions because of the art."

"I can't think of a better reason." In fact, I can't think of any other reason to change one or even have one. Art and fucking, those most private of divertissements, seem the only transcendences. Everything else just keeps you glued to the procrustean loam.

"So where is she?" he asks.

"There. There. There." I point to one painting after another.

He turns from the wall. "I mean where has she gone, this wife of yours? You said she's gone. But she hasn't left you. She isn't dead. And she's not with another man. Where is she?"

He is aggressive in his questioning. He refuses to believe she exists.

"Come."

I go to the bed. He follows me, though I still cannot feel him through the floor.

I sit. He stands before me. I notice for the first time that his shiny, shapeless pants are held up by a piece of rope. I remain so forlorn at Clara's absence that I think again of the hangman.

"Sit, please." I even pat the quilt.

He does sit. Not near me, but at least I finally feel his weight, like some discrete quop of rain on the vast inland sea of my being.

He is the first person, Elspeth aside, who has touched our bed. He is no fantasy, this one, but a real if insubstantial man who's all I have left. I look at him and want him to be Clara, but I know he's not. I want to take him in my arms and bury myself within him, my entire being, but I shall not. He is afraid of me, he seems almost to cower. This is so unlike Clara, my malapert, who beckons me with every glance and gesture, knowing, as she does, that I cannot get enough of her and would wither and die if ever I did.

I reach behind me for Clara's Week-at-a-Glance.

"Come closer."

He inches toward me, and to mask his fear he says, "This is the biggest bed I've ever seen."

I picture his own bed, as narrow as he, chaste in his purity, but it's Clara I see in it, naked, knees apart, floating away toward the horizon, watching me disappear.

"What size is it?" he continues.

"Do you know what piece of music first had the cadenza written out?"

He understands, but he seems to find it fatuous. "This is your empire?"

"I live in this bed. I listen to music. I read. I think. I wait for Clara."

"How long?"

"Nine feet."

I think he's going to ask me where we get sheets for it and is it actually square, but he says, each word distinct, as if I were trying his patience, "How long have you been waiting for her?"

I look at the clock beside the bed. "Almost four hours."

He shakes his head. "That's all? I thought you were going to say all your life."

"Almost four hours," I repeat.

"That's nothing."

"It's not the time." For it isn't.

"Then what is it?"

I open Clara's Week-at-a-Glance and point to the empty space that's now, this minute we are sitting here together on the bed.

"What the hell is that?" He puts his finger down into the thicket of her words.

I feel him touching her. His eyes follow his fingers over the tortured scordatura of her writing.

"Her appointments."

"Can you read this?"

"Yes."

He looks at me with the same perplexed expression with which he's been trying to read her writing. "So what does it say? Where is she?"

"It's what it doesn't say." I point again to the empty space.

I can see his narrow eyes working to avoid being caught within the net of her language. They struggle to escape but cannot. I wonder what he sees. Etymologically cognate here are Oriental and orientation. Mankind looked to the East, as it were, to find out where he stood, to locate the truth.

"There's nothing there," he says.

I nod. "'The depths lie on the surface.'"

He looks up at me, surprised. "Buddha?"

"Nietzsche."

"There's nothing there," he repeats, as if to tell me that he finally understands.

I feel like sobbing. Had I expected him to supply her there, to bring her back to life, manifest within lines pressed from her pencil? Instead he merely corroborates the truth. It's as if she's stepped off the edge of the earth. I can feel her gone. I am filled with the absence of her.

How can I make him understand what this emptiness means?

"The Lamas," he says, "have what are called their elegant sayings. One of them's about the astronomer who can calculate the movements of the moon and the stars, but he doesn't know that in his own house the women are misbehaving."

Why do I take such delight in this? It is so distracting an image: the sky is so vast, it must be the only thing in nature that we may speak of as full and empty at the same time, plenum and vacuum, unless it is the heart of one whose love has gone; the misbehaving woman is so tight before the eyes. I can almost see her.

"Maybe she doesn't want you to know where she is," he says. "Or maybe you don't even have a wife."

He is frustrated, so he strikes out at me. He persists in thinking I'm some vecordious husband with no wife to his name sitting here alone at the top of the city in the midst of music and the smell of Chinese food that's colliquating in the sink.

"Maybe I don't," I say. "But I did."

He looks again at the empty space in her datebook. He touches it now and looks up at me.

"Yes," he says, as if he finally comprehends. "Sometimes people just go away. They disappear. Most people you see you see for the last time in your life. Like me, for instance."

With that, he rises from the bed.

"Where are you going?"

"You were my final delivery. I've got to take my bike back."

More quickly than I have ever moved—for I am a man who is nothing if not deliberate in what I do and say, as it is wise to be in contention with a culture in which speed is valued over depth, and action over thought—I am on my feet and have pushed him back toward the bed. As he falls from my hands with so little resistance to the air he seems no more than air himself, I am given an image of him flying back up with his body like a deadly letter *E*, a martial artist fulfilling the stereotype of his race. But as he hits the bed, he curls up so tightly I think he is going to fit completely into one of the wedding rings on the quilt.

"Don't." His voice remains surprisingly manly, given his embryonic attitude.

"Don't what?"

"Hurt me."

"I won't." I see him try to look at me, but his glasses are askew with the side of his face pressed into the quilt.

"Where are you going?" Apparently he can see me. There is desperation in his voice, as if now it is he who does not want to be abandoned.

I walk away.

"Why did you throw me down?" he calls after me.

I say nothing until I return. He remains voluted on the bed, encased like a snail in his virtue. "Here."

His eyes are closed. "Where?" He doesn't know what I'm talking about. He shifts his body uncertainly.

"No, *here*."

He opens his eyes now and squints at the violin case I'm

holding toward him. As if he can't believe what he sees, he pushes himself up with one arm and with his other hand adjusts his glasses on his tiny nose. "You can't be serious."

"You promised," I say, putting the burden on him to play and removing from me the much simpler one of bequeathing him this violin in what he perceives to be, to judge from his last words, the zaniest of xenial gestures.

He stands up. He straightens his shapeless pants, tucks his colorless shirt beneath his rope, and in so doing seems to regain his dignity. "No I didn't."

He's right. "Nonetheless," I say, "we have a deal."

"No we don't."

"Yes, we do. You have to play it for me."

"And then what?" He is still uncertain.

"And then it's yours. If you want it, of course. Go ahead. Open it up. Take a look at it. Here. I'll take out the bow."

I put the grip of the violin case into his hand. I can see he thinks of laying it down upon the bed, but instead he carries it over to one of the flame-bark worktables.

I follow him and walk around to the other side of the table so I can watch.

When he sees the violin, he closes his eyes and brings his palms together at his breast.

"It's so beautiful," he whispers.

"Here's the bow," I find myself whispering in turn.

He opens his eyes and parts his hands and holds them out to receive the bow.

"Where did this come from?" He is whispering no longer.

"From me to you."

He smiles slyly, as if he's caught me out. "I mean its provenance."

"German," I answer. "From the 1650's. The violin is Italian, of course, and younger—1773, a mere 220 years old. The bow had a fixed frog originally, but after a hundred years that was replaced with this Cramer nut. Otherwise it's no different from how it was three and a half centuries ago. It's older than Bach."

"What a stick." He holds it straight out in his right hand. "It's heavy."

"Snake wood."

"Not Pernambuco?"

I shake my head. "Snake wood."

"It must be stiff."

I see my anguine cock slithering up the inside of Clara's thigh. I'm tempted to make a play on those words but remain musical: "Polyphony was all the rage."

"Perfect." His narrow eyes shine.

Just like a violinist to pay more heed to the bow than the box. Just like a man as well, now that I think of it.

He puts down the bow and carefully takes the violin from its case. He holds it to his ear and plucks a string. Then he looks at the strings and plucks them all. "Gut E and A," he pronounces. "Wound D and G."

"Yes." As if I didn't know.

"How long have these strings been on?"

"Forever." Like everybody else, I reduce eternity to my own span. "Since I last played."

He picks up the bow and resins it and draws it across the strings. "Can I adjust the tuning to $a' = 415$?"

"Be my guest."

As he tunes the instrument, I wonder what he's going to play. I wonder also if he will be worthy of this gift, the sight of which has awakened in me memories of jubilation and longing and embarrassment and failure. I remember screaming for my mother to come rescue me. I realize for the first time that when I stopped playing the violin, I stopped doing, acting, and began being. It was the beginning of my downfall and my salvation. I shut the door into the world and opened the door into myself. And no one has walked through that door but Clara. And now this boy.

He surprises me by putting the violin back in its case and the bow on the table. I prepare to throw my arms around him to keep him here when he says, "Is there some place I can wash my hands? They get all greasy from my job."

I can't let him wash his hands in the kitchen, for the bag of food he delivered is still sitting there in one of the sinks, and I don't want him to have to suffer the humiliation of confronting what he's forced to do to support his music. So I point toward the closed door of my bathroom.

"Be right back," he says and goes into the bathroom and locks the door behind him.

Little does he know what privacy of mine he has invaded. No one but Elspeth has ever been in that room, except for Clara on several occasions when she's surprised me by coming into the shower and soaping me. There is something, she implies—and it is obvious—particularly exciting about the sight of semen flying off in its pure, inspissated whiteness into the lean, cleansing clarity of water.

While he's gone I listen again to the music that's playing. I know I must turn it off but cannot bear to just yet.

"Excuse me."

I have not heard him return. He is standing next to me with the violin and bow in his hands.

"Listen," I say.

"I know the piece. I told you."

"Listen," I say again.

We stand there next to one another, listening. The quartet is coming to an end with an almost deviant waltzlike rhythm. Tears come to my eyes.

Silence.

I put the machine on Pause. "Shostakovich wrote that the year I was born, 1960."

He cocks his head and looks at me over the angle of his glasses. His gaze might be considered prurient were I not entering him at a diagonal. Or is this some Buddhist way of skewering the flesh over the coals of oblique curiosity?

My eyes go dry. My skin tightens. It has taken him this long to notice me. I feel sucked into his languid being as through a straw. He sees into me and finds beneath my stolid clothes the emptiness that I've been left in Clara's wake.

He could bring me to my knees by lowering his head, so caught up am I in how he looks at me, but he straightens his neck and levels off his eyes and lets me go and says, "I thought you were older."

I don't know whether to interpret this as praise or insult, but I'm delighted nonetheless to find he'd thought me anything. I cannot have him go out into the night with just the violin and nothing of the man who played it years ago when he was innocent and yet to become a living dissonance.

I pretend to ignore his remark and return to the music. "Shostakovich wrote it in memory of Nina Vasilyevna. His wife. It's felt by some that the piece marks the beginning of his withdrawal into himself."

"He must have missed her."

Finally! He knows now that I have told the truth, and he accepts it.

"Victor Ledin described that waltz at the end as Shostakovich's last dance with his departed wife."

"Yes."

In his concurrence I can feel my own wife in my arms as we dance near the abyss. I close my eyes and stare.

Then the music begins.

It is the chaconne from Bach's D minor partita.

I realize that when he'd said, "Perfect," he was referring not to the bow but to the piece he had chosen at that instant to play for me.

I have never heard anything so beautiful in my life. The music leaves him and enters me. I am one with it and him.

I open my eyes and see that his are closed, even as he makes his way through this longest by far of the movements Bach wrote for the solitary violin.

His ears move as he plays, as he listens to himself playing.

So involved is Sonny in the music he makes that he doesn't see or hear me go to the closet or return with the 2-Pound Camp Wonder.

And when I bring it forth against the back of his neck, he doesn't know what hits him.

Who does?

I HAVE HIT him not with the blade of the hatchet but with the hammer on the opposing side of the blade.

There is no blood. The force of the blow itself has delivered him from this world of unrest to the world of peace.

I carry his almost ethereally light body into my closet and place him gently on his back on the floor. Then I return and get the violin and bow, neither of which has suffered from the fall out of his profoundly accomplished hands.

I visit him once more in the closet and place the violin and bow across his breast. I smile when I see his glasses fallen one last time to the end of his nose, and I push them up to cover his eyes, behind which, closed, there might still sound the music he was playing when he died.

I am aware of being watched as I do this.

The bust of Nietzsche gazes upon me as I kneel beside this lonely, gifted boy.

Tell him, I want to say, tell him what you know: that dying is

149

not a slander. That one should make a feast out of one's death. That all that is ripe wants to die. That all that is perfect wants to die, and he became perfect. Tell him and tell me too that since one is certain to die, why should one not be gay?

In the silence that once again invades me and surrounds me, I rise and leave and go back to the lighted closet of my life.

12 A.M.

I am lying in bed, waiting for the music.

The remote is at my fingertips. Clara's diaries are spread around me over the quilt. The phone is on my stomach.

I may, on the one hand, seem the very definition of cunctation—indecisive, lazy, dilatory, as if I have all the time in the world to choose my weapon—but on the other I am a virtual paradigm of communication: music and writing and speech are all, literally, within my grasp, and what, after all, is the essence of life if not communication, or at least of my life? It is not praxis that makes perfect, as my father would have it; rather periphrasis, as long as it may take, the circling around of the truth until it is bound up inescapably in knowledge and acceptance and its own expression of itself.

We are here to tell each other why we are here. There is no higher calling.

Nor any more painful. So to ease the vivisepulturial nature of this vocation, we are given music and love.

With love flown, I choose music. A remote control is the penis on the body of aestheticism: hold it, touch it, press it, and it delivers immediate pleasure.

Releasing the Pause (if only human beings came equipped with same), I hear again the perfect music at the perfect time: the joy and tragedy of life contained within a single evening to the perspicuous accompaniment of congruous sound.

In the opening duet of Pergolesi's *Stabat Mater*, the soprano and alto sing of a mother's tears mingling with the blood of her son as she stands beneath the cross on which he hangs.

The *Stabat Mater* is sung today today. Or yesterday, as it happens, September 15, on the Feast of the Seven Sorrows, and I would be hearing it yesterday and not today, the brand-new September 16, if I had not spent so much time with the boy who delivered my dinner, for which I have no stomach at this moment, or if Clara had come home on the day she left or never left at all.

The Feast of the Seven Sorrows is also known as the Sorrows of the Blessed Virgin and is celebrated as the Feast of Our Lady of Sorrows. Among her seven heartaches, all having to do with her son, were, of course, those relating to the Passion; the days she was apart from him when he was a rebellious teenager among the Jews in the Temple; and the prophecy of Simeon, during the circumcision, when Simeon proclaimed her boy was destined for something monumental. Aside from the fact that, like Sonny, I'm not Jewish myself, although I am circumcised, I doubt very much that the doctor who presided at the ceremony burdened my own mother with a similar vaticination. Nothing much seems to have been expected of me. And until today—yesterday, as it now turns out—I had done virtually nothing that would attract attention.

Even Pergolesi had accomplished more, and he was surely not much older than Wun Gon Jew when he died, at twenty-six, and nearly as poor and obscure, for like Schubert's, Pergolesi's fame was posthumous. This very *Stabat Mater* was written on his deathbed. And as I listen to it on what I hope will be my own deathbed (for this is where I want to spend, and end, my days), I think of Sonny's mother, whoever she may be, and of my own mother, whoever she may be.

I am rehearsing my phone call when the phone itself explodes on my stomach. Its dry gargle joins the lament of this woman for her bruised, derided, cursed, defiled son.

It does not stop. It rings and rings and rings.

I turn the music louder until it sings away the sound of the phone. But the phone goes on quavering through me from heart to groin.

I press it into my gut, to smother it, but this only joins my hand to the trembling. My fingers librate, like Clara's, numb, moving side to side between her legs.

"Who is it?" I ask.

I can only imagine. I won't pick it up.

It's Sonny's mother, come back from the dead to protect her son.

But it's too late for that. Besides, he never told me whether she is dead or alive.

So it's Hang. He's looking for his delivery boy. And if I pick up the phone, he'll say, "Hang, mister," and I'll say, "Yes, I probably shall," though of course that will be metaphoric only, for in New York State we are so benightedly kind as not to kill our killers but to give them the rest of their lives to sit in their rooms reading and thinking and listening to music.

But Hang has only my address, not my name or number.

It's not my father. It never is. Though how fitting it would be for him to call tonight before I call him, when I've finally done something, rather than nothing, to earn his condemnation.

It must be Clara. Who else would call me? The others have no reason. Or, if they have reason, they are ignorant of it.

But Clara would not call. She knows I never answer the phone, for what need have I had of other people when I have had her?

But it is Clara, calling to tell me what I already know: I shall sleep alone for the rest of my nights.

I can feel her through the very twitching of the phone, which I move down to my groin like some pitiable man in the haptic vacuum of his solitude.

"Oh, Clara," I say to the phone. I bring the entire thing up to my cheek as the soprano in her aria sings, *"Vidit suum dulcem natum morientem desolatum,"* most apposite, with its image of a man hanging in desolation for the sins of his homeland.

As the phone pulses against my face, it throws off like a vein at her neck the sweet smell of Clara. And as I kiss the body of the phone, it finally comes dead upon my lips.

I am ready to make my own call.

So I turn down the music and punch out the number and hold my breath as the phone purrs in my ear and don't let it out until he answers.

His voice is hoarse. I can tell instantly that I have awakened him, but I can also tell that he doesn't want me to know this. He cannot bear to appear vulnerable. He was never one to admit that he needed, or indeed ever indulged in, sleep.

"I'm sorry if I woke you up."

"Who is this?"

I'm delighted he doesn't recognize me. I take it as evidence not that he's forgotten how I sound but that a year of silence and four years of happiness have given me a new voice.

"It's John," I confess.

He cannot hide the deep breath his body demands of the air around him, for it wheezes through his sleep-dry throat.

I wait for the crash of his phone in my ear.

"John?"

The tone in which he whispers my name is ambiguous: has he

forgotten who I am or is he merely surprised to hear from me?

"Dad?" I say back and try to invest the word with like equivocation. And such a peculiar word it is, so abrupt yet chummy, so fraught with affection for a sound so close to *dead*. And why these palindromes: DAD, MOM? Are they meant to imply some eternal return, or that mom and dad get you coming and going and that there simply is no escape from them?

"John," he acknowledges, though still in an almost intimate whisper, as if he's not planning to talk for long and is afraid of stimulating himself too far out of sleep with the sound of his own voice. "Where are you calling from?"

I nearly hang up on him. If I tell him where I am, I'll end up in his courtroom, where he'll say he needn't recuse himself because in fact he doesn't know me at all.

Impatient as always, he simply asks another question when he gets no answer to his first: "What time is it there?"

I look at the clock on Clara's side of the bed. It's still a new day. Not too late for her to be out, if she were merely out in the city and had not stepped off into the void, though late enough for me to have begun to become concerned and to have felt that strange mixture of worry and desire that is brewed in one's mind at the rim of loss.

"It's late," I answer.

"It's later here."

I don't understand him. Has he grown old and lapsed into metaphor?

"No, it's not." Even if he's talking about death, he's no closer to it than I.

"Aren't you calling from California?"

I think of Clara, leaving California as little more than a child, turning her back on her parents as I, clearly, have been unable to do. Heading east like the weather from what Jack London had named the Valley of the Moon, to be flooded by men.

I think of her in her trickery arranging to have him sent that Christmas card from there. How enticing I found such deviousness then. How unnerving it seems to me now.

"I tried to find you there." Once again, he speaks through my silence. "I must have had my clerk call every little town within a hundred miles of San Francisco looking for you. Are you unlisted?"

Who isn't?

"Yes."

"That explains it," he says dismissively. Once more, he understands the world.

"Why were you trying to find me?" I cannot imagine why. But, then, I could never have imagined I would have wanted to find him for the reason I have now found him.

"I wanted to invite you to my wedding."

Since his wedding preceded my birth, not to mention my conception—I am, it occurs to me, an illegitimate child in every way but the consuetudinary—his inviting me to it strikes me as the equivalent of erasing me forever from the annals of time. Does every child wonder, as I have, whether his parents in the private depth of night have ever said, "Don't you wish we'd never had him? Think of how our lives would be . . ."? But who else's father would ever abort through time travel? I am erased even in his fantasies.

"Mom's dead," I hasten to remind him.

"John." His voice, though still in whisper, fills my name with concern.

"Why?" I ask.

"I felt you should be there."

"Where?"

"At my wedding." Even at these years' remove, I recognize the old impatience in his tone.

"No. Why," I explain, "did you say my name that way?"

"What way?"

"As if you care for me."

He clears his throat. "Listen, I know I can be an eristical son of a bitch," he hisses in what sounds like confession. "I know I tried to make you do things you didn't want to do. I know I tried to make you see the world the way I see it. That's what fathers do. But I was wrong. I was right. But I was wrong. I'm getting taught how to say that, John. I was wrong. You're my son. You belong in my life. Our life. I have a new wife, John. That's what I'm trying to tell you."

"Where is she?"

"Asleep. It's after midnight here."

"Where?"

I can feel right through the phone his shaking his head. The phone moves against my face so that my head shakes with his. "New York. Where do you think we live? *You* phoned *me*."

"I meant where is she sleeping?" I say deliberately and softly against his bluster.

Is it too intimate a question, particularly from what he thinks is his bachelor son? "Where?" he repeats uncertainly.

"Is she sleeping," I remind him.

"Here," he confesses.

"In the same bed?"

"Of course in the same . . ." He stops. He locks into the memory I've forced upon him. He remembers that he and my mother had separate beds. For as long as I knew them, they had separate beds. But before I knew them, they had shared a bed. My mother told me that after I was born they had started to sleep apart. She didn't mean to imply that I had destroyed their marriage. They had a good marriage. Only that after me they had wanted no more children. I was enough. I was sufficient. I was pretty and bright and showed no interest whatsoever in living in the world as they interpreted it. I was irredeemable.

157

Now that I know what marriage is, I cannot imagine my father married to anyone. Not to my mother. Not to someone new, whom I can't help but picture as Clara, the very idea of wife, and in what I suppose is some strange variation of the primal scene, I see them lying next to one another and look to the right of me and look to the left of me and feel myself floating alone on this gargantuan boat of a bed and know that I am condemned forever to drift away from my existence.

"You know that I will always love your mother until the day I die," my father whispers. His rare redundancy escapes either his notice or his censure, and I imitate him in the latter.

"Can she hear you?"

"No. She's a very sound sleeper."

"I meant Mom."

What must it be like to lose your wife? I think of Clara dying, and as painful as that is, it seems preferable to this. If she's dead, I'll always know where she is and be able to make my way to her. Alive, she evades me.

I have never felt such sympathy for him. His wife died. It must be worse, even, than losing your mother. He is unable to speak.

So it is my turn, finally, to tell him about me.

"I got married too."

I expect him to bellow out his disbelief, but he says, "I would love to meet your wife."

What a novel idea. I don't see it. She hates him. "That's impossible."

"Don't ever say that to me, John."

"It's impossible," I repeat, because it is.

"No, it's not," he insists. "If you can't come East, then we'll come to you. My calendar's full, but I'll make time. Just say the word, and we'll be there. I would love to meet your wife. What's her name?"

"Clara." Saying her name to him—to him, of all people, who

pushed me away, who made the world uninhabitable—almost makes her real again.

"Clara." He gives forth the word with such authority I actually look toward the door as if he's called her forth and brought her back. "I like that. And do you have—"

"I have nothing."

"—children?"

"Never."

"Oh, I would like for you to have children, John."

"So would I. To make up for being yours."

He breathes deeply. He is unaccustomed to attack. He is, after all, judgment itself, and those who dare malign him he pronounces contemptuous.

"That's a terrible thing to say about yourself."

He makes me laugh. This is something new indeed. "I was saying it about you."

I can feel his anger. I can see his eyes narrow and his jaw tighten. The phone bites into my ear. "Me?"

"It's no more terrible than when you said, 'God help you if you ever become a father.' "

I'm a lawyer in his court, and I've just put forth the evidence that condemns. It's quite exhilarating. Perhaps I could have a career after all. Prosecutor. He always loved prosecutors. He used to tell us at dinner that the only good attorney was the prosecuting attorney. When you believe the world is evil, the possibility of innocence is annihilated.

"I did say that," he admits. "I remember saying it. I was in grief over the death of your mother. But that's no excuse. I was trying to blame you for something that was my fault."

"Her dying?"

"Your living."

Has he ever said anything so contemptible? "Didn't you even want me to live?"

"Of course I did!" he whispers emphatically. He is trying not to awaken his new wife, who sleeps beside him. Can marriage have redeemed him too? "But not in this world."

"Then what about my living was your fault?"

"Hurting you so."

When he says that, all the pain I have ever felt seems to rise within me. I double over on the bed until, supple like Clara, my chin is at my knees. My cheek rests on the cold blade of the 2-Pound Camp Wonder. I blubber like any other fool at long-awaited triumph over injustice.

My head is on her pillow. The mouthpiece of the phone is crushed beneath my ear. I can hear my father calling to me. My name pips from his mouth like the diminishing call of a migrating bird. It is as if he is speaking to me in my mind, as I had so often spoken to him in mine, before I found Clara lying in the street and learned to talk to her.

Still bent in half, I put my mouth against the phone and interrupt his search for me by saying, "Do you want to know the truth?"

"Do I have any choice?" he asks wearily. "It's my job to know the truth, John. But as Nietzsche says, truth is ugly."

"And you love it," I say with as much bitterness as I can muster. I had thought fathers were supposed to be their sons' heroes, not usurp them.

"Yes, I do." I hear in his voice his relish for iniquity. If mankind weren't damned, he'd be out of a job.

"Can you live with the truth?"

"Of course I can."

"But Nietzsche said it's impossible. Nietzsche said—"

"Don't you quote Nietzsche to me, John!"

This is very funny. This is wonderful. This is the best conversation I've ever had with my father.

"He said that the only thing that keeps the truth from killing us is art."

"Well, he's wrong about that! I don't believe in art, John. Art is what gets in the way of truth. Art is what stands between man and God."

"Then why did you want me to play the violin?"

He laughs. "Oh, my," he says. "Oh, my. Because you were lousy at sports. That's why."

I laugh too. "Do you still want to know the truth?"

"Please," he says graciously.

"I have nothing."

"You said that before. What are you talking about? Nothing. What do you mean? Do you need money, John? Is that why you're calling me in the middle of the night? Can you possibly have spent all your mother's—"

"I have nothing," I repeat, wondering if he can grasp how empty I feel and what a heroic feeling this is.

"That's not true," he pronounces softly. "You have me. You have your wife."

I can't tell him Clara has left me. Not when I have just presented her to him as evidence that he and I finally have a kind of perversely coparcenarial relationship so far as the sharing of matrimonial status is concerned.

So I say, "My wife is dead."

"What!" Does he grip his own sleeping wife's arm when he hears this?

"I told you it would be impossible to meet her."

"Oh, John," he whispers now. "Oh, John." There is such pathos in his voice, I realize that he, too, has come to know the rapture of marriage.

I have him where I want him. I uncurl my body. I don't say a word.

"How did she . . . ? When did she . . . ? How long were you . . . ?"

"It doesn't matter," I soothe him. "She's gone now."

"May she rest in peace," my father intones.

"And one other thing . . ."

"Yes?" His voice is wary, not out of distrust but compassion for his viduitous son.

"I killed somebody."

"No," he pronounces.

"Yes, I did. Really. And it wasn't an accident. I didn't drop one of my books on someone's head. I didn't bore someone to death humming Praetorius. I murdered a man. With an axe."

"Like hell you did!" he bellows.

I hear a voice. A woman's voice. I look toward the door.

But it's not my wife I've heard. It's my father's wife. He's awakened her finally with his yelling at me, and now he's trying to soothe her with an explanation. "It's my son, darling. It's John. He's calling from California. Go back to sleep now. I'll tell you about it in the morning."

I hear the sound of a kiss.

Strangely, my own lips pucker. I think of when I was little and my mother would read to me the story of a boy who sucked lemons, and my lips would pucker as did the lips of all the people in the story, and every time my lips would pucker, my mother would lean over the top of the book and kiss them.

And now my opsigamous father is kissing my new stepmother. It's a dismissive kiss, I know—he merely wants her to go back to sleep so he can come back on the phone and tell me I am incapable of what, in fact, I have proved unequivocally able to do— but as it is transmitted to my own lips it becomes rather more passionate. And while this is hardly the primal scene either (one's stepmother is a wholly legitimate object of desire, whereas one's true mother, however genuinely exoptable, is priggishly interdicted), I am embarrassed for both my father and myself. I am aroused. He is not. That I should feel triumphant makes me shameful, to say nothing of the fact that the woman I am deosculating is his wife, not mine. Mine is as good as dead. Though the phrase should be, should it not, as bad as dead.

My father returns to me. I hear his newly quick breathing. I feel sorry for his (I'm guessing) young wife. She's the one who should be hearing it. If it were Clara next to him, he'd be on her and not on the phone with me.

And then I see her. I actually see Clara, whole, handsome, looking quite herself, lying there beside my father.

No wonder my kiss was so affectionate. I was trying to win her from that thrasonical bastard, who comes back at me—"John, I don't believe a word you've told me"—with disbelief. His voice is stately, controlled. "This business about a wife, dead or otherwise. A murder. You don't have to traduce yourself to get my attention. I know you're not married—nor should you be. And I certainly know you haven't killed anyone. If there's anything I know, it's murderers, and if there's one thing you're not capable of, it's murder. And lest you mistake my meaning, I say that with approval."

"Thank you," I reply, having waited thirty-two years to be told that what's admirable about me is I'm not capable of murder. "I have to go now. Something smells. Something awful. Maybe it's the corpse."

I can't help chuckling and hang up to the sound of my father calling my name.

I'm glad we talked, though I'm not sure why I phoned him. It may have been for something as complicated as condemnation or approval or as simple as a betrayal of Clara, who would rather hear me whisper endearments to some strange maiden than touch voices with the man who had made it so painful for me to become who I am and whom she married. But in abandoning me, she's made me seek him out, if only to confess. And in seeing her with him, though only in my mind, I betray her more fully than if I fucked my father's own new wife.

Whatever the reason, I feel better. Confession must indeed be good for the soul.

Enough, then, of this lugubrious *Stabat Mater* with its thorns and wounds and *inflammatus et accensus*. I shall leave the bed, though not before I carefully place the 2-Pound Camp Wonder on the floor beside it, lest I accidentally axe my own neck with it and not before I punch out of (or is it into?) the remote that other Pergolesi, love poet. And as I go in search of that disgusting smell, I am Orfeo, singing, "*Nel chiuso centro*," which Charles De Brosses declared the best Italian cantata of them all. Alas, he so pronounced in 1739. Poor Pergolesi had died in 1736. Not unlike your father calling you to his bosom after you've committed the deed for which, along with your having been born, he would lock you away forever.

When you don't believe in life after death, the word *posthumous* becomes the most malignant in the language. But when you don't believe in life before death, that distinction belongs to *love*.

"*Euridice, e dove sei?*" I recite with the soprano in search of my lost love. Where are you, Clara, light of my eyes? "*Chi farà che torni in vita? Chi al mio cor la renderà?*" Who can bring her back to life? Who can bring her back into my heart?

Pergolesi wrote this piece when he was working for the Princess of Asturias, whose name just happened to be Maria Barbara. This strange coincidence encourages me to think that somewhere in the world I might find another Clara Bell, to replace the one I've lost. Or shall we die together? I'm not afraid of death so long as I'm with my beloved.

"*Non a terrore per me la morte, presso al mio amore . . .*" I sing as I step fearlessly out the door and discard what smells so bad.

It's not Sonny. Sonny is too frail and fleshless and freshly killed to smell.

It's the food he's brought. The smell of it has made me nearly sick to my stomach. I've removed it from the kitchen sink and thrown it right into the can outside the back door. I regard it not as evidence but as garbage.

I should think I'd be absolutely tabescent, but I'm not. I feel strong and whole and hungry for nothing but knowledge and revenge.

On my way back to the bed, I call to Dalsigre and sing, "*Torna, deh torna, o cara!*" and on the bed I sing, "*Torni volando a serenarmi il ciglio, che non ho piu consiglio, pace non ha il mio cor.*" Return, my beloved . . . return flying to give peace to my eyes, for I have lost my reason, and my heart knows no peace.

Not true, but I like the mournful tunes. I am at peace.

And so, lying in bed, I turn off the music and turn back to the diaries.

Cross in the Square

I go through periods when there's a piece of my body missing. It's not a limb or an organ. It's something that doesn't exist but that I need back. Orgasms rip me apart. They put me back together. But I don't want to have them alone. I need someone to watch me.

Tonight there were 2 of them.

Ron I've been with before.

Ron talked me into this. He said, "I want my friend to see you."

"See me what?"

I knew what he meant. But Ron didn't know how to say it. Men are not good with words.

"I told him you don't fuck," he said.

"What else?"

"I told him he'll have to get himself off."

"And?"

"He's game."

I've never done this before. I've thought about it. When you can't find 1 man it's perfectly natural to think of more than 1. I've pictured them over me and under me, top and bottom, front and back. I've thought about the tips of their dicks meeting somewhere inside me. After that they have a lifetime bond. They go off and leave me alone.

I was a little nervous. 1 man is usually no trouble. But I was worried that 2 would feed off each other.

I should have known better. They were docile. Ron was possessive, first of all. He didn't even tell me the other man's name. So I had to ask. "Stan." "Clara." Ron had kept that to himself too.

He also tried to orchestrate. "Go ahead, Clara. Show him." "Watch this, Stan. Watch what she does."

I started on myself. My eyes were closed. Someone I could not see was making love to me.

"No, don't touch her!" It was so sweet. Ron was my protector now. I came without opening my eyes.

"Your turn."

It was too late for poor Stan. He'd come just watching me. Listening to me. I was sorry I hadn't seen it.

We got to watch Ron labor over himself. He seemed very self-conscious, which he'd learned not to be when he was alone with me. But Stan made him nervous.

"Please," he said to me. He knew better than that. I wouldn't touch him.

"Close your eyes," he said to Stan.

Men are so unevolved. Each one exists in his own little world. They see nothing.

Stan actually obeyed.

So there they were, the 2 of them with their eyes closed. While I watched them both.

Stairway to Heaven

It was raining when we got out of the concert tonight. There weren't any cabs. So we walked down Lexington and there still weren't any cabs and I said let's take a subway. Johnny said the rain wasn't going to last, "Let's go in here." He didn't wait for me to agree. He pushed through the doors of HMV, which is not like him, he's usually such a gentleman. "I'm going downstairs," he said. "Want to come or . . ." The ground floor made him very uncomfortable. I've gotten him to listen to some pop music, but when he's in that part of a record store he gets nervous. The names of all the artists make him squint and scowl. "I'm not letting you out of my sight," I said. So I followed him downstairs. His hair was wet and dripping on his collar. But he doesn't own a hat or an umbrella. He's always hoping he'll never have to leave the loft again.

Even though I went with him downstairs he still took almost an hour. I can never figure out how he does it. He rushes from one part of the room to another to another to another. He flips through discs and either talks to himself or sings to himself and then suddenly leaves and dances over to another bin and flips through those discs. He looks like a bee in a field of flowers. He doesn't go alphabetically by composer. Or by artist. He doesn't stay at new releases. Maybe he hears music in his head and then goes to look for it. Maybe he thinks of a piece of music and goes to see if they have a particular recording of it. All I know is I love to watch him. Even if not for a whole hour. I particularly like it when he stops in his tracks and listens to something they're playing over the speakers in the room. He stands there stock still. Frozen in the middle of an aisle. I get to stare at him in public. I get to see him in ecstasy from across a room.

Tonight he ran up an aisle to me waving a jewelbox practically over his head. "Look!" he said. "Clara!" he said. "Das Marienleben!" he said.

"Buy it and let's go."

"Glenn Gould!" he said. "Hindemith!" he said.

"I hope it's better than those sonatas."

He stopped waving the jewelbox. "You don't like the sonatas?"

"It's not me. It's my ears."

He didn't laugh. He just said, "Maybe you'll like this more. Roxlana Roslak is the singer."

"Somebody sings?"

Somebody sings for sure. It's been playing ever since we got home, and I have to say I really don't think the Virgin Mary would want to get up and sing these songs.

So it was still raining when we left HMV. Johnny's hair got wet again and dripped again, but he still stood out there waving for a cab. He kept dashing from one corner to another. He'd stand on Lexington. He'd stand on 86th. No cab.

"Don't be afraid."

"But I've never taken the subway. You know that."

"There were a lot of things you hadn't done before you met me."

"Not as dangerous as this."

We waited on the local track. Going down to the express level would have been just too cruel.

The 6 came and we got on. The windows were fogged up from the rain. There were puddles on the floor. Johnny had hold of my hand and was practically pulling me into a seat. But I wouldn't let him. There was a puddle on the seat too. He couldn't understand it. "Does the rain come right through the surface of the earth?" "No. The train runs outside before it goes underground." "Then they shouldn't call it the subway."

I looked down to the far end of the car. "The seats look dry down there." "Let's just stand here," he said.

So we stood there. The doors were closed but the train took a while to move. When it finally did, Johnny took off in the opposite direction. I grabbed his wet sleeve and pulled him back to me. "You have to hold on," I told him. I pushed his hand up to one of the metal straps. I watched it close over it. With hands like those, I thought, we're safe.

"Who are all these people?" Johnny hollered. He was looking around. Every time he caught someone's eyes, they looked down.

"How should I know who they are. Don't stare at them."

"But I could feel them staring at me."

"Maybe that's because we're the only people standing in the whole car."

"What did you say?" He leaned down to bring his ear to my mouth.

"Nothing."

"I still can't hear you. It's incredibly noisy in here."

"It's the subway."

But he only shook his head. How come I could hear him and he couldn't hear me.

"I don't like it," he said.

He seemed relieved when we pulled into 77th Street. "Is that it?"

"That's only one stop, Johnny."

"Let's get a cab," he said, but by that time the doors had closed and we were on our way.

I could hear him start to sing as the train sped up. Not words. Just music. Something we'd heard at the concert. The faster the train went and the more noise it made, the louder Johnny sang.

I was worried he would keep singing when we stopped in the next station but his voice dropped into a hum.

"Is that the Haydn?" I asked him.

"The Schubert." He started to sing it again as the train pulled out. But now he sang it so loudly I knew everyone could hear it. People sitting near us got up and moved to the other end of the car. At 59th, people who got on the train didn't sit near us because they could hear him humming. By the time we were pulling into 42nd we were completely alone in our half of the car. He drove the last person away by singing so loudly that he drowned out the screech of the wheels on the curve into Grand Central. And that's the way we rode all the way down to our stop.

We walked home from the station through the rain. "You can stop singing now," I said. "You're safe."

"But it's such a beautiful piece."

"I recognize it from The Hunger," I told him.

"What's The Hunger?"

"It's a movie. Starring Susan Sarandon and Catherine Deneuve. They're lovers. And vampires."

"Vanessa and Virginia. They had that look. And the Schubert was used?"

"I didn't know what it was until tonight. But I did remember it. It was inside me this whole time."

"I don't care for movies."

"I know."

"But I did see a movie once with another French actress. Jeanne Moreau. I'll never forget it. She had sex in a rowboat while the first Brahms sextet was playing. I'd never heard it before. It was incredible."

"How was the sex?"

"I closed my eyes."

I stopped him to give him a hug. We were both soaked through. The rain had flattened his thick hair.

When we got home we stripped and dried each other off

with towels. One thing led to another. We made love to Das Marienleben but even that couldn't stop us. In the middle of it he said, "Admit it." "Ok, we'll never go on the subway again." "Not that. Admit you couldn't stop thinking about Sharon Robinson and Jaime Laredo making love." "You read my mind," I said.

Lawyer's Puzzle

It's amazing, but every boy I had there, every single one, said just the way Kevin did "What about your parents?" I mean, the door was closed. What's the problem. Not that my parents were ever home in the afternoon. And not that I would have done it if they were. Because then they would have known. And I didn't want them to know. Not because I thought it was wrong. But because it was private. This was for me to do. This was me becoming me. This was innocent. I was innocent.

Eagles with Cigars

A man comes into the shop. He says, "What can you tell me about your quilts?"

"Nothing."

"Nothing?"

"Nothing."

He's disgusted. "If I ran my business the way you run yours, I'd be out of business."

"If you were out of business then you wouldn't be in here telling me how to run mine."

"How's that?"

"You wouldn't be able to afford a quilt."

"What makes you think I'm going to buy one? You won't even tell me about them."

"That's right. I won't."

"Now I know why stores open and close on this street before the ink's even dry on the lease."

"Do you see one that appeals to you?"

"What are you talking about?"

"A quilt."

"That appeals to me?"

"Yes, a quilt that appeals to you."

"How would I know?"

"Look around."

I go back to my paperwork.

"What about this one?" He points.

"That's a pieced quilt. Cotton. It has 48 white blocks. As you can see, 24 of them have red quarter circles in the corners and the other 24 have red pinwheels in the middle. When the blocks are pieced together they give you that wandering design. That's why it's called Drunkard's Path. It was made in Missouri during the Depression."

"And that one." He points.

"That's a Cape Cod Bridal quilt. It's much older—early 19th century. I see you like red on white. Those are appliqued oak leaves. Oak leaves represent longevity, at least when they're on bridal quilts. Are you married?"

"Was."

"Then don't buy this one."

"But that's the one I like."

"It doesn't speak your language, sir."

"You mean you won't sell it to me?"

"Right."

"And that Drunkard's Path does?"

"Does what?"

"Speaks my language?"

"I wouldn't know."

"Will you sell the Drunkard's Path to me?"

"Of course."

He throws his gold card down on my desk.

"I don't understand you," he says.

"Why should you."

He ignores that. "When I came in here you refused to tell me anything about your quilts."

"Of course."

"But then you . . ."

"You have to be specific."

He signs. He leaves.

"Close call," I say to the Cape Cod Bridal.

Crescent Moon

I was sitting here with nothing to say when I noticed the Crescent Moon cover I put on this book and thought about how it symbolizes virginity.

I love being a virgin. Almost as much as I love sex.

I'm not going to fuck anybody until it's my husband. And I'm not going to marry anybody until I find someone I can trust my secrets to.

It's probably too late for me. I'm 21 years old. I have a bunch of quilts. I'd love to get more and sell them and get more and sell them. I'd love to have them pass through my hands. Every beautiful quilt ever made. But I don't want to make one myself. I have no desire to do that. Even if I did, it's probably too late for me.

> At your quilting, maids, don't dally,
> Quilt quick if you would marry.
> A maid who is quiltless at 21
> Never shall greet her bridal sun!

Underground Railroad

I'm always in heat. Or almost always. Or I can be warmed up. Easily.

My sex is all over me. In my hair. On my ears. Toes. A finger in my nostril. (Not my own finger!) My spine. My ass parted to the air. Fingertips on my teeth. And my lips. My lips are impossible. They burn my mouth. My waist. At the sides. Like I've got nylon zippers there and when they're down I open up. There are times when one man's not enough. I swear I think I could fit them all inside me. Then they'd have nothing to talk about but me. Sing my silly praises to the guys. The skies. Disguise. The insides of my thighs. The skin there must be what God is covered with all over. And Its final creation was cheerleaders in their little skirts. The backs of my knees. If I don't let it tickle, I bliss. And when I'm on my knees, I pray. Even the pain is plush. My throat's a waterfall. My eyes are bigger than my mouth. And my eyelids. How could I ever tell anyone what it means to have them touched.

Streak of Lightning

This is the first time I've ever been faithful to anybody. I like that I didn't choose it. I didn't decide to be faithful. I didn't swear off other men. I just found I didn't need them. I can get from 1 man what it used to take 10 to fail to give me.

We're together all the time. We're obsessed with ourselves. The sex is spectacular. And I'm finally at peace with myself. I can't imagine ever wanting anyone else. Even my fantasies are less intense. I'm no longer interested in getting fucked by phantoms.

I told him: "I've stopped seeing other men."

"So have I, Clara," he said.

Robbing Peter to Pay Paul

Johnny told me Julia Duckworth used to lie for hours on her dead husband's grave.

After she married again and had Vanessa and Virginia her son by Mr. Duckworth used to explore Virginia's private parts.

"How did she say it?" I asked.

"Just like that. "He explored my private parts." Vanessa's too, I gather. But Vanessa didn't write about it."

"Read it to me."

Johnny went into his closet and came out with a book. He didn't come back on the bed with me. (I made him give me the book afterward so I can copy down what he read to me) "I can remember the feel of his hand going under my clothes, going firmly and steadily lower and lower. I remember how I hoped he would stop; how I stiffened and wriggled as his hand approached my private parts. But it did not stop. His hand explored my private parts too."

I could see Virginia with his hand down her clothes. A girl like me, posing for pictures while my hand explored some boyfriend's private parts. The Bell girls who aren't real Bell girls get violated. Why does it arouse me all the time?

Johnny knew me too well. That's why he stood at the end of the bed. He shook his head at me.

"She was only 6 years old," he said.

And I was only 15! I want to scream at him.

True Lovers Knot

Ike told me he wanted me to make a studio visit with him so we closed the gallery and he called a car to take us downtown and asked for a limo because he said that's what artists like to see. I have never been in a limo before and from the way Ike was looking at me and I found myself looking at him

I could understand how dangerous they are. You feel everybody's looking at you but at the same time you feel you have a separate existence. You can do anything. Not that we did. But I spent the whole time on the opposite seat looking at Ike with my hand halfway up my skirt. He had to drape his raincoat over his arm when we got out.

"Let me do the talking Clara," Ike said as we climbed the metal stairs to the studio at the top of the building.

Fuck you I would have said if I had been permitted to speak.

The artist was brilliant. Fortunately so was some of his work. His name is Franco Rothberg, or at least that's what he calls himself to take advantage of this year's ethnic sales pitch. He's kind of Marquez meets Chagall in the suburbs. Nothing is grounded in his huge canvases. People such as they are bungee by. All human movement is vertical. Which to me means you can be buried in the ground or in the sky. You can believe in the earth or in heaven. But not in both. Industry encroaches from the periphery. Grass and flowers grow, Franco says, "excrementally."

"What do you call this one?" Ike asked.

"The Jewish Community Center Cannot Hold," Franco answered.

"Yeats," said Ike.

"Oh please," I said to stop him from making a fool of himself.

Ike shot me a dirty look. But it was too late.

"I'm joking," said Franco. "I'm from Newton Mass. So everything I do is called Newton. With Roman numerals. Who cares? Fig Newton. Isaac Newton. Titling makes me self-conscious. It's like having to give names to your fingers."

On the way back uptown Ike said he wasn't going to represent him.

"Why?"

"You know why."

I didn't but Ike did. Franco called me late this afternoon.

"Come back by yourself," he said.

I went in to Ike's office. "Reconsider," I told him.

"Was that he on the phone?"

"How did you know?"

"I'm not going to take him on just to keep you away from him, Clara."

"I won't see him if you do."

"Just which one of us are you bribing, me or him?"

"Myself."

"Go," he said. "I'm not interested in his work."

"What about me?"

"I'm not interested in you either."

"I meant what about my interest in his work."

"Go and indulge it."

Ike picked up his phone.

"Don't you dare call him."

"I'm not." Ike smiled. "I'm just getting the limo back for you."

So I went. Franco made love to me. From the periphery. I don't know if Ike's jealous. But I know I am.

Daisy Chain

I just got around to reading Lancelot by Walker Percy, which I can't remember where I got it and I found in a stack of old books in the back of my closet. It's about a very strange marriage and has "hard-ons" and "cunts" in it, which are words I'd rather think than read, and the hero, whose name is John, puts hidden cameras around to catch his wife fucking. I would like to see me and Johnny doing it. But there's no way we're going to get a camcorder. We don't even have a TV or a

VCR to play it on. We don't even have the kind of still camera my father used! Johnny reminds me of the John in the book, who says all you need is a room with a tiny window and one other person. As soon as you add the world, he says, like other people and TV and the news, you go crazy. While I was reading it I asked Johnny because this comes up in the book, "Would you say you're John the Baptist or John the Evangalist?" He shook his head at my book and said "Neither." But later when I told him how the hero of the book stops talking just the way he did, Johnny said, "Oh, well then, you tell your Mr. Percy that he should have used Juan de la Cruz—toda sciencia transcendiendo. There was the John who understood what Steiner calls the abandonments of speech as ancient as those of the Stylites and Desert Fathers. Anything else I can be pretentious about?" I told him that this man said that when his wife wasn't with him it was like being without oxygen. "And when you're not with me," Johnny said, "it is like being without . . ." He stopped. "What?" I asked. "There is no way to describe the emptiness," he said. I closed my book.

Beloved Flag

Truro. Johnny watches me from the bed the way he does at home. The room's so small, I can feel his breath between my shoulder blades. I love to write in here with his eyes on me. I love to feel him try to see right through me.

The ocean sounds like traffic. When you live at the top of the city, it feels like the whole world rushing by between your legs.

We left New York early this morning. Johnny had not been out of the loft for a couple of weeks. That's how strong he is. He wouldn't go pick up the rental car without me. He won't go anywhere without me. Except when he buys me a present I guess. He loves me so much he'll do things he never does to do them for me.

We took 95. You have to get past New Haven around Guilford before you feel New York let go of you. Everything until then's a suburb. You think you might die at any moment. Then around Guilford you smell the sea. Or you hear it. Even over the music. At least in your mind. This morning we played Mozart flute quartets and George Thorogood. Traveling music we call it. We never listen to it at home. Johnny likes Bad To The Bone. Everybody who hears it ends up singing it. They probably don't even know what they're singing. But Johnny does. That's what he does. He takes things apart. He always says, "But don't call me a deconstructionist." "I wouldn't dream of it. You're a diaskeuast." He makes me laugh. He makes me laugh at him. When a man does that, he kills my fear. I've never for a second been afraid of Johnny.

We hit traffic going over the Cape Cod canal. For a while we just sat there on the swell of the bridge. I looked down and thought about dying. Actually, I looked down and thought about our car falling off into the water. When you're on it it looks like the highest bridge in the world. But I don't die. Johnny makes his way to me through the water and claws open the window and presses me against him and we swim up into the sunlight.

I look at him while I'm seeing this. He's in the driver's seat. I won't drive over these bridges. One of them has a sign about calling the Samaritans if you're thinking of killing yourself. It's on the side of the bridge leading back toward the city naturally. Johnny knows. He's just staring straight ahead with his hands on the wheel. But he knows he rescued me.

6 was crowded all the way. When we hit the single lanes past Hyannis with all the white crosses bunched together it got even slower. If I died in an accident on that road, and

somebody insisted on sticking up a cross to make an example of me, I'd want it on the spot where I went.

We still got to the flea market before it closed. Homer was there. "Clara," he said. "John." He remembers everything. "How's that Hole in the Barn Door you bought 5 years ago?" he asks me. "And that shirred rug with the flowers?"

"Sold them," I tell him.

Johnny gets interested because we're talking about a time before he knew me. I could feel his heat come out of the heat of this huge drive-in. No shade. But he was hotter. He wants to possess me possessed. He creates me for himself. Other people just erase you. They want to make all the difference to you. They don't. This guy would watch me getting nudged around by my father's dick in my mother's womb if he could.

"How do you remember these things, Homer?"

"I can picture her buying them."

Johnny wants to be Homer now. He wants to be standing there 5 years ago looking at me.

I was just happy to be standing there with him today.

He was in awe of Homer. Just like of me. We see things. Johnny can't. He has nothing in his mind but words and sounds. He taught me how to hear. I'm teaching him how to see. But he won't. You can learn to see things outside but you can't learn to see things that aren't there.

He has other gifts.

Don't you Johnny?

I went through Homer's old van and found some pieces. I knew I would. Homer goes back to the midwest every winter and scours the farms. Quilts rise from the earth as people are buried in it. He likes to get them before they make it into the inventory of the estate. He won't wholesale them, but New York prices are so high it would shame me for Homer to see them. So I never haggle. People in New York will pay anything for something "authentic." Anything.

He's got a Circular Album buried near the floor of the van. The van's so hot I sweat on the quilt.

"You found it," he said.

"Where did you get this?"

I could tell he'd been saving it for me. I told that later to Johnny.

"You adore it when men save things for you."

Of course I do.

"See you next year. Or whenever."

I like Homer. He's a vagabond. Once a year's enough for most people. My husband's the only one I want to see repeatedly.

When we got to this motel I spread the quilts out on the bed. Johnny knew I would. He was patient.

"They're beautiful," he said.

"I hope I can find the right people to sell them to."

I barely got them folded when he gathered me up.

Pinwheels

Possible Names For My Store

Quilts USA	Take Me To Bed
America The Beautiful	Is Never Done
Ladies Delight	Trapunto
Sew Sew	Stairway To Heaven
Quiltuplets	Quality Quilts
Quiltessence	How They Hanging
Manhattan Pavement	American Artistry
Hole In The Barn Door	Quilts For Quickies
Quilt Pro Quo	Lying In Bed
Handjobs	American Treasures
Native Born	Fragility

A Stitch Out Of Time

Grandmother's Flower Garden

Fuckable Fabrics

Call It Quilts

In Stitches

Virgin Territory

Crosses and Losses

Pieces On The Ground

Counterpain

Dead Women Don't Sew

Belzidas

How Can This Bee

Bell's Bottoms

Public Hangings

Ike And Clara's

Contemplations

Quilt And Innocence

Farmer's Wife

A woman came into the shop. She looks around. But I know she's not here to shop. She doesn't touch a thing.

Finally she must figure enough time has past.

"Are you married to John Chambers?"

She isn't bad looking. Too much silk but not too much flesh so the silk lies flat. She takes care of her body. Her shoes are fine, they shine like a black apple. With straps that start up her calves because she knows she's got good legs. She's not my type. I mean she's not one of me. But I can see Johnny with her. East Side. Short hair too but blond. This is definitely not Cosima who I picture with curly hair and unenviable eyebrows and by this time, 12 years after the fact, a fat ass.

"Yes," I say.

She looks at my left hand. Don't you just love women who can't help searching for the evidence. If God came down like Zeus for a quick one they'd ask It for a sign. Make the wind blow. Calm the seas.

"Poor thing," she says,

"Why do you say that?"

"I used to date him."

"Oh really."

"If you could call it that."

"I wouldn't know. I never dated him. I just married him."

"So I heard. It was very fast. I don't suppose you're pregnant."

"Not yet."

"I wouldn't think so."

"Why?"

"He's hardly the most virile man I've ever met."

"Did you try?"

Finally she touches a quilt. She rubs the back of her hand along it the way her mother must have done with her. "I don't see what business that is of yours."

"It's not."

Now I think she's about to touch me. "Admit it. He's the strangest man you've ever met."

"Absolutely."

She does touch me! Her cardinal nails come to rest on my sleeve. "I knew it! God, how can you stand him?"

"Sometimes I can't."

"Oh you poor thing."

"Sometimes he's too much for me."

"For me too! A friend of mine fixed us up. He's rich, she said. He's handsome, she said. He's got 16 rooms in the 60s, she said. Great, I said. I was ready, believe me. Aren't we all. I should have listened to my father. Before he died he ran a bro-kerage house and the only thing he ever taught us because he said it was the only thing we'd ever have to know was if some-thing's too good to be true it's too good to be true. And of course he was right. He drove me crazy."

"Your father?"

"Of course not my father. Him. Your husband. John Chambers."

"How so?"

"How so! How can you of all people ask me that! He's from

183

another planet, that man. He's up in the stratosphere. He's so busy looking for the meaning of life that he doesn't have a life. I tried everything. I cooked meals for him. I went to Merkin Hall with him. I opened up a charge at Brooks Brothers. I spent hours sneezing from the dust on the bottles at Garnet. I read Thus Spake whatever his name is. I even asked him to marry me."

"Why did you do that?"

"To see what he'd say."

"And what did he say?"

"He said he couldn't."

"Did he say why?"

"Oh yes he certainly said why. He said he couldn't because he'd already had sex!"

I shouldn't have laughed.

"It's not funny," she said.

"Maybe it wasn't then but it is now."

"I pity you," she said.

Not as much as I pity you.

"Why did you come here?"

"I thought you might need someone to talk to."

"I have someone to talk to."

"A shrink I hope."

I thought that was her exit line until she said from the door, "So what is he like to be married to?"

"Too good to be true," I said.

Union Square

I showed my diary to Ike.

"What the hell is this, Clara?"

"My diary."

"What happened to it?"

"What do you mean?"

"It looks like you wrote it with your toes."

"That's my handwriting."

"Just keep using the computer, Clara."

"Don't you want to read it?"

"Nobody could read this, Clara. It's sick. I don't know what it says in here but you ought to marry the first man who can read it. You'd be meant for each other."

"That's ridiculous. I want to marry you."

"That's impossible."

"Why?"

"Because I love you too much."

Tree of Temptation

Is it possible to be so happy that you want to destroy either yourself or the person who makes you so?

Johnny told me the story of a political philosopher named Louis Althusser who strangled his wife to death. He said he had always loved her.

Johnny says he can't understand that. But I can. There is something about being married that sometimes makes me want to kill him. I don't know if it's to make him go away or to keep him forever.

I look at him next to me and I try to imagine life without him. I blot him out. I don't see him. He's not there. And I feel a terrible mixture of sadness and relief.

I gave myself to him forever because I thought he was the only innocent person left on earth. I am haunted by him. I am in love with his suffering. And his silence. No matter how much he talks there's always that silence, somewhere behind his voice. I can climb inside my husband and find peace. He's my grave.

Why is it so painful to love somebody? Why is it so easy to imagine losing the most precious thing you have that you think you would rather destroy it than lose it?

Goose in the Pond

I stopped on the way home today at Crotch Veneer on West Broadway and bought Johnny some new underpants. They're plain. They're white. They're briefs.

"I can't wear these," he said when he unwrapped them. I could see from the pain in his eyes l. that he was trying hard not to hurt my feelings and 2. that he was frightened of his new underwear.

"Why can't you?"

"Because I've never worn anything like this in my life. I've always worn the same kind of underwear."

I couldn't stand it any more. He is so conservative. He is so old-fashioned. He is so unaware of how beautiful he is. All I really wanted was to see him in a normal pair of underpants with his buns outlined and his basket full.

So I said, "Well I hate your underwear."

"You hate my underwear?"

"Yes. I have always hated your underwear."

"You have? But why?"

"Because they're so drab. So boring. So ugly."

"I see." He looked down at himself with a painful expression in his eyes. Like he can see his underwear right through his pants.

"At least try them on."

"Am I allowed to return them if I don't care for them?"

"Of course not! God, are all rich people like you. Don't worry. If you don't like them, I'll wear them."

The fear left his eyes. He smiled. "Now I understand what this is about."

"What?"

"You know as well as I."

"No I don't. And get that smug look off your face."

He kept right on smiling and put on the underpants. "These are monumentally uncomfortable," he said. "I think my testicles are becoming one. Here, you wear them."

He put them on me. "How do I look?"

"Ridiculous," he said. "May I?"

He put his hand in through the fly. Oh my.

"I'm sorry," I said.

"But you're a woman."

"I meant that we had our first fight."

"We did?"

"Over underpants no less."

"I like these," he said.

"But I thought . . ."

"On you."

"So do I." The fly is like a door that's meant to be opened from the inside only. Why don't they make these for women.

Shoo Fly

This guy knows more things. He thinks I'm a Bell so he tells me about the Bells. I know I once read A Room Of My Own by Virginia Woolf just because of the title. But now I don't remember anything else about it. That's what happens to me with books. It's completely different with things I see. Or even things I think I see. Or things I see on the inside that don't even exist on the outside. I see them once and never forget them. Beautiful things, I mean. Ugly things I don't see even once. I can stop them between my eyes and my brain. They never register. But beautiful things last forever. I remember every good quilt I've ever seen. Even ratty ones. If you ask me about a pre-Depression Bullseye made in Pennsylvania by Alverba Herb I can tell you that it's got a green and red little circle in the middle that's a bullseye exploding into either 8 or 9 concentric circles of diamonds and triangles. What I like best about it is the contrast of the simple appliqued flowerpots in the corners. It has a cyan blue ground and a rope-stitched murrey border. There are hearts in the ground quilting. It will go with me to the grave.

I don't remember words the same way. He does. But he doesn't seem very good with images. His mind's a blank. Which I notice is what scares him. Blankness, I mean. Like the quarter he told me about with nothing on it. Like the silence he went through. He talks a mile a minute now, but it's that silence I keep thinking about. How it must have purified him. He's like a saint. I want him to save me.

After Virginia Woolf's sister Vanessa married Clive Bell, Virginia said, "God made her for marriage. And she basks there like an old seal on a rock."

"She makes it sound so comfortable," I say.

"Well," he says, "Clive Bell was in love with Virginia. His sister-in-law. They had an affair. And Virginia was in love with Vanessa. Her sister. And Vanessa encouraged Clive and Virginia in their passion. But they never actually made love."

"Vanessa and Virginia?"

"Virginia and Clive Bell."

I love these stories he tells me. Where do they come from. I wonder if a mind can hold all these things and still have room for me.

Slave Chain

Johnny freaked when he unfolded his new quilt.

"It's a swastika!" he screamed. "We can't put this on the wall!"

"Why not?"

"A swastika? What will people say!"

"What people? Nobody ever comes in here except Elspeth and delivery boys."

"I wasn't referring to other people. I meant ourselves."

It is so like Johnny to make the world out of nobody but us. Is it any wonder I feel so safe with him.

"Help me hang it," I said.

He did. And while we hung it, I told him all about it. That it was made in the 1890s and was an Indian symbol and was supposed to signify good luck. All it is is a cross with arms, but it was a shape that went back far earlier than the time of Christ. It has appeared in many cultures. Quilts like this go by many names. The Chinese 10000 Perfections. The Battle Axe of Thor. Wind Power of the Osages. Favorite of the Peruvians. (When I mentioned that one he said that his favorite of the Peruvians is our little man with the big dick) The Pure Symbol of Right Doctrine. Even Heart's Seal, whatever that may be, the best or worst of things, depending on when you seal it.

"How do you feel about it now?" I asked him when we got it up on the wall and adjusted the lights.

"Confused."

"Good."

I wanted him to know that pictures can be like words and destroy their own meaning.

He's not the only one here who longs for something stable.

Devil's Claws

It's funny how you can be married to a guy and live with him sleep with him eat with him talk with him laugh with him cry with him joke with him shop with him drink with him drive with him suck him off in the shower and you still don't know who he is.

Thank goodness.

Base Ball

We went up to the Cloisters today. It's still his favorite museum in the city. I tell him that's because after I've been dragging him around to every art museum big and small in the city for the past 2 years so he can learn how to look at art what he still likes to do most is lie down on the grass and neck and how many museums in the city can you do that at. (Outside the Egyptian Room at the Met is one place!) But he told me today that the reason he likes to go to the Cloisters is because it has his favorite work of art.

"And what might that be?" I ask him.

"St. Jerome Tempted By Visions Of Maidens," he answers.

It was done in the early 15th century and looks a little like the Cloisters with its arches and columns. St. Jerome is a narrow-eyed man with women's hands. The maidens are in the "city" (in other words the place of sin) and wear beautiful dresses low on their tits and tight on their hips. One of them is looking at another one like a woman about to get it on with a woman (St. Jerome was not very original with his visions!) And the second one is looking right at old Jerome, P. F. as we used to say in junior high ("Pussy Forward"). I point this out to Johnny. "That's called lordosis," he says. "You mean it's something religious," I answer. He laughs. "Not precisely. Lordosis is the name for the pushing forward of the genitals, the

offering up of one's edea, one's <u>sex</u> to a desired partner." "So it
<u>is</u> religious" is what I offer. "Not to St. Jerome," says Johnny.
We neck on the grass.

Buggy Wheel

This is the first time we're reading the same writer at the
same time. I'm reading The Stranger. He's reading The Notebooks. The day we met he quoted Camus to me. I wonder if
he remembers. I do. I also remember that one of my first
boyfriends in New York read Camus. In French. I loved the
way those books looked. They were white paperbacks with
black and red printing. I used to borrow them and pretend to
read them on the bus. It was a good way to meet other boys
but only on certain buses. Fifth Avenue practically anywhere.
Lexington but only around Hunter. Broadway near Lincoln
Center and then up around Columbia. And the crosstown
buses through Central Park, always the crosstown buses,
except you had to work a lot faster than you did on the
avenues.

This boy Daniel said that in 1981, which is when we were
going out together, nobody came up with ideas any more.
Nobody made you feel they understood you by telling you
that life was pushing a huge rock up a giant hill and when you
got to the top the rock rolled back down and so you pushed it
up again, and that's all you did your entire life over and over
until you were dead. Daniel's favorite phrase was "no exit." He
loved to make out with me. He never gave me any trouble
about my demands. He even took credit. He said, "You have to
separate yourself from things to see them." He still didn't like
looking at my vagina. I think it was the first one he'd ever
seen. But he loved to watch his hand on his dick. He could
hypnotize both of us with that motion. He could go on for-

ever. And he never came. I think he was afraid his penis was too small and he didn't want either one of us to see it unerect. But to me having sex and not coming is <u>exactly</u> like pushing a boulder up a mountain over and over.

Johnny read to me tonight. He usually does that only with Nietzsche. It's never more than a sentence or two. An idea. "Listen to this," he'll say. But he won't read to me until I look at him.

"An intellectual is someone whose mind watches itself. I am happy to be both halves, the watcher and the watched."

That's what made me remember Daniel. Daniel read Camus to me too. Whole long passages. Then he went and killed himself. He hanged himself in his dark little bedroom on Morningside Drive.

The person who told me said he was wearing a beret. I try to remember Daniel without the hat. But I can't.

He died in vain.

Just the way he would have wanted it.

I wonder what he's trying to tell me. Johnny I mean.

Whig's Delight

When I got to the shop this morning I read in the Times that Ike died of aids. There was no picture of him. As if he'd never existed. I should write a letter to the editor.

It was a tiny obituary. Isaac Labrovitz, Gallery Owner. Represented several artists of immortal inconsequence. No immediate survivors. No companion. I wonder if that was my fault.

I haven't seen him in 8 years. Not since the day he fired me. But I have seen him in my mind. I see him taking off his suit. I see his body. It's the most perfect body . . . God, Johnny would kill me for that . . . the grammar, not what I said . . . but it is, the most perfect body I've ever seen. It's not more beautiful than Johnny's, but Johnny's is mine, Johnny's gets so close it disappears from sight, Johnny's gets buried inside me. Ike's was like a work of art. I could stare at it for hours. So could he. I mean he could stare at me staring at him. He told me I was like a mirror. He could look at me and see himself. He once joked we were the opposite of Galatea and Pygmalion because I'd taken a living being and turned him into a statue. "Just a maquette," I kidded him. "I trust you're not referring to my cock," says Ike.

He was the most important man in my life before Johnny. Not just because he gave me the money to start my business. Which I paid back to his lawyer Barry Weiss and still didn't hear from Ike. Because he was my greatest lover. He was my ideal man. I was never so safe in my life. I could close my eyes with his eyes on me and know that no one would touch me but me. I could lie there in my little studio apartment with him on my tiny twin bed and me draped across my wonderful old wing chair and sink deeper and deeper into myself until I came and exploded back into the world. And there he'd be. Kind of aghast, I guess. He told me my orgasms lasted longer than The Low Spark Of High Heeled Boys.

After he fired me I didn't do what some girls do I guess and what I would have thought I'd do. I didn't find more men. I didn't bury my sorrow in the oblivion of vengeful dick gathering. Instead I started to have fantasies about men actually fucking me. And I learned how to make my fingers numb so that way I could be completely alone and yet have someone with me. Watching me. Watching over me. Isn't that what girls want? Someone to watch over me. A father. A husband. But Ike was the best.

I went 4 years between Ike and Johnny without seeing a man's body.

Now I've been 4 years with Johnny without seeing a man's body. When he holds me, I am reborn.

I don't know why I haven't told Johnny about Ike. He's the only man I'd bother talking about. Besides my father. Andy was just a boy. And Ike brings no shame. But I love my secrets. I mean, I love having them. I don't want to tell them. I want them to be found out. I want to be spied on. I want it illicit. I want a sin to be committed.

I wonder if I'll be stoned if I go to Ike's funeral.

Blindman's Fancy

Where are you Monica???

I should never have waited a week to call her. I guess I wanted her to call me. By the time I did, her phone was disconnected.

I got Mr. Labrovitz to let me take the checks to her apartment. He was going to mail them. Or so he said.

I went there after work today. She lives on Lispenard Street. Or she used to. Somebody answered her bell and said she moved out. She didn't know to where.

She's the only friend I ever had here. I told her all my secrets. It's like this city just chews people up and swallows them.

Horn of Plenty

I have this fantasy that I take Johnny home and introduce him to my parents.

He isn't what they expect. He doesn't look like the men who grow out of the boys in the Valley of the Moon.

"Is he a professor?" they ask me. "A lawyer?"

"No."

"Well, what does he do then?"

"Nothing."

"A ne'er do well," says my father.

"More like a ne'er do anything," I tell them.

They don't get my joke. They look at me like it's a pity I didn't have the sense to marry a local grape grower.

"He's the only person I've ever met who's in harmony with the world. He doesn't have to do anything. He's kind of like an ecological miracle in the realm of the spirit." (That's how they talk in California) "He takes nothing and he contaminates nothing. He's pure. On top of that he loves me to complete distraction."

Now my mother understands. She nods. She smiles. If a man loves you he could be a mass murderer for all she cares.

Then she says, "Perhaps he'd like to see photographs of you when you were younger."

I'm about to scream No! when I realize Johnny would like to see nothing more. The only thing he mourns is his absence in my past.

I look at my parents. They're frozen in time. It's 1979. The year I left. My father is 38. My mother is 36. Now they're both in their 50s. If they're even still alive. But I see them like me and Johnny. And I begin to understand those pictures. I was 15. They'd been married since just before I was born. I am the evidence of their teenage lust. Who better to inspire them.

So we all sit around looking at pictures of me.

"Isn't she beautiful," says my father to my husband. "Look at what her hair does to the light."

"And what a nice little figure," says my mother.

"Well we know where she gets that," says my father to my mother.

"Oh you make me blush." To distract attention from her own embarrassment my mother turns it back to me. "Look how nicely she holds that boy's penis in her hand. How reverential."

"Do you recognize him?" my father asks me.

"Oh, sure. That's Billy Zellerbach."

"How about this one?" My father shows us all a photo of me with my eyes closed and my lips kissing the tip of a very long, very narrow dick. (It wasn't until Andy that I actually put one in my mouth. Or all of one anyway)

"That's Stan MacIver."

"Wasn't he on the basketball team?" says my mother.

"No. He only looks tall."

Everybody laughs.

"And this? Jeez, that must have been fast film!"

The camera has captured what must have been the first shot of semen out of the thick dick I had in my hand. It looks like the white of an eye at the top of an arc. "Frank Bagnani."

"Looks Italian," says my mother.

"How would you know?" says my father.

They both start to laugh. And while they're laughing they face each other grasping hands in front of them, fingers interlocked in fingers.

"Stop it you love birds," I say, but I'm very happy for them.

Johnny must be impatient, because he turns over the next picture. I'm holding a supple dick against my cheek. My lips are glazed with come. "Johnny Agoston."

"He's dead, you know," says my mother, who's still looking into my father's eyes.

"What!" It's hard to make the jump from junior high to death, especially when you're looking at the handsome cock and silky come, alive with sex. "I can't believe it. Can I have this picture?"

My parents look at Johnny. "Do you mind?" I ask him.

I know what he's going to say before he says it. "Of course not." Then he adds, "I thought you never knew another Johnny."

196

"I lied," I say.

My mother turns the photo over and hands it to me upside down. Then she quickly flips another picture up. She looks at it and her eyes go wide. "My God what an enormous pecker! I forgot we had this, Carl."

"So did I." I am turned to as the expert. "Who is this?"

"Timmy Wetzel."

"That's Timmy Wetzel!" My mother takes a closer look. "But he's so . . ."

"What?" asks my father.

"Nondescript," answers my mother.

"Not any more," says my father.

"Of course he's gotten quite fat," says my mother.

"Ain't that a shame." My father smiles with relief.

We go through the pictures one by one. I know every boy by sight.

"Isn't she amazing," my father says to Johnny.

"A prodigy," adds my mother.

"She's positively eidetic," Johnny tells them.

"If you say so," my father says to him.

"You are a strange man," my mother says to him.

My wifely instincts kick right in. "Not compared to you two."

"Why would you say a thing like that?" says my mother.

"I think she finds us quaint," my father tells her. "We're a long way from New York here, Lillian. She's traveled far from where she was born and raised."

I don't want to argue with them, so I change the subject. "Do you have any pictures of Andy?"

"I don't know one boy from the next," says my father. "You're the expert. You tell us."

He hands me what's left of the pictures. I throw them aside

one after the other until I come to one I know is him. All you can see is my head, my hair, with his graceful fingers arched within it. I start to cry.

My parents both together gently take the picture from my hand. They look at it. They shake their heads.

"He loved my hair," I say. "He loved my hair."

"Not as much as I did," says my father.

"His picture of it won a prize," my mother tells Johnny.

"Claret," says my father. "Isn't that what I always called it, Carla? Claret."

Johnny, who'd been wiping away my tears with the soft sides of his huge hands, stops and says, "Don't your own parents even know your name."

I take his hands and hold them against the sides of my face. "There's something I've been meaning to tell you, Johnny . . ."

Storm at Sea

Tonight we had another baby discussion. I'm still afraid to tell him the truth. If I tell him how much I love him will he turn against me. I am betraying you every minute of every day, beloved husband.

We were lying around after dinner. He was reading. I was reading. The tip of his tie was wet from doing the dishes. Music was playing. He told me what it was but I've forgotten. Vocal. 4 Last Songs. 7 Last Words. (But definitely not 8 Days A Week or Sweet Little 16 or 19th Nervous Breakdown) We can both read with music on. It doesn't seem to disturb the silence. The way a television would. We don't own one. We are probably the only 2 adults who ever met and got married and neither one of us had ever owned a TV. My parents used to watch it all the time. I don't think Johnny's did. He says he's never seen TV, except when he was walking by one. He's never actually <u>watched</u> it. It frightens him. He says it doesn't bring the world to you. It takes it away.

I was reading a novel by Milan Kundera. It was recommended to me by one of my favorite customers. She comes in once a year and buys a quilt. She makes me dictate into her little micro-cassette tape recorder everything I know about the quilt she's chosen. But only after she's chosen it. She says it's very important to fall in love with something or somebody before you know anything about their past. But once it's yours, no matter what it is or who it is, you have to discover everything you can, everything there is, good or bad, the truth. She's a particular fan of Graveyard quilts.

Johnny never reads fiction, ever. He says it disturbs him too much. Because he believes it. He told me he was born without the ability to tell fiction from fact. "I receive everything as the truth," he said, "so I avoid the imaginary. Of course the truth turns out to be notional anyway."

That doesn't stop me from reading things to him. Not whole books. God forbid. Little passages. You have to share what moves you. Otherwise live alone.

It's very boring, but I'm going to copy down what I read to him. I hate to interrupt my own thoughts. Every time I copy something it makes me feel like I'm in school. And I left school the day my father froze me in time.

"A child is the very essence of love. Yes, the essence of every love is a child, and it makes no difference at all whether it has ever actually been conceived or born. In the algebra of love a child is the symbol of the magical sum of two beings."

"What are you trying to tell me?" John asks. He's on the bed as usual. He's put his book down on his lap. That's one thing I love about him. Even if you interrupt him he pays attention. He doesn't try to sneak peeks at whatever it was he was just doing. He's a saint that way compared to me.

Was I trying to tell him something. I didn't think I was. Until he asked the question. I thought I was just reading something interesting. Passages in books about having children always make me stop. I'm not a freak. I sometimes feel like a garden where children should grow. But I still don't want one. I still don't need anyone else in the world to love.

But I can't tell him the truth. So I just sat there with my eyes on my book again.

"It does make a difference. Children aren't symbols. Whoever wrote that is lying. Or having his character lie I should say. You never know with novels, do you. You never know to whom you're really listening. But whoever says those words you read sounds like someone who doesn't want to have a child at all. Not at all."

Why can't I tell him? Why do I think it would break his heart to find out I love him so much I don't want to have our child.

I know he cares. But he doesn't blame me. I don't think he blames himself either. We just keep making love. That seems to sustain him. He trusts me. He trusts nature. He's an idiot. Holy. But an idiot.

"You see why I prefer philosophers. They write about the same things with just as much beauty but a great deal more truth. In Nietzsche children are redeemers. Derrida calls pregnancy holy. He says the way you behave even before you have a child influences the child. If you suppress your anger and you offer the hand of conciliation your child will grow out of what's most gentle. But if you're caustic and abrupt with one another, if your love is bitter and untrue—listen to this—it will pour a drop of evil into the dear stranger's cup of life. Tell me that isn't a beautiful vision. The triumph of goodness in the unborn child. We could have a world of saviors. We create a world of scum."

If anyone had told me I'd be married to a man who goes around quoting philosophers and whistling classical music, I would have pictured myself tied up to a bed and not for fun. What I didn't know was how he would connect me to everything he knows. Some men just give you their dicks and the latest crap to enter their minds from Daily Variety or Business Week. Johnny all dressed up in his suit and his big glasses communicates this pool of pain of people trying to figure out what it means to be alive.

What it means to me is to have him to myself and fuck you scum! (I'm the angry one in this family. Johnny is the one "most gentle")

Kansas Troubles

Sometimes when he's fucking me I don't even know who he is. I could swear he's somebody else. I don't know how he does it. I look down there and it's not his dick in me. It's fatter or it's thinner. It's darker or it's even paler than that pale it gets sometimes from the cream I sometimes make not just before I get my period but just before that. He knows I sometimes like to grab hold of it and feel it slide along my palm while it's going through me, but it even feels different sometimes, it's someone else's dick. I don't mind that. He knows I don't. He does this to me and I don't know how. It's not just the dick. Though it starts there. He feels different all over. His shoulder's in a different part of my neck. His hand's not in my hair the usual way. His finger's not on my lips or in my mouth. His breathing's not the same. Even his voice is someone else's voice. It drives me wild. Also he comes faster. But I think that has to do with me. I have this other man on top of me. I can't contain myself. Johnny's behind this, I know that, but it's not Johnny who's doing it to me. Johnny's watching—thank God!—but this stranger has his dick in me and I want to push him off and pull him in at the same time. Mostly the latter.

Flying Geese

A man came into the shop and said he had my diary. He found it in the street. He was holding it behind his back like a bunch of flowers. I asked him if he read it. He said he couldn't. So I plucked out his eyes.

A man came into the shop and said he had my diary. He found it in the street. He was holding it behind his back like a bunch of flowers. I asked him if he read it. He said he had. So I opened it up and we stood together reading.

Johnny never comes to visit me in the shop. He used to come in to learn about quilts before we actually got married. But once we did, he just stayed home. So I sometimes imagine that I see him enter as he did that first day. The only quilt I still have left from then is the Broken Star. It needs work. But that's not why I keep it. I keep it because it's the first thing we ever looked at together. I believe that whatever eyes look at they leave something of themselves upon. So we are joined forever on that quilt. And when I look at it now I can see Johnny. He comes through the door and he's the most beautiful human being I've ever laid eyes on. He hands me my diary and I open it up and we read it together.

I'm sorry, but it's the sexiest thing I can imagine. I am split open like a plum and all the tears I've never cried fly out.

Rising Sun

Johnny was telling me about how Nietzsche and Strindberg wrote letters to each other. In Latin, Greek, German, and French. This was in 1889, when Strindberg returned home to

Stockholm after years of traveling and Nietzsche went crazy. Nietzsche lived 11 more years, but he never recovered. That's when his work became known. He might as well have been dead, Johnny said, just like Schubert, who never got to hear people humming his pretty melodies. Strindberg lived on for many more years after that and gave up socialism to carry on Nietzsche's ideas and then became a mystic. Johnny calls my diary my mystic pad. To me that sounds like a sanitary napkin. But he always wrote about sex. August Strindberg I mean. I once knew a girl named April. There was someone named January in a Jacqueline Susaan novel. And I've heard of Mays and Junes. But never anyone named July. And I never heard of a man named after a month except for August Strindberg. Most months don't fit men. Though maybe March would be a good name for a man. For a woman too. A woman can be named anything really. Words just fit us better. August Strindberg was married to a writer and to actresses and when he wasn't married he jerked off. But he said he couldn't live on masturbation and charity. "I don't want to fuck any more children into the world"—I didn't know people spoke like that then, which they'll probably say about us someday—so he tried to find a woman who already had children, because he said he couldn't work without the sound of children's voices.

Johnny made him seem real to me. I could see him sadly jerking off into a handkerchief and could hear the voices of children as if they were my own.

There was a time Johnny said when Strindberg couldn't make his wife come and he thought it was his fault. So he went to have his penis measured. Johnny read to me from one of his letters. "I arranged a cock inspection at 3 o'clock one summer morning, in the presence of witnesses, including a whore. The whore gave me her approbatur, except sine laude."

"What does that mean?" I asked.

"It means, you pass, but without honors."

I laughed.

"What about mine?" asked Johnny.

"Your what?"

Johnny got up from the bed and came to stand beside me where I was sitting. He unzipped his pants.

"You want me to measure you?"

"No. Just tell me. You know. You've seen so many. You've seen a flood of men."

"True."

"So."

His penis was before my eyes. I could have stuck out my tongue and touched it.

"I'm sure Mr. Strindberg's wasn't growing during the examination."

"That's probably because his wife wasn't there."

"Big dik-dik," I said, to make him laugh. According to Johnny that's the name of one of the only animals who doesn't cheat on his wife.

"You think so?" He wasn't laughing. Men. I should have known.

"Big."

But it isn't. From what I know, which I guess is something, it's about average. But it's very beautiful. It's the most beautiful thing I've ever seen. And when it's inside me, it's as big as I am. It is all I am, and so is he.

Old Maid's Ramble

Johnny took me out to Bouley tonight for our 1st anniversary. When he told me where we were going, I said, "How did you get a reservation?" "Oh, I had to make it long before I met you." "Did you tell them it was for our anniversary?" "Of course."

It can't be true. But I believe him.

Dinner took 6 hours. We both had the chef's tasting menu which means we ate whatever they brought us. 9 courses. But only 2 bottles of wine. And 1 of champagne of course. And now I sit here not full and not tired waiting for Johnny to come out of his bathroom. We have no windows to the east but I can hear the morning light on the roof above.

We talked the whole time. Even for us 6 hours is a lot.

Johnny said, "I'd like to make a toast." He raised his glass. "Don't worry. I won't quote Nietzsche." I laughed, and he said, "This year with you has been an eternity of joy for me. Life was given to me, but only you could have brought me to life. Thank you for marrying me, Clara. I love you with all my mind."

What other man could have made me cry and laugh at the same time. And what is it about a man who can make fun of himself that makes him so unbearably desirable. We touched glasses. I sniffled and wiped my tears on my sleeve and raised my glass and said, "Fuck me, Johnny. You're the only one." Little does he know how true that is.

Later on we tried to figure out how many times we'd fucked. I suppose that's what couples do on their 1st anniversary.

"I remember every one," said Johnny, which I wouldn't put past him.

I don't remember every one. I wouldn't want to. I don't even bother to mention most of them in here. To me fuckings aren't separate events. They accumulate in you like knowledge.

"Do you think we do it too much?" I asked. Ingenuously. Disingenuously. What's the difference? I'll have to ask my husband. What kind of husband would a husband be if he can't answer a question like that.

"Well," he said, which he never says unless he's about to make a speech, "there are contradictory instructions in that regard. Methodius as well as John Chrysostom say that if you don't do it too much you can still go to heaven. So long as you're married of course. The church itself says you don't have to do it but you're allowed to do it. It took 5 long centuries of painful debate for this to be decided. Nuptius non concubitus sed consensus facit. But only if you're married. And not that often. Sundays, no—the resurrection. Saturdays, no—the Virgin Mary. Fridays, no—Christ's death. Thursdays, no— Christ's arrest. That leaves Mondays and Tuesdays, except for certain periods of fasting and commemoration—the week before communion, the 40 days before Easter, before Christmas, before the Pentecost. Otherwise, fine, if you can bear the animus of the saints. Jerome said it's dirty. Arnobius said it's debased. Tertullian said it's opprobious. Methodius said it's indecent. And Ambrose said it's debauched. Of course they knew this from experience. They were all reputedly great lovers in their time. Augustine prayed for chastity—but not right now. Such a tired, anticipated sentiment. Like people on diets—just let me eat this one last creme brulee. I prefer what Napoleon wrote to Josephine: I'll be arriving in Paris tomorrow—don't wash."

I laughed and asked Johnny, "Would you prefer me not to bathe?" (God, I was starting to sound like Josephine. It must have been the champagne)

He looked at me over the top of the shaky little lamp on our table. "Would you prefer me to be Napoleon?"

I shook my head and felt the bubbles wash over my gums onto my lips. I looked at him learning how to make jokes and thought to myself that I wouldn't prefer him to be anyone but himself. Except in bed, where lately he sometimes seems to be someone else, no one in particular, just someone else. No one has ever done that with me before. Most men try so hard to prove who they are. Johnny seems willing to sacrifice who he is to whoever I might want him to be. He can do this with a different touch. Or a touch timed differently. Or a sound he'll make that doesn't sound like him exactly. Or the way he'll move his body. Or maybe it's just an illusion. Maybe I'm just recreating him. But if I am, he knows it. I can tell he knows it. And he becomes who I want him to be. Not anyone in particular. I don't have fantasies about people I know. But I do like to be seen for the first time. I enjoy the beginningness of it.

I remembered how I told Johnny the first time I met him that I felt religions crushed women. Everything he'd just said made me feel the same way. What all those saints thought was dirty wasn't sex. It was women. And Johnny knew it. That's why he told me the Napoleon story. "Isn't that right?" I asked him.

"Well, the Jews were different," he said. "But aren't they always. My father hates Jews because he never knows what side they're on. They defend. They prosecute. They think they are the people of the law. He railed against them at every opportunity. And he so rarely got a chance to put any of them away. He used to say that a Jew would be the only person he'd rather sentence to death than to life in prison. Why would I give a Jew a chance to sit and think? he would say. It's like throwing B'rer Rabbit in the briar patch. But the Jews didn't tell their people when they couldn't fuck. They told them when they had to. The writers of the Talmud were able to face what other religious scribes could never acknowledge—that women's desire is greater than men's. So they told men it was their duty to satisfy their wives. Workers who lived at home were instructed to do it twice a week. Salesmen once a week.

Camel drivers once a month, no matter how far away their camels took them. Students of the torah had to do it every Friday night. And the rich every night."

"Are we rich?" I teased him.

"Even if we aren't we certainly pretend to be."

He's in bed now, waiting for me. It's a new day. A new year for us. I don't think I'll bathe.

Crown of Thorns

Health club after work today. I skipped aerobics and did 20 minutes by myself on the Nordictrak. I put the leg meter up to 8. Then I did free weights. Then I did another 20 minutes on the stair-stepper with the climbing attachment. Then I did crunches. Then I went for a massage.

I didn't care who did it. I never request. I don't want to get too attached to anyone in particular. Except I did say I wanted a man. That's my only requirement.

I stripped and lay down. I put a towel over my ass and kept adjusting it like a tablecloth. Then I closed my eyes.

I didn't open them when he came in. I listened for the door to close and his footsteps approaching me.

"Hi," he said. "I'm Rolph."

"Is that spelled like the therapy?"

"Thanks for asking. Most people call me Ralph. It's R-o-l-p-h. Rolph. But I thought therapy started with a t. Or t-h to be exact."

I opened my eyes. All I could see of him was from nipples to knees. Some of them wear white pants with a belt and a t-shirt. Some of them wear tank tops and bicycle shorts. Rolph was in the latter category. His shorts looked like he'd stuck a turtle down the front. Or maybe it was his brain. (Why do I get so sexist when I'm getting a massage!)

"I'm Clara."

"Hi, Clara."

"Hi, Rolph."

"Oil?"

"No thanks. Use my sweat."

"Just my preference." But I could tell from his voice he wished he could smear me with something lemony.

He put his hands on my shoulders. His doubts flew away. "You're right. No drag. No friction. Hard butter on a warm plate."

As he moved around my body, he kept naming things. On my shoulder blades he said, "Tight scapula." On my joints he said, "Let's unfreeze that synovial capsule." On my arm he said, "Strong humerus." And on my face he said, "Nicely defined zygomatics."

I couldn't stand it any more. I said, "Please work on my sacral vertebrae."

"First the thoracic." He sounded a little testy. I guess I had invaded his territory, which only happens to be my own body.

So he worked his way slowly down my back. There was little pain. I'm supple and I don't resist. Besides, I concentrate on the towel. I see it and my ass beneath it and his hands moving toward it. I want him to lift it off me, but he won't. They never do. You have to do that yourself. And I won't. But when he reaches the valley of the shadow of ass I rise from the table. It never fails. I can feel my pubic hair release the vinyl like velcro.

"Coccyx," Rolph explains. For the first time he doesn't have a hand on me. We've lost contact. I've made him nervous.

I lower my ass. The towel shifts. He can see me.

He moves the towel back up very daintily. Without touching my skin. I am very disappointed. But I still leave him a big tip. And when Johnny hugged me when I got home I reached behind me and put his hand down right where Rolph refused to touch. "I had a massage," I say. "Oh, good," says Johnny and he sticks both hands right down the back of my tights.

Bridal Stairway

I was reading A Room Of Your Own again and stopped to read this to Johnny: "Women have served all these centuries as looking-glasses possessing the magic and delicious power of reflecting the figure of man at twice its natural size."

"What do you suppose she means by the figure of man?" he asks.

I pointed. "That."

The Road to California

Tonight I had my best chance ever to tell Johnny my real name.

We were sitting around after dinner. Johnny pushed all our dishes to one end of the table. The bones from our lamb chops made question marks on our empty plates. The loft smelled like somebody had put rosemary on our pulse points. We weren't listening to music. We were listening to the wind. And to the sleet tapping messages on our huge windows. "Hold each other tight tonight. Keep each other warm." Johnny put out a thick hunk of Parmagiano Reggiano and opened a bottle of Amarone. The label was handwritten. I thought how lucky I was to have handwriting no one can read.

Johnny watched me take my first sip. I always love it when his eyes are on my lips. When anyone's eyes are on my lips. I feel transgressed. There's no other part of my body that arouses me so to have someone stare at it.

"It's bitter," I tell him.

"That's where its name comes from. It's also high in alcohol. You should sip it slowly. It's meant for a night like this. Chill. Blowy. It's meant for contemplation."

"Of what?"

He tapped his glass against mine and took his first sip. "Whatever."

"God?" I asked him.

I enjoy provoking him. Provocation is important in a wife. Before I met Ike I went out with a criminal lawyer who told me I provoked him. I told him I didn't know what he meant. He told me that in the law provocation means something said or done that leads to murder in hot passion and without afore-thought. "You want to kill me for something I've said or done," I asked him. "Something you haven't done," he says. I not only never fucked him. Or touched him with so much as a nail clipping. I wouldn't even see him again. He tried to break down my door one night. Then for a while he left strange messages on my machine: "If I can't have you nobody will" sort of thing. Finally I called him back and told him "nobody will." He made me promise, so I did which was no big deal because I didn't think anybody would, and he told me if any-body did he would sue me. So sue me Sigh (which is how I used to spell his name in my mind even though I knew it was Sy which is short for Seymour) A few other guys who I refused tried to force me but I always escaped by finally get-ting them to touch themselves. I talked them out of having me. But there were times when I thought about Sigh and his "provocation" and thought I might die. Not that I think Johnny would ever kill me. But I love to provoke him to the same kind of hot passion. I don't want rage. He never gets angry at anything anyway. I just want murder turned into lust. I want to be desired as much on the day I die as I was on the day we married. Who doesn't.

211

"I wish there were a God," he said.

"Why?"

"So we could have something or someone to blame. The absence of God puts the burden squarely on ourselves. Most people can't live with that."

"So what do they do?"

"Pretend to believe."

"I believe."

He looked at me as if I'd suddenly become more precious. Then he poured me more wine. "Your God is an It, as I recall," he said.

"Of course."

"What's an It?"

"Something that sees."

"Sees what?"

"Everything."

"And . . ."

"That's all. It just sees."

"It doesn't do anything? It just sees?"

"To see is to know."

"So what does It know?"

"Everything."

"What does It know about me?" He pounded the side of his wine glass against his chest.

"It knows you hate It. You hate It and don't believe in It at the same time. But don't you see—your hatred makes God real."

"You're right," he said. So much for provocation. "I wouldn't hate what I don't believe in. God the Father. I'm always afraid He's going to abandon me, so I disavow Him. Perhaps that's why I didn't speak for so long—to confront silence with silence. But He's so very hard to rid oneself of."

"Try mine," I said.

"God the camera."

Johnny laughed, but I nearly spilled my wine. How does he know these things about me.

He filled my glass quarterway. "You clarify things for me," he said. "Have I ever told you that? With an a. Clarafication. You make everything clear. Perhaps that's why I married you. That. And this."

I let him take me to bed. And the whole time, as he lay atop me with my lips at his ear, I wanted to say I am not Clara but instead it was his name I called.

Barn Raising

When I handed Johnny the van Meckenem engraving and said Happy Valentine's Day, he closed his eyes and then buried his face in his hands. "But I don't have anything for you. I didn't know it was Valentine's Day. I've never celebrated Valentine's Day in my life."

Should I laugh or cry.

"Didn't you exchange valentines in grammar school?"

He lifted his head. "Actually, I did."

"And didn't your mother ever give you a valentine?"

He smiled. "Yes, she did."

"So what's the problem here, John?"

He takes both my hands. "I forgot I had a life before you."

"Well, you've made me forget the life I had before you. And that's the best Valentine's present I ever got."

"May I have it?"

I know he's not referring to my gift. It's still on the table, wrapped. "Have what?"

"The life you had before me."

"If you can find it," I say. "In the meantime, open this."

He does. I watch his face. I wonder if I know him well

enough yet to know if he really likes it. He stares at it intensely. "Teach me how to see it," he says.

So I tell him all about it. And that's his true gift to me: opening his mind to let mine in.

Wheel of Chance

I did it! I got Mr. Labrovitz into bed! I've never seen a man so frightened. Even the boys back in junior high didn't shake as much as he did at first. He said, "I don't do this. I've never done this." I said, "Don't worry. You won't have to do anything you don't want to. I just want to see your body." That relaxed him a bit. And it was true. Every day he wears a suit to work and every day I want to break through that suit. Even if it is Armani and looks beautiful on him. I've never spent so much time with one man before. Except for my father of course. I really just wanted to see him. It was driving me crazy not knowing what was under there. He's my boss. How can I go on working for him if I can't see him. So I invited him home. "Whatever for?" he asked. I lied. "My boyfriend wants to meet you." He didn't seem to care about that. He wasn't interested in my life at all. "I'll take a raincheck," he said. So I said, "I quit." That got his attention. "You can't quit, Clara. I'm not tired of you yet." "I'll quit if you don't come over." So finally he came. And when we got here I gave him a glass of wine and told him to get undressed. He looked around. "Where's your boyfriend?" "I don't have a boyfriend." That's when he started to shake and said, "I don't do this. I have never done this." But when I told him I just wanted to see his body, he said, "That's all?" "Yes." Because it was true. "Why?" "Because I like beautiful things." Aren't I shameless. I couldn't take my eyes off him while he took off his suit. His shirt. Everything else. He kept talking the whole time. But his words couldn't stop me from seeing him. "I'm only doing this because you're appealing to the narcissist in me. And there's not anything in me but a narcissist. But you seem to know that already, don't you, Clara, you shameless thing you." Now only his fingers were shaking, as they opened up his clothes. When he was completely naked, he held his arms out like Jesus and said, "Ta da." His dick wasn't hard but it was pretty. I couldn't stop staring at him. He stopped talking. My room has never been quieter. Finally, after how long I have no idea, I said, "You look wonderful." "Do you really think so?" "Yes." "Inside every narcissist there's a pessimist struggling to get out." "Well, he should be optimistic." Isaac laughed. (My rule in life is: once you've seen someone's dick you're allowed to use their first name.) "Tell me what you see," he said. "Pretend I'm sculpture. Something Greek. Greco-Jewish." His arms were at his side. He rotated his wrists so his palms faced me. Then he stood still. He was no longer shaking. "I see green eyes. Long lashes. I see your nostrils moving. Nothing else is. Your lips are red from the wine. The top one's mean. The bottom one's kind. Your neck is thick, but the sinews stand out, so it looks slender and strong. There's a pulse going in it, I can see it through the skin. Your shoulders have veins in them. Your chest is so tight it looks bulletproof. Your nipples are small and clean like a little boy's. And they almost point down because of the muscles in your chest. Your ribs make you look like someone's hands are holding you together and your stomach has those grids in it. Your belly button's a little white grape. You don't have hips to speak of. We used to have cheerleaders in junior high who wore kneesocks and short skirts so all you got to see of them were their thighs. I didn't go broadcasting it around, but I used to think those thighs were the most beautiful single things in the world. They were smooth and pale and strong and I used to long for them, I don't know what for. I thought I could stare at them for hours on end, but of course you never got to see them for more than a few seconds at a time. Your calves bulge out at the sides like parentheses. You have very long toes. And your toenails are pristine. Also, I like your hair a little messed up like that." His eyes were closed tight. I supposed he was trying to see himself. "And?" he said to keep me going. "And," I said, "I've never imagined a cock like that. It's very beautiful and very hard and pointing at yours truly." "It's the narcissist speaking. Not the man. Can you understand that, Clara? I don't care for women. I don't like their equipment. On an intimate level, its aesthetics are off. On the other hand, to give the devil her due, the macroaesthetics are superb. I could look at you forever. Which is to say, at least a year. But I'm never going to touch you. Is that clear. And you're never going to touch me. I won't permit it. Do we understand each other." It wasn't a question, exactly, but I said, "I understand." I didn't tell him what I understood—that he is the perfect man for me. And my boss all rolled up into one! We can be together all day every day and we can have sex with ourselves and he will let me watch him to my heart's delight. "You can take off your clothes then," he said. "Not today." "Are you sure?" "I just want to watch you." "Watch me what?" "Put your hand on it." There's no more beautiful sight than watching a man getting himself off. My breath starts coming in the exact rhythm as his stroking. I feel more connected through my eyes than if that thing was all the way inside me I guess. Just before he came, Isaac started saying, "Richard, Richard, oh Christ I'm sorry Richard," and I said, "Now darling, now darling, now darling." His semen gushed out just like any other man's. All those babies flying through the air. I got him tissues. It's not just gay men who get so fastidious right after they climax. "So who were you apologizing to," I asked him. "This Richard because you're with me or me because you were thinking of this Richard?" "You. I didn't want your feelings to be hurt." "They weren't." When he was clean and dry he looked down at himself. "I feel funny." "You look beautiful." "What do you want from me, Clara?" "Nothing." He reached down to get his underpants. But before he put them on he swiveled around on his heels so his back was to me and said, "So how come you never mentioned my ass!" Then he laughed so loud he couldn't hear me praise it.

He left very quickly. I'm sure he's worried about confronting me in the morning at the gallery. Next time I'm going to let him see me.

Courthouse Steps

Sometimes I think the best thing that ever happened to me was my father taking the pictures. Because if he hadn't I wouldn't be a virgin. One thing would have led to another and I would have started fucking those boys. Beginning with Andy. Even though I loved him I know I would have fucked others. My mind is too full of fucking even now, and I haven't fucked anybody. I don't even know what it's like. Sometimes when I'm watching a man touch himself, I feel my eyes are magnets and they aren't just attached to him but they pull him toward me, into me, and I can almost feel the flesh I'm watching disappear within my body. But what does it really feel like. That's the mystery.

I don't want to know. My curiosity is not as great as my contentment. I feel so pure. I feel like a heroine. I am what American girls are supposed to be. I am untouched. I am innocent. I am immaculate. I am alone.

I don't mean I'm lonely. I mean I stand alone. I'm apart from everybody else. Here I live in this city where when you just walk down the street you bump into strangers with your shoulders and your clothes brush and sometimes the backs of your hands touch and still my flesh is not tangled up with anyone else's. That's what I mean by alone. I am totally unto myself.

Everyone should be a virgin. Forever.

Cookie Cutter

When we were making love tonight, Johnny said, "Clara."
I didn't know if it was a question or what.
"Clara," he said again.
What does he want?
"Clara."

It was my name, and it wasn't. I mean, Clara, Carla, both of them are my names and they're not. Nobody's born with one. It isn't like a nose. It's no more attached to you than a scarf. It isn't <u>yours</u>, not even when you chose it for yourself, like me.

If I were the only person in the world, I wouldn't have a name. I wouldn't need one. And if there were only 2 of us in the world, we wouldn't need names either. When he spoke, I would know it was to me.

He and I are the only people in the world, when we make love. There are no others, except as we imagine them, and they aren't real. So each time he said my name as he said it over and over, he took my name from me. He pulled it from my body, from my skin, from my lips. Clara. Clara. Clara. Clara. Each time he said it ground me deeper into the mattress. And pulled him deeper into me. My name was leaving me. It was a bird above the bed. I didn't want to let it go. I turned beneath him, side to side. I shook my head. I struggled. But he said, "Clara. Clara." It became a name I didn't recognize. A sound I didn't know. It wasn't me. And that left only me beneath him, a stranger, nameless, new. It was like being born. It was the most exciting, joyous feeling in the world. And the world was empty, truly empty, of anyone but us.

When Johnny fell asleep, I got out of bed. I don't usually do that. I usually stick some tissues between my legs and hold him in my arms. I write in here before. But tonight I got up and sat down here to write about this. I wanted to think about what happened to me. I wanted to try to understand it. I wanted to describe my ecstasy. I wanted to say this about it

Wild Goose Chase

He asked me, "Would you rather love someone more the first day you meet or the last day you're together on earth?"

"The last day we're together on earth."

He held out his arms to me and we danced. No music was playing.

Lazy Daisy

I finally have a girlfriend. (Not to mention a new job) I lost all my girlfriends when I got interested in boys. I thought I'd have millions of girlfriends when I got to New York. I pictured myself leaving boys behind and walking down the avenues holding arms with girls. But that turned out to be a hair commercial. First of all, I didn't leave boys behind. I just don't let them touch me. And I don't touch them. Secondly, I had forgotten how to talk to girls, if I ever knew how in the first place.

Then I get hired to work at the Labrovitz Gallery and I walk in to start working this morning and there's another girl sitting at what I figure is my desk, since it's the only desk there. It's the only place to sit there.

"May I help you?" she says.

"I'm starting today."

"Starting what?"

"Working here."

She looks bewildered.

"What are you supposed to do?"

"Reception. Catalogs. Hang paintings. Artist relations, whatever that is."

"I'll tell you what that is. It's telling painters that their latest work's the best thing they ever did."

"What if it isn't?"

"They're artists. You lie. It's the only language they under-stand. Except money. Money talks."

"What does it say?"

"Fuck you."

I didn't know if she was saying that to me or telling me what money says when it talks. So I didn't answer.

"So who hired you?"

"Well I went through an agency. But—"

"Have a seat." She got up.

"I don't want to take your seat."

"It's yours now."

"What about you?"

"I'm fired."

"How do you know that?"

"Because the same thing happened to me."

"What?"

"I walked in here and told the girl sitting here that I was starting. That's how he does things."

"Who?"

"Labrovitz. He doesn't like confrontations."

"But it isn't right."

"Tell me the truth."

"What?"

"Do you really believe in right and wrong?"

"That's . . ."

"Complicated?"

"Yes."

She came around the desk and put her arm around my shoulder. "You'll do just fine." Then she took my arm and walked me to the back of the gallery. There were 3 doors. "That one's storage and supplies. Canvases. Coffee filters. Plastic cups and barf bags for openings. That one's the W.C. Customers only, needless to say. Watch out for art connoisseurs among the homeless." She knocked on the third door and opened it before anyone answered.

There was a young man in a beautiful black suit sitting behind a desk. We seemed to interrupt him staring off into space.

"Isaac Labrovitz," said the girl.

He finally looked at us. "I see you two have met. If you're who I think you are."

"She is," said the girl.

"What's your name again?" he asked.

"Clara Bell."

"Clarabell what?" asked the girl.

"I believe that's her name," said Mr. Labrovitz, if that's who he was. I had imagined someone much older.

"It is," I said.

"From Howdy Doody?" asked the girl.

"Yes."

"You must have strange parents," she said.

"Very."

"Don't we all," she said.

"Isn't it remarkable," said Mr. Labrovitz.

"I like her name," the girl told him.

"I was referring to how much alike you 2 look. You give the impression of being willowy without having the gall to be taller than I am. I detest towering women. Have you noticed how many more of them are being made that way these days? And you both look a bit like boys without giving up a dram of your femininity. That's very important. It's 1984 after all. We must challenge conformity in every way. I tell you, that agency is first-rate. Are you sure you aren't sisters? Now Monica, why don't you show Clara the ropes and then take her out to lunch. On me. Just bring me the receipt. I'll reimburse you.

And by the way, you were magnificent. The best assistant I've ever had."

"Then why are you firing me? I need the work, you know."

"Need you ask—because I get tired of looking at the same person day after day."

"Turnover," she said.

"That's the key," he answered. "In life as in art. As for you, Clara, the same thing will happen. About a year from now you'll look up from that desk out there and share a precious moment of bewilderment with someone who I can only hope is as fetching as you. In the meantime, you will be the most important person in my life. Goodbye."

Monica took me for lunch to Da Silvano on Avenue of the Americas. I refuse to call it 6th Avenue. To me New York City is America. The rest of it's another country.

"Spend a lot," she said.

I looked at the menu. "It's very expensive."

"Yes, it is. But put that down. You should never order from a menu, especially in an Italian restaurant. The waiter wants to seduce you. The chef wants to cook something he didn't cook yesterday. The owner wants to be able to charge you something unprintable. And Ike won't be happy unless you bring him back a huge bill. Let's have a bottle of wine. An old one."

We ended up having 2 bottles. It was like a date, and I fell in love with her.

"What will you do now?" I asked her.

"Work for the competition."

"Another gallery?"

"Don't be silly. An artist."

She told me artists were always asking her to work for them. "Some of them are the most disorganized people in the world. And the rest of them are the most organized people in the world. So they all need all the help they can get. What about you? Are you organized?"

I told her about my diary. I have never told anyone about my diary. I showed her my handwriting (not in my diary!) I told her my life story, or at least the interesting parts. I told her about the photographs (after a lot of wine)

"That's sick," she said.

"Yes."

"It's a form of rape."

"Yes."

"It's almost incest. By both parents."

"Yes."

"But how lucky you are."

"Why?"

"To be such an object of desire."

I told her I was a virgin.

All she said to that was "I wish I were."

I asked her if she'd slept with Mr. Labrovitz.

"He's gay."

"Did you try?"

"Of course."

"What happened?"

"He told me to go practice my sgraffito on someone else." (I just looked that word up so I know I spelled it right. I also know Monica really does know what it means)

"What does that mean?"

"Not to try to scratch beneath the surface."

She paid our bill with a credit card. She gave me the receipt and told me to give it to Ike and tell him to mail her the money along with her last paycheck.

"Aren't you coming back?" I asked.

"I'll walk you to the door."

I gave her my phone number.

She gave me hers.

We walked arm in arm through Soho.

Thank you for being my friend, Monica.

Hozanna

He says, "Have you ever been fucked like this before?"

"Oh, yes," I lie. "Many times."

Which only makes him fuck me better than I've ever been fucked before.

Rolling Stone

Today I closed the shop for lunch and took Johnny shopping. For somebody with so much money he never wants to buy anything. All he gets are CDs and books, usually through the mail. Sometimes he splurges on a fancy bottle of wine. And presents for me. The only time he goes out of the loft without me is when he's going to buy me something. He says the reason for that is this is where he lives, not out there. I kid him that he meets one of those strange maiden girls he's always looking at when we're out together and that's why he buys me so many presents.

I love to be out in the streets with him and watch him watch women. He doesn't do what men do when they put that stare on you like they were capturing your image on some film that loops behind their eyes. It's more that he watches them leave. Even when they're walking right toward us. I can almost hear him saying goodbye to them. It's not that I want him to have them. I don't want to be the only woman in the world, the way he said I was. I want to be them all and then for him to have them.

I took him into Armani. It was very crowded because it's lunchtime but there must be something about Johnny that makes people think he's got money to spend, because we had a boy and a girl on us right away. They were both almost as tall as Johnny and looked like incestuous siblings. Their clothes were the color of eels. I was about to make some excuse for what Johnny was wearing when the boy said, "That's an amazing look." And the girl said, "Your shoes are presumptuous." "I'm square," said Johnny. "Exactly," said the boy. "Fadulous," said the girl. What a ditz, I thought, but Johnny said, "I like that word." She said, "It means . . ." Johnny held up his hand. "No need." She was his forever. He could read her mind. Which would take all of 2 minutes, and that's with a bathroom break. "Let's get out of here," I said. But they wouldn't let him go. "Do you model?" asked the boy. "Oh no," said Johnny. "You should," said the girl. "You look . . . you look . . . you look . . ." "Gifted," said the boy. "No," said the girl, "not gifted." "What then?" said the boy. "Wholesome," said the girl. "Exactly," said the boy. "Your clothes are unapproach-able. Your shoes . . . well, Shibboleth told you. And your glasses . . . they remind me of my favorite professor. He was like a father to me. Are you a teacher?" "Good heavens no." "Well what do you do then? Don't tell me you're a designer." The girl thought she had it. But Johnny said, "I'm a husband." "Don't I wish," said the girl. "It goes with the clothes," said the boy. "I'm glad you like them," said Johnny. "But Clara admires your wares. What might you have for her?" That son of a bitch, he bought me 4 thousand dollars worth of things. He called me his little onion in front of those 2 dummies.

So I took him up the street to Barnes and Noble and told him I'd buy him any book in the place. And what does he buy? A blank book! And he gives it to me. I can't believe it. "Did I ever tell you about my first day in New York?" "Tell me again. Over lunch." I tell him I have to get back and open the shop. But he takes my arm and pulls me a couple of blocks south to Union Square Cafe. Even though it's late, they don't have a table. So we sit at the bar and we both order tunaburgers and I tell him how I got a room at the Martha Washington Hotel and I threw my bag down and walked out of there and through some park and got to Fifth Avenue, which I couldn't believe they actually let you walk on, and came to this bookstore and bought a blank book. "Isn't that amazing," said John. I asked him what. "You told me that story, but you never told me what you bought that day." So the book he bought me becomes all the more precious to him. He takes it out of the plastic bag and opens it up and leafs through the blank pages. I don't know if he's trying to read what I'll write there or he's just trying to see me at 16 with a book like this one in my hand. He wants the impossible: me before he met me.

Snail's Trail

I never know what to say when I'm about to come. Whoever I'm with's looking at me and as soon as I get close I start to talk. I say I'm there. I say help me. I say do it. Where do those ridiculous words come from. I don't talk like that. What am I trying to say. Whoever I'm with doesn't know what to do. I'm not talking to him. But there has to be somebody somewhere to help me. In the meantime I sound ridiculous. Someone should publish a book with instructions. What to say when you're about to come. At least when I'm actually coming I don't say anything. I just scream and moan as Jonathan Edwards says. Words fail me thank God.

Log Cabin

I just put the last piece of grandma Belzidases quilt on the cover of this book. I remember I used it on the very first book I bought on the day I started my diary which also happened to be my first day in New York. A lot has happened since then. You can read about it in my diary. Except you can't. I don't even know who you are. So go away. I like the idea that the first and last thing I used the quilt for is my diary. I also made pillow covers from the quilt. I am lying on those pillows now. Actually, I'm not lying on them. I'm lying against them. Today I moved into my own apartment finally. If you can call it that. It's one room. Nobody lives like this in the Valley of the Moon. But I wouldn't go back there if it was the last place on earth. Which is exactly what it is. The last place God would ever visit if It visited earth.

No one can find me now. I have my own apartment. I cut my hair. (You should see it short. I never knew how pretty I really am) I changed my name. Clara Bell. It's almost like my old name, which I used to love. One of the branches of my family even changed their name to Bell but that was because they didn't think Belzidas was American enough. They were trying to fit in. Me, I'm trying to fit out.

Some guy in a bar told me it was a clown's name. Yes, I said, isn't it awful. What kind of parents would give a kid a name like mine? I told him I ran away from home because of my name. "Isn't that a little extreme?" he said.

Not compared to the truth.

In the Valley of the Moon where the Pomo and the Wappo Indians once roamed there was a beautiful girl named Carla Belzidas. She lived in a nice house on a nice street in a little town with hills all around and grapes growing everywhere. Her mother was a bookkeeper at a winery, but it was in the next county over, on the Silverado Trail. Her father was a commercial photographer who was supposed to take pictures of nothing but things. His claim to fame was how he could capture the sunlight that had just broken through the fog from the west in a glass of wine so that the sunlight seemed to be

228

part of the wine itself and came out of the page (if it was glossy enough I guess) and actually landed red on the lips and eyes of anybody looking at it. At least that's what somebody said about it when one of his photographs won a prize from an ad club and they all went down to San Francisco to see him get the prize and he made a speech and said he was inspired to capture the color of the sun in the wine from the way he had seen the sun in her hair. "That was the color I wanted," he told everybody. "The color of my daughter Carla's hair." "Oh, you've embarrassed her," her mother said after her father had come back to their banquet table with everybody applauding him and her hair, but she said, "No he didn't. I wasn't embarrassed at all." Nothing embarrassed her by then. She was 14 years old. She was opening up to everything. That's how she felt. She was exploding. She would see herself lying on the ground with her arms stretched out and her legs apart and her eyes open and mouth open and ears open and forehead open and she'd say take me, hold me, shake me, burn me, twist me, grab me, kiss me, fuck me. Just walking through the air was a thrill. Her sheets were criminals. Wiping her ass was a whole new kind of love letter. Nothing embarrassed her. She was born again. She was naked and unashamed and ready to get handed around. The boys got a whiff of her fast enough. It wasn't anything she said. It wasn't anything she did. She was just a wine-headed column of want. At first she just kissed. That was enough. It happened on her lips, but it involved every living cell in her body. She was a pool with one finger stuck in it and the whole thing boils. Her lips ached, her eyes burned, and rain fell in her panties. Then it was her skin. Touch me, touch me. Not her body parts. Just her skin. Under her arms. On the back of her neck. Her throat. Her shoulders. Down her sides. Her waist, where she'd put boys hands because they never thought of that themselves and they preferred her breasts, naturally, though what she liked best about them was to look down and see them in a boy's hands. She liked them to hold her breasts from underneath, not cover them up and start grinding them into her chest. It took a while for her to pay attention to whoever she was with. It took months. She even forgot sometimes that anyone was there. She made them all into pieces of herself. While they were touching her, her own hands held on for dear life to the air around her. But once she started touching boys, she saw them. And once she saw them, she started telling them apart. That's when she got boyfriends. The first boy she took her pants off for was her first boyfriend. His name was Paul. It's the first name I remember. He kept his own pants on. He didn't touch her. He just looked. He kept blinking, and staring through his blinks. "You can touch it," she said. "No thanks." He blushed and went back after her breasts. She never said goodbye to him but she got other boyfriends. They knew how to touch her, or she taught them how. The first time she came unalone was in the middle of a lesson. She curled up like a snail and trapped his hand between her legs. When she finally opened her eyes, she couldn't speak. There didn't seem to be anything it would be possible to say. So she smiled at him instead. But he looked frightened and pulled his hand away and looked at it like he'd shot somebody with it and wiped it on his underpants. After that she went for older boyfriends. Not much older. In the next grade, maybe 2. They took their pants off and that was something. The first time she saw a penis she looked around her room. The boy got scared. Roger Stare. He covered himself up. His eyes followed hers. "What are you looking at? Who's there?" "Sorry," she said. She tried not to laugh. He got dressed and left. She didn't tell him she'd been looking around at all her stuffed animals. She sees a penis for the first time and wonders what her animals could possibly be thinking of this development. But it was her who the sight of Roger's penis haunted. So from then on she didn't worry about her animals. She concentrated on her own shock. And she never got used to it. Not to this day. They are such a surprise. They take up so much space. Not because they're big but because they don't look like they belong anywhere. Certainly not on a person. Their color never matches. It's like somebody's mother never taught him how to dress. They're never the right shape, though maybe they would be if they didn't have balls hanging off them. And they're all out of proportion. They make men look ridiculously beautiful. She couldn't keep her eyes off them. Or her hands. The first time she touched a boy he came. She'd read about it but who could possibly describe anything like this. All she did was put the tip of one finger against the side of it, just to kind of test reality, and the thing jumped up and away, and Kevin said something like "Oh no" or "Uh oh" or "Oh oh," and his penis for one split second stood completely still in the air, and while it was like that, completely still, out of the end of it flew a round white little moon that landed halfway across the bed on her pillow. Then there was no stopping it. His penis moved up and down all by itself while white ribbons streamed out of it and came down one after another on her bare skin, each one a little farther down her body, starting with her lips and chin and then right in the space between her breasts and into the crease in her stomach and onto her thighs, her knees, the toes of one foot. It was hot when it landed, almost burning. Then it cooled very quickly and made her shiver. But she didn't move a muscle. She just sat there before him watching how his penis rested now among the tufts of her bedspread. It was still swollen, but it looked soft instead of hard. And very slowly it was crawling away from her, back to him. She reached over and put her hand under it. It weighed less than it looked like it would weigh. He said, "What about your parents?" Kevin had never been here before. They'd never done this before. Did guys get fearful of the consequences only after they'd climaxed? She never worried about her parents because she never once thought there was anything wrong with what she was doing. But to make Kevin relax she said, "My mother's at work in Napa, and my father's over in Dry Creek Valley. You know that." "Are you sure?" "Kevin, I do this all the time." "You do? Who with?" "Boys, of course." Kevin came again. He seemed much happier with himself this time. Before he left, he offered to make her come. She said no. This seemed to relieve him. He said, "Please don't do this with anyone else." She said sure. And she didn't do it with anyone else. She did it with everyone else. Well, not everyone. But everyone she could. Why not? She was curious. It was fun. And it was the best way to get to know boys. It's how you learn that people lie when they say boys are all alike. Boys aren't all animals. Boys aren't all pigs. Boy's aren't all crude or awkward or insensitive. Boys don't all want the same thing. Unless it's getting their penises stroked. And who can blame them about that? So she invited them over. After school. One at a time. They couldn't believe their luck. They figured they were going to have to borrow a car and take her out necking to Nuns Canyon or Moon Mountain Drive. And she leads them right into her own bedroom with the furry little animals and no place to sit except the bed so they didn't waste time trying to break down the terrible space between human beings who have never touched before. It was the greatest experience of her life. Nothing had ever brought her more peace than to lie on her bed with a boy on their backs or facing each other with her hands on him and his hands on her and their bringing each other off as slowly as the light of the sun dripped down her window before it fell behind the hills to the west. Some of the boys were as happy with that as she was. A few others really wanted to fuck. But she wouldn't. She told them they were both too young. But that wasn't the reason. Age had nothing to do with it. If God hadn't wanted kids to fuck, It wouldn't have given them such fuckability, not to mention such miraculous equipment. And a desire so great it and it alone could make you believe in God. No, the reason she didn't want to fuck was she couldn't bear to let anybody's penis out of her sight for that long, however long it takes to fuck, which is something I'm not sure about since I've never done it. Also, if the truth be told, there wasn't anybody she wanted to fuck. Until Andy. When Andy showed up, all the others just dissolved—in her hands, in her eyes, in her mind. He never told her to get rid of them. It wasn't his decision. It was hers. But he knew all about them. He said, "Sometimes when you're holding my cock I picture another cock in your hand." He smiled both shyly and slyly. He was proud of being such a worldly boy. "Me too," she said. Oh, how that made him laugh! He did what lovers have to do to be true lovers. He made the whole world their world. He locked them both up within it and threw away the me. They had nothing to hide from each other, so she didn't mind losing sight of his wonderful penis. They talked about fucking all the time. They planned for it like a summer picnic when it's still winter. They probably would have done it, too, if they hadn't enjoyed talking about it so much. For the first time, she felt her age. She was young. There was plenty of time. Besides, in the meantime she'd hide his penis in her mouth and close her eyes and nod her head upon him yes yes yes until he came. She could always tell when he was about to come because he'd put his hand in her hair. He would just kind of slip it in. He didn't grab her hair or push up and down on her head. She could feel his fingers spread upon her scalp and her hair standing up between them. When he came his hand would arch so he seemed attached to her only by his fingertips and the cock that bounced against the roof of her mouth. And when he finished and the last squirt was out, which sometimes took a heck of a long time, his hand would melt back relaxed into her hair, and his penis would shrink and plop out of her mouth, and so the only place he'd be touching her was right on the top of her head, in her hair. Even if he took a little nap then, his fingers would keep moving in her hair. It was like one of his gestures. She never asked him about it. She didn't even know if he knew he did it. And she didn't want anything to make him stop doing it. It was almost better than the sex itself. It was impossible to think of having sex without having his hand end up in her hair. She didn't even know if he liked her hair until one fateful day when he sat up and leaned over her head in his lap and looked down at his hand and said, "You have beautiful hair." "Oh, thank you." "What color is it anyway?" "I don't know. Red?" "Not red. You're not a redhead. I can't stand redheads." He laughed. "So obviously you're not a redhead. But there's red in your hair. What do they call this color? Name some reds. Auburn? That's one. Brick?" "Oh please!" "Carmine? I love that word. What else? Come on, Carla, help me out here. Scarlet? What's another kind of red? Crimson? Cherry? That's a good one. What's on your learner's permit? Cherry hair. Grape eyes. I'd love to see that." "Claret," she said. "That's what my father calls my hair. He says my hair's the color of wine with the sun shining through it. And claret's a kind of wine. I'll show you a picture he took. It won a prize." She jumped off her bed. "Where are you going?" he asked. "Come with me." He reached for his underpants. "Don't worry. Nobody's home." They went out naked into the hallway. He had his hands over his groin. She remembers how she spread her arms out and danced a little jig or whatever. "Where are we going?" She opened the door to her parents bedroom. "Excuse the mess." It wasn't just a bedroom. It was sort of an office too. Nobody except some rich newcomers building houses up in the hills had very big homes around here. Her father had made the little downstairs bathroom into a darkroom. But this was where he kept all his photographs. And he was never very neat about them. "I don't like this," said Andy. He was looking at her parents bed. It wasn't made, as usual. This gave her a dirty idea, but one look at Andy and she kept it to herself. "What are we doing here anyway?" "I told you. Looking for a picture." There were photos everywhere but she couldn't find the one she was looking for. She was beginning to think maybe her father kept that one in a special place since it had won a prize. And maybe he did. She never found it. She stopped looking when she found real pictures of her hair. Not a glass of wine. Her hair. Her head. Her neck. Her shoulders. Her breasts. Her back. Her ass. Her knees. Her thighs. Her pussy. Her feet. Her fingers on a penis. Her fingers on penises. In the midst of her despair she couldn't help wondering whose penis was whose. She didn't recognize a single one of them. Except Andy's, and that was because her mouth was over half of it, so it had to be his. All she knew was her own hand. Touching them, holding them, grabbing them, stroking them. They were all so familiar when she was with them, watching them as they grew and shrank and shivered and shot. She would have sworn she would never forget a single one of them. That they were burned forever into her memory. But except for Andy's, she didn't know whose was whose. She couldn't connect a single boy with his own dick. She couldn't connect herself with a single boy. What had she done, she wondered. What was sex if everyone you had sex with remained a stranger? "Is that the picture?" Andy was upon her. "Yes," she said. There was her hair, spread out on some boy's stomach while his dick rose before her face like a traffic light. All she saw were her eyes. They bore into that dick as if she would never want to forget this moment as long as she lived. "This is sick!" Andy threw the picture down and picked up another one. "This is sick!" She watched him watching her as the photos passed before his eyes. She wanted to say I don't know who any of these people are, but she realized that made it even worse. "Who took these?" he said. Then he looked at where she'd found them. "Your parents use these to get off." "No!" she screamed. To this day she won't believe that. To this day all she knows is that her father took them. Andy dragged her back to her room and almost tore the place apart and found the cameras. "Let's fuck for them." He was angry. He threw her on the bed. But she was closed up, dried up, dead. He didn't force himself on her. When his dick shrank he hid it from the cameras and got dressed. "See you," he said. But he never did again. Carla Belzidas packed up all the photographs of herself she could find. That was her message to her parents: Look, I have found myself. Look, I have disappeared. She knew they could never try to find her, because if they did, she would show the photographs and their shame would become public. Besides, she likes those photographs. She keeps them right here in her diary.

I turn the book upside down and crack it open like a lobster tail and out into my lap and upon the quilt drop little pictures of my noctivigant wife, a girl, such a beautiful young girl, ripe in her pucelage, with beautiful fingers and lips and nose and eyes and cheeks and chin and hair. I can hardly bear to look, not out of jealousy but envy, of these boys, that I should not have known her then. Oh how I would have swept her in my arms away and never let her go. She would not have been forced to give herself another name nor I to lucubrate over these photographs of her, a ghost now, gone, nothing left of her but these puisne, pistic pictures (as if I needed them!) and these unbearable words. These words— my own, which choke me, blind me, deafen me, these ugly, indefinable words, and hers, which break my heart.

Job's Tears

A man came into the shop today and asked for the Stars Within Circles quilt begun in 1850 by John Brown's mother. I happen to know the quilt because I've seen it in a book.

"I don't have it," I told him. "Can you get it?" "No. It's part of the Lenice Ingram Bacon collection. Perhaps there's something else I can show you. I have a number of quilts with small, contained stars. There's a Sunburst from 1850 as well. Listen." I grabbed Robert Bishop's book to read him something about Sunbursts when he exploded. "I didn't come here to buy some design. I am not looking for a pattern. I am not decorating." He spit not only his contempt but also his spit. Why does it always seem to land in my eyebrows. "I want that specific quilt. I want Mrs. Owen Brown's quilt." "I'm sorry then." And I was. He left me. His skin was that bruise-purple you sometimes find in Amish quilts as if a few drops of blood had fallen into the dye. He's a severe man. I'm attracted to his intense concentration.

I unfolded the Sunburst and studied the quilting. Then I read what it took to make one of these: "It took more than 20 years, almost 25, at night after supper when the children were all put to bed to make that quilt. My whole life is in that quilt. All my joys and sorrows."

I wanted to call Johnny at home. I wanted to read this to him. But he doesn't answer the phone.

When I got here I told him the story. I thought he might be

interested in discussing why black people hardly ever come in or how the woman in Ohio working on her quilt reminded me of him. But all he said was, "Imagine what it must be like, not looking for a pattern."

And I thought I worked long hours!

Bow Tie

Tonight Johnny told me the story of a girl who decided to call herself Cosima. "The one girl you ever had," I said, "and you don't even know her name." Make that the 2 girls he ever had.

"Why Cosima?" I asked. I am interested in what name a person chooses when a person chooses a name.

That got him started on Nietzsche. I should have known. Here's what I remember.

Cosima was the name of Franz Liszt's daughter. First she was married to Hans von Bulow. He was a great pianist too. Like Cosima's father. But he was a lousy composer. So she left him for Wagner. Nietzsche and Wagner were friends. Nietzsche was in love with Cosima. Everybody was. She had a little overbite. Just like me. Otherwise I am vastly more beautiful to quote my husband. But Nietzsche's problems weren't about love. They were about art. He believed that art is what keeps the truth from destroying us. That art is the only thing that redeems humanity. Not love. Not religion. Not philosophy. Art. Johnny quoted Franz Kafka about art being an axe for the frozen sea within us. I like that. It reminds me of marriage of all things. Anyway, what did old Nietzsche do? He tried to make art. What kind of art? Music. He wrote little romances like the piece for Cosima's 33rd birthday party and when she played it Nietzsche sat there beaming with pride and Wagner left the room. People thought he was either jealous or ill. But when they found him he was lying on the floor nearly puking with laughter.

I got him to tell me how he had her. I could see him in his big clumsy shoes running out to buy another condom. I never heard them called safetys before. You can use all the safetys in the world, you still can't make sex safe.

My favorite part of the Cosima story is how he came right into the condom. When you love somebody you want to possess them all the way back to the day they were born. Every day they lived before the day they lived with you is a day lost from your life. But at least I have that: my Johnny as a boy so excited that just a touch drives him wild.

He has no shame over his inexperience. Most men like to boast of all they've done. Like me. Or lie. Not that I lie exactly. But I certainly don't tell him the truth.

Tree of Life

Tonight we danced. We were clearing the table when Johnny said "What's that?" and I said "It's Ornette Coleman. Just For You is the name of the song, I think," and he put down his dishes and took my dishes out of my hands and put his arms around me and we danced.

I never danced with anyone before when we were all alone. No, that's not quite true. Men who'd never touched me used to put on music and say let's dance. To try to get to hold your hand and maybe touch your waist.

I'm very sensitive on my waist. Even somebody's fingertips when I'm going through a door and a shiver goes up me through my breasts all the way up the sides of my neck.

But to dance with your husband, unexpectedly, when you're all alone, home, and there's nothing of you left for him to explore, there's no intimacy he hasn't enjoyed with you inside or out, and it's over as quickly as it began, when the song ends, and you go back to the dishes or whatever you were doing . . . it's the most intimate thing I can imagine, just his hand on my waist and not a word to be spoken.

Barn Raising

For Valentine's Day, 1990, our first Valentine's Day together, or married, or both, which is tomorrow, I'm giving him a copy of Israhel van Meckenem's engraving of himself and his wife Ida. I wanted something special for him. Something symbolic. This was done before Columbus discovered America. Johnny will understand the meaning of that. He told me I have made him an American. That I have brought him home. That we are the great American couple because we embody all the best ideals of our society. "We live in peace. We promote beauty. We honor the mind." "And we fuck our brains out," I had to add because Johnny can be such a pompous asshole sometimes.

It's supposed to be not only the earliest known self-portrait ever printed but the earliest printed portrait outside of Asia. Israhel and Ida don't look like me and Johnny (thank goodness) but I love to think of this man so in love with his wife and of how this emblem of their marriage has survived for so long. He's got a nice smile. The most wonderful deep furrow in his skin from the side of his nose to just below his bottom lip. His eyes are sleepy—from art or sex? She however looks like a nun. Especially in the eyebrows—they are arched but fuzzy. I'm sure she didn't like what he did with her chin. It looks like a golf ball glued to the bottom of her face. "I know I look like that, but did you have to be so realistic!" What she doesn't know is that he would never have drawn her exactly as she is if he didn't love her completely.

Ladies Delight

I walked to work today. It took me nearly 2 hours. I didn't care if I was late opening the shop. I went all the way up Avenue of the Americas into Central Park and came out at 72nd Street and stopped to look into the courtyard of the Dakota and went into Nancy's to buy a bottle of wine for dinner. Sometimes I do that—walk. Usually I take the subway, though Johnny thinks I take a cab, because he says if I take the subway he'll be unable to concentrate on anything all day out of worry for me. He says his father always took the subway down to court because it put him in the mood to lock people up and he took a limousine home because by then he'd smelled enough humanity for one day.

I love to be out in the city. I could never stay home the way Johnny does. Where does he find the strength to spend so much time by himself. He doesn't belong to anything. Nothing. Not even a book club. He doesn't have a religion. Or a political party. A home team. An away team. He's not part of any generation. He's the most alone person I've ever known. Nobody on earth has a harder job. No distractions. Nothing between himself and himself. He calls music a divertissment. But I don't think it is. Neither is sex. Johnny doesn't want to get lost. Johnny doesn't want to wander through the city. Not any longer. The day I met him was the day he stopped. Since then the only thing he's explored is his own mind.

I'm not as strong as he is. I need to be away from myself. I need to stop thinking. I need to feel the city in my legs. I need to hear it scream. I need to rub my eyes against the world.

Today I wondered what would happen if I just kept walking. Out of Manhattan. Over the Hudson. Out of my life. I could disappear so easily. I could go back to the Valley of the

Moon and lie in my old room with swollen, panting, grateful boys. I could be a child again. Because now the only place I am is in my father's pictures. I wonder when I stopped hating him for taking them. I wonder when I became grateful. Is that perverse. I was never so innocent as when I touched those boys and let those boys touch me. I'm glad my parents got to see it.

And I realized that when I think of leaving here, it's not to escape the city or my marriage or Johnny. I don't just want to go back. I want to go back in time. And I want Johnny to follow me. I want us to have our past together.

White House Steps

We were lying on the bed as usual just reading. Johnny had vin santo on his side with bisquits. He'd dip a bisquit in and shake it off and tap me on the shoulder and bring it to my lips. I'd suck some wine in and give the thing a little bite. My lips were all it took. The wine and spit had saturated it. It made me want to blow him but not right away. I was reading a new novel about quilts by Whitney Otto and feeling very discrete the way a book can make you feel. I love that word even though Johnny would kill me because I couldn't say if it makes a homonym or homograph or homophone with discreet. He likes to put things in my mouth or on my lips. Sometimes when he's fucking me he sticks his thumb or his first two fingers in, and I can always make him come if I start sucking on them hard. It's funny how we read most nights, together on the bed, one of us in one book, one of us in another, worlds apart, the only thing connecting us whatever music's playing and the way we touch. The way we touch is usually the way we'll fuck. As with the bisquit. We're like 2 telegraph machines talking dirty across the ocean when our books and minds are continents apart. So when I got to a point in my book where I didn't mind stopping and to tell the truth didn't want any more bisquit dipped in vin santo, I closed my book and smiled because I didn't care where he was in his book and put my head on his stomach and opened up his robe and lifted up his dick and glided it over my lips like lipstick. But before I could put it in my mouth, he cupped his hands in my armpits and pulled me up to him and said, "One must cease letting oneself be eaten when one tastes best," and I thought O my new husband, you've outdone yourself this time. He'd rather kiss me than have me suck his cock. He'd rather look into my eyes than watch my hair wave in the southern sea. And he did kiss my eyes. But then his hands slid down to my waist and closed upon me there and lifted me up so for a second or 2 I was completely off the bed. And put me down. On my stomach. The first thing I thought of was how to tell him I was too impatient to have him in me for a backrub when he swung his leg over me and straddled me and rose up on his knees. It still might be a backrub till he put a hand under my stomach and scooped me up so I was on my knees and forearms and my ass was pressed against one side of the circle of his dick. Forget backrubs. How was I going to tell him not to stick that in my poor little heinie. Just the picture of it in my mind brought tears to my eyes. Could he possibly think I had done this with all those men he thought I had done this with. "Don't," I said. But did I mean it. I was very comfortable. My eyes were closed. My face was in my palm. My ass was open to the air and much more sensitive than I'd have thought. But I could tell he was confused. I'd never refused him anything before. And now he'd stopped touching me. So I took one arm off the bed and rose up on my other hand and reached around behind me and pulled his dick back onto my ass. I rubbed it along the crack. I could feel it tighten on me. I'd like to feel him come all over me in there but I still certainly didn't want him buried in me. So I pushed him down and aimed him at my lips and pressed him up against them and told him "In." His hands went around the sides of my ass. I was in a vice. His fingers stretched around my front and hooked into my pelvic bones which I always think of as the ears around my pussy. He pulled me back and forth onto his dick. I shoved a pillow under my face and buried my face in it. I never felt so blind. I thought I wanted to see him. I thought I must be missing him. But when I pictured what was actually happening John was gone. It was like God came down and put a hand on John's shoulder and tossed him aside and looked at me like I was in prayer. Which is what I felt like. I was all stretched and humbled. I was blind. I was whispering things into the pillow. I didn't even sound like myself. I didn't know who I was. Or who was behind me. I was wiped out. I was in ecstasy. Fuck me, I said to It. Fuck me. More. More. More.

Sunshine and Shadow

I want to have a child.

I never wanted one before. Never.

It's not that I'm lonely. I don't want companionship. I don't want someone else to love. I have everything I've ever wanted. Everything. That's why I want to have a child.

In other words there's no reason. And there's no better reason than that.

Bear Paw

I don't understand his body. It never changes. Just like his clothes. Sometimes I want to sneak into his closet to see if he's got bodies lined up there the way he's got suits and different pairs of those peculiar shoes. It's strange how I've gotten to like those shoes. I don't know what I'd do if he suddenly turned up in those loafers that are cut back so far on top that socks show. It looks like a fish got into someone's shoe. When a man walks into the shop wearing shoes like that, I won't sell him a quilt. Johnny's shoes look like blocks of solid mahogany nailed into the earth. That's how stable he is.

I couldn't believe it the first time I touched him. I put my fingers up his sleeve. It was like feeling a rock with skin. I could hardly breath. But he never exercises! I work out hard in the health club like everybody else in New York and I still think my ass is falling. He does <u>nothing</u>. Some days he barely moves. I find him in bed right where I left him. In his suit, of course. But when he takes it off at night he is always the same. He has no fat on him. His muscles are defined. I turn the lights down just to watch the shadows crawl up through them.

I once asked him how he stays so fit.

"Am I?"'s what he answered.

Maybe if you don't live in your body, your body will never change.

But now I remember something else he once said. "Thinking about some things is harder work than anything you can imagine. And not thinking about some things is even harder."

Maybe he's a man whose body is carved out by his brain. My Apollo. My Mr. America.

He looks eternal. If I stay with him maybe I won't ever die.

Ice Cream Bowl

"What do you see in me?" he wants to know.

I make up some things I think he'll want to hear. They aren't lies. They just aren't true. At least not yet.

245

I hardly know him. But I know him well enough to know this: what I see in him is me.

And me in him.

We're both virgins in a scumy bed.

New York Beauty

I was planning to cook tonight but when I got home Johnny said let's go out to dinner.

I thought we were going to stay in the neighborhood as usual, but when we hit the street Johnny hailed a cab and said "Carnegie Hall."

On the way uptown he talked to me about his day and asked me about mine. He told me he'd been listening to Robert Schumann's piano music. How Schumann had crippled his hand in a device he'd built to try to stretch his hand so he could reach more notes. I told him about a woman who came in and looked around and asked how much something cost and when I told her screamed, "Are you out of your mind! It's second-hand!"

"What a marvelous story."

I put my head on his shoulder and held his hand.

I thought how different it was riding in a cab with him than how it used to be. Other men always seemed to be talking for the benefit of the driver. Or they didn't talk at all. Johnny talks like we're the only 2 people on earth. And he listens like I'm the only person on earth. Everything we do is private, no matter where we do it.

Johnny told the driver to let us off in front of Trattoria dell Arte. I asked Johnny if we had a reservation and he said we didn't need one because we'd come just when the Carnegie Hall crowd was leaving for the first bell. Sometimes I wonder how a man who sits at home all day can know so well how the world works.

This is where we usually eat when we leave our neighborhood. Johnny likes the body parts on the walls. The noses over the bar. Last year they gave us a solid chocolate nose for Christmas. It was so hard we couldn't cut it with our knives. What we needed was a chisel. All we had was a kind of hatchet Johnny ordered through the mail because we talked about going camping. Us! He used it to smash the nose apart. He was like a little boy eating the nostrils and making a big show of it. "Nostrils are holes," he said. "They should be chocolateless."

Sandra greeted us. "Hello, Mr. Chambers." "You are so beautiful," she said to me.

"You should work the gates of heaven," he told her.

Sandra looked like she wanted to put her head on his shoulder. "At least no one could lie about having a reservation."

We followed her to a table. We watched her legs. Johnny always said she was the only woman who had more beautiful calf muscles than me. I'll never get to see mine the way we get to see hers.

Sandra said, "Unless you'd prefer a booth. It's more private. It's quieter."

This was the first time she'd offered to put us where the celebrities sit, up on the next level against the wall. I'd seen Sting there but Johnny didn't know who he was. And David Geffen. "He's richer than you," I'd teased him. "But did he get it for nothing?" Johnny competes only with those who do nothing but ask questions of the void.

"No thank you," he tells Sandra. "This is perfect."

Tonight we ordered broccoli rape and the Monday blueplate duck and fish and wine. We sat and drank and ate and talked. There's never nothing to talk of. I don't know where we find the things that interest us. I don't have to plan what I'm going to say. I don't have to save up things. Anything I say becomes a part of me offered up.

People are afraid of us. We're like newlyweds on a cruise ship. My customers are always going on a cruise somewhere. Peace at any price.

At the end of the meal our waitress pours us grappa from a huge glass jar with pale berries bunched at the bottom. "Sandra wanted you to have this," she says. She holds the jar like one of von Zichy's women with a dick in her hands.

We look around. Other couples watch us sip. My bottom lip feels swollen and oily.

This is our social life.

Birds in the Air

I think Dr. Leslie's in love with me.

I certainly hope so.

Not that I want him to suffer. But I figure that if my gynecologist's in love with me, I must have a very interesting mind.

If he's not in love with me why does he insist we have dinner after every appointment? He says it's because I make him see me in the evenings, after I close the shop, and he gets hungry when he works late. But I think he just uses that as an excuse. I think it's because he's in love with me.

I know I'm in love with him. I tell him so when he's examining me. "I love you. I love you."

"Oh, stop it, Clara!" he says. He's got a gruff voice and a little white beard like a psychiatrist.

I just got back from seeing him. He took me out for rognons. I paid for the wine. That's our deal. He said he'd be willing to bet he was the only doctor in New York who had the courage to eat innards.

"I guess it goes with the territory," I told him.

He groaned. But it was one of those groans where you're telling the person you're groaning at that you not only forgive them but you embrace them for their folly.

I went to him for birth control.

"What have you been using?"

"You should know."

"But I assumed . . ." he sputtered.

"Assume nothing." I've been waiting for a chance to say that ever since Johnny told me about the sign on his father's desk.

". . . that you were using condoms. I'm sure we've had this discussion." He frowned at my chart. Then he shook his head.

"So what have you been using?"

"Nothing."

"Good for you." He might be in love with me, but he still likes to keep things out of women's bodies and the babies coming. "So are you worried that you're not pregnant yet?"

"No. I'm worried that I'll get pregnant."

"What's wrong with getting pregnant? You're married now." This is the first time I've seen him since I met Johnny. I was worried he wouldn't ask me to have dinner with him. I needn't.

"My husband wants to have a baby. I thought I did too. But now I don't."

His stubby little fingers . . . and let him believe they inspire me to cry out my love . . . they start pulling on his stubby little beard. "Uh oh."

"That's something a doctor should never say."

"What?"

"Uh oh."

He puts his hand back on the desk. "You're right. The only truly brilliant teacher I had in medical school lectured us on precisely that. Never say "Oh my God!" Never say "Mercy me!" or "Holy shit!" Never faint at a patient's feet. But what's the matter, Clara? The marriage is no good? You come in here and tell me you got married 3 weeks ago? 20 minutes later you tell me the marriage stinks? Of course people know a marriage stinks usually in the first day."

Only a kind soul could be so cynical.

I told him, "It's the opposite. The marriage is so good I don't want to have a child. I'm already scared to death I'm pregnant."

"You're not," he said.

He gave me the prescription. What am I going to have to tell Johnny to keep him from fucking me until I'm safely on it. I was so ignorant that Dr. Leslie had to tell me at dinner that I couldn't start until after my next period.

He was still shaking his head when he asked me what I did about birth control before I got married.

I told him my husband was my first fuck.

He opened his mouth so wide a kidney rolled out.

Contained Crazy

I cut the piece for the cover of this book from a Contained Crazy quilt whose stitching had given out. Almost every little piece of fabric was coming up. You'd never know from what I put on here how the black bands made a grid over the whole thing to contain the pieces within regular squares. There must have been nearly a thousand scraps catstitched and French-knotted onto the cambric. It should have been tufted. Not quilted. Then it might have held together and wouldn't have ended up on this book. But I'm glad I got to cut it up. Sometimes you have to destroy something to learn its secrets.

This Crazy has the common velvets from dresses and satin from ribbons and silk from neckties. But I also found small pieces of silk underpants in nearly every square. Each one of them is cut in a **V** and stands like a **V**. No other shape is so consistent in its placement. Johnny would call it a leitmotif. Triumph of the Vagina. Whoever made this knew what she was doing. I wonder where she got all the panties. They are the softest things here. I rubbed them with my finger. I thought of making a woman come across the centuries. Sometimes I wish I weren't such an innocent.

I told Johnny I might get him a Contained Crazy. Not one with underpants. Even I couldn't have dreamed that up. But I can't help wondering if he shouldn't get out of here more. We've been married almost a year and the only times he went out without me was to buy me Il Parmigianinos. The Collo Lungo for my birthday. I couldn't figure out the significance of that so he reminded me I'd mentioned it the day we met. I fall for things like that. Sentimental fool. Who'd have dreamed I'd end up with a storybook husband. Then the circumcision for Valentine's Day but late because he didn't know it was Valentine's Day until I gave him the van Meckenem. Simeon's doing the honors. He's looking at Christ's penis (thank goodness) Christ's looking at us (nobody else is) Simeon's bald. Christ's halo is a burst of white light. Their heads are together so that's what you see in this. The knife and penis are of little regard. And everywhere else you look, HAIR. Nobody's head is covered, the way they usually are, like in the Tucher Altarpiece, and there's no reverence in the styling. The Virgin's got a messy French twist. Everybody's a little on edge. Except for the bald prophet and the radiant savior. I pointed this out to John. He said it probably represents the triumph of the mind. "Over what?" I ask. "Sex," he says. He points to the rabbit at the bottom of the painting. "And emotion. Fear. Anxiety. Dread. Anguish. Death. Like you and me." "So that's why I get a picture of a circumcision for Valentine's Day!" "Because you saved me," he says.

"Wait here," I said. I went into my closet to get something else for him. I had been saving it for another occasion, or for no occasion but I don't like to be the last one to get a present. I lived on my own too long to be able to give up control all this quickly.

I handed it to him. I deliberately hadn't put it in a box. That way when he tried to unwrap it the dick broke through the tissue paper. He gasped. I was giggling in anticipation.

"What can it be?" he said. He pulled the paper down around the huge dick. "My goodness." He was blushing. "It's a little man. With a funny hat."

It was an early Peruvian Mochica pitcher. Maybe 400 AD. Johnny poured some wine into it and then we both drank from it. I got excited to see Johnny with that dick in his mouth. Then he put it against my bottom lip and moved it back and forth. I could feel the wine dripping behind my lips and soaking my teeth. Some of it spilled out over my lip and dribbled down my chin and under my shirt and down the skin of my breasts. The thing didn't hold much wine anyway. When it was gone Johnny closed my lips over the penis and moved it back and forth in my mouth. It was cold and hard and small and tasted clayey. But when I couched it in my tongue and washed it with my spit I felt it was alive. Johnny took it from my mouth. He spread my legs. "May I?" "Only on the outside." He touched that little guy to my clitoris. "Happy Valentine's Day," said Johnny. "But that was a present from me to you." "Precisely."

"So are you trying to tell me I'm a contained crazy person?" is what he said when I mentioned the quilt.

"Don't you want to go anywhere?"

"Not without you."

"Don't you get bored?"

"Not with you."

"Aren't you lonely here day after day all by yourself?"

"Not with the promise of you."

"Don't you ever want to go out and chase one of those strange maidens you're always looking at?"

"Not when I have you."

"But I thought you said I'd made you into a philogonist." Hello, am I spelling that right.

"You have."

"So?"

"This is the world. And you are the only woman in it."

I realize why he's home. It isn't easy. It isn't lazy. It's not escape. There's no distraction here. The others are distracted. I see them in the shop. They know that everything they do distracts them from themselves. Their jobs. Their games. Their toys. The things they say. The lies they tell. The money they spend. They think there's magic in a quilt. Peace and quiet. History without headlines. Sleep without dreams. They buy them from me. But they don't have the courage to become one.

Johnny's a quilt. He took years to get sewn together. He cried out with the pain and time of it. He is all of a piece and perfectly ordered. He is worn down and fragile and all the stronger for the way life has rubbed against him. He is beautiful. And now he lies here on our bed, my husband, my hero, waiting for me.

Wheel of Mysterie

"Have you ever had sex in a church?" he asked.

"Of course."

It wasn't true. But God knows I'd wanted to. When I first got to New York I used to wander into churches all the time. I didn't have a job. I was either too warm or too cold. The streets were so noisy. I couldn't believe how many churches there were. Back in California when I pictured New York it was a big city just the way it really is but it didn't have any churches. I didn't think they would allow them. But they're all over the place and most of them are just another building on the street. I knew I was in them for peace and quiet but after a while I'd always get horny. Without fail. There was something so serene about them. They'd always deliver me unto myself. So I'd end up standing there behind a bench with my fingers on me. It wasn't a religious thing. Or the thrill of transgression. Transgress what? It was like being at home except I felt safer. But you have to be discreet. Churches echo. Once I came and heard myself a thousand times. I felt like the choir. I couldn't stop rubbing and singing. I went down on my knees. When I left going up the aisle an old man looked at me like I'd had an epiphany. I was embarrassed more than anything else. I had my hands over the bottom of my face like a veil.

I didn't tell Johnny this. I never do. It's better for him to imagine me than know me. So I just said, "Why do you ask."

"Purely academic."

"Yeah, right."

"I was reading in Peeps diary. You remember I told you about Peeps writing in shorthand. He tells how he finds a girl in church and puts his hands on her and wants her then and there but he doesn't get her because she nearly sticks a pin in him. He describes her as a pretty maiden. A modest maiden. And it reminded me of Bach having sex with the strange maiden in the church at Arnstad. Of course most sex in church is with oneself. The penitentials even set out punishment. 30 days fast at most for a monk. 50 days for a bishop. It was apparently very common. There is something about a church that makes people . . ."

"What?" I said because he stopped speaking.

"Most human," he answered with a look on his face of surprise at his own words.

"Would you like to do it with me in a church?" I asked.

"Oh please."

The way he said it I didn't know if he was begging or just begging off. Not that it mattered. I stretched out on the bed and opened myself to him.

Country Husband

Ike fired me today. He didn't do it by having some new girl come in to take my place. He was not afraid to confront me himself.

He asks me to come into his office. There are people in the gallery. Only once or twice did we have sex with people right outside. I wanted us to do that more often. I wanted us to do it someday with the door open. Ike wasn't ready for that yet. But I was unbuttoning my blouse when I closed his office door behind me.

"Don't," he says. "No, Clara."

I stop. Something's wrong. We have been lovers for 8 months. Because we never touched I had learned from my distance to see him like a painting. I knew the shadows his lashes made when something saddened him. I could tell from the bounce of his lower lip how grave might be the words from his mouth.

"What's the matter?"

"I don't want you working here any longer."

I don't say anything until I do the math in my head. "My year isn't up." I tried to make it sound light. Inside me I felt like I'd swallowed something heavy and bitter.

"This has nothing to do with time."

"So you're not sick of . . ."

"When I say I can't stand the sight of you, it only means that the sight of you is too much for me to bear."

You'd never know it. He was staring at me intensely while he talked. Maybe he actually thinks he's never going to see me again.

"I used to be a nice gay boy with lots of friends and a very stable life. By that I mean I was in full control of the disorder. I said I was a narcissist. But I wasn't really, because I had a life somewhere out there beyond the boundaries of my own flawed beauty. It's one thing to hit the gym every day or to twirl your dick around a few times in front of a mirror when you hope no one is watching. Or everyone. It's another thing to end up with no friends and no lovers but just your own hands giving you pleasure and to do it while the first woman you've ever loved—pacem Mom—is watching you. And you watch her too. And she even convinces you that vaginas have more to recommend them than their pretty name. But I can't touch you, Clara. You don't want me to anyway. And you don't want to touch me. So I end up making love to myself. When what I need is some other guy's dick in my hand not to mention up my narcissistic ass."

I don't know what to say. I went out to my desk and got my bag. I probably should never have left it there anyway. I'm too trusting. I go back to Ike who is just sitting there staring at the space I'd been standing in. I open my bag and take out my purse and pull out the one photo I carry around of me and Andy (the rest are in one of these books) His golden dick is in my hand. My lips are spread open on the top of it. That's all you can see: hand, dick, lips, and the blood of my hair. It's like the perfect ad for cocksucking. My father should blow it up and put it in his portfolio. I hand it to Ike. I see he sees it's me. He says, "What's this?" "For inspiration," I tell him.

"Which one of you am I supposed to be inspired by?" he asks.

It's my revenge. I know what he'll do with it. Long after I'm gone he'll look at that at night. I want him to be as alone as he's leaving me.

"I have something for you too," he says.

I remember Monica's last day. "I'm not interested in lunch."

He hands me a business card.

"Who's this?"

"My lawyer."

"I'm sorry," I tell him.

"For what?"

"I refuse to sign a pre-nuptial agreement."

Ike knows a good joke when he hears one. Maybe I should marry him. How many people do you meet in your life who know when you're kidding.

When he gets done laughing he says, "I want you to go see Barry. Not today. Tomorrow. I'm going to call him this afternoon to tell him I want to set you up in business. On 2 conditions. I don't want a piece of it. This isn't an investment. But here they are. 1: not this business. I don't want you competing with me. And 2: I don't ever want to see you again in my life."

Don't worry you prick. You won't ever see me again. Not with your eyes open.

Tobacco Leaf

"What was your first orgasm like?" he asks me.

"It was . . . I don't remember."

"Try. Please."

"Why?"

"I want to understand."

"What."

"What it's like to be a woman. To be you. How am I going to learn these things if you don't tell me?"

"I don't trust you. I think you just want to get aroused." Like my parents. Images of Carla in heat.

"No. This is purely intellectual."

"Right."

"I want to understand what it's like when you've never felt such a thing before. How could anyone have imagined it? What does a girl think when this thing happens to her? When it rolls through her. Such ecstasy. It must change your life forever."

"What about yours."

"It happened while I was asleep. I didn't even wake up. I thought I'd wet my pajamas. I dried my sheets with an entire box of tissues and stripped them from the bed and carried them secretly to the laundry. I was ashamed."

"Not me."

"I wouldn't think so."

"You're right."

"How so?"

"It was ecstasy."

"I thought so."

"And I was never the same."

"Yes."

"You're right about that too."

"Yes. Thank you. And how old were you?"

"Not as young as some girls say they are. 11, I think. Maybe 12. I wasn't riding a horse. I wasn't bouncing on a see-saw."

"Were you alone?"

"Of course I was. It wasn't sex. I didn't know it had anything to do with sex. It was just me. I was totally alone. I was as alone as I've ever been in my life."

"Were you touching yourself?"

"I was looking at myself. My body had begun to change. Just a little bit. More on the inside than anything else. I wasn't bleeding yet. But there was something going on under my skin. I could feel it. All the time. I was nervous. In an excited kind of way. I felt like soil, the earth, with sooething growing in it. Waiting for the sun."

"By the window?"

"No. On my bed. At night. The moon was out. My bed was by the window, yes. I was naked. I used to lie there looking at myself in that light. I thought it made me pretty. My breasts were tiny. But I'd lie so they made shadows. And I'd watch them grow. The moon was turning me into a woman. I was growing soft little hairs. I couldn't see them. But I could feel them. And I loved my waist. I'd put my hands on both sides of it and push them in."

"Trying to get a figure."

"I suppose so. They weren't like my hands at all. I was very sensitive there. Then I learned to move them to the top. My stomach. I'd move them round and round over my belly-button. And the night it happened I moved them down. I didn't know what I was doing. When my fingers got between my legs I pushed my legs together and trapped my hands there. It was like a struggle between my hands and my legs."

"Who won?"

"My hands. What else. My legs opened up and I spread them as wide as I could. I had my feet flat on the bed and I remember I was looking at my knees. They were shiny from the moon. They looked so little and so far away. But my fuzzy little pussy seemed to get closer and closer. I was pushing it toward me with one hand practically under my backside and caressing myself with the fingers of the other hand. I was amazed. It wasn't like in the bathtub. I usually washed in a jiffy. I wasn't ever very curious. But now I was learning so much. My hands kept moving faster while the rest of me felt like it was slowing down. My mind was racing. I had thoughts and pictures running through it and bumping into each other. I couldn't tell the words from the pictures. And then I heard myself go Oh. I took a breath so deep I thought I saw the whole world come sucked into my head. My mind went blank. Everything in it just disappeared. My legs came together and trapped my hands again and wouldn't let them move. But all the rest of me started to shake. The light was bouncing off my knees. My hair was tearing at my pillow. My tiny breasts were trembling. My stomach rose into the air. And the greatest feeling I had ever felt came rushing through me. Or over me. I didn't know if it was inside. Or out. Or both. Again and again and again. Again and again and again. I thought it would never end. I thought I was going to die."

"Were you frightened?"

"Only that it would end."

"And when it did end?"

"But I have no memory of that."

"Did you fall asleep?"

"You must be kidding."

"What did you do?"

"I prayed."

"For what?"

"Forgiveness."

"You felt guilty?"

"Yes."

"For what?"

"For not knowing."

"Not knowing what?"

"How wonderful it could be."

"Sex?"

"Life."

Prickly Pear

I think I'm pregnant.

My period isn't late. I don't have strange appetites. My breasts aren't tender. I feel fine in the morning. My sex drive hasn't intensified. My weight's stable. My saliva hasn't thickened. My legs don't tire. My bowel movements are regular. My hair conditioner still works. Nothing smells different. My palms are dry. I don't want to leave work early. I've shed no sudden tears. My shoes fit. So does my skin.

But I think I'm pregnant. There's someone inside me. I don't feel it in my womb. I feel it in my eyes. Nothing looks quite the same. The air is tinged with color. My quilts and paintings give off light. The dark's no longer black but transparent. I lie awake at night and see the morning long before it comes. The moon is in the streets in the middle of the day. I look in the mirror and see my mother. I look at my husband and see him as a child. Everything comes together in what I see. There's a baby in my eyes. I just can't see him yet.

Drunkard's Path

I'm giving Johnny a Broken Dishes for our first anniversary. It was made during the Depression by an Amish woman in Ohio—western Ohio most likely because it's cotton. The guy who trucked it in called it a Pinwheel. I asked him if he was married. He said, "Sort of." He probably thought I might want to fuck him and he couldn't decide if I'd be more likely to if he was free or taken.

"Did your wife ever throw anything at you?"

"Not really."

"Did you ever throw anything at her?"

"I've got a nasty temper."

"Did it break?"

"It always breaks. I make sure it breaks. That way I stop. I smash something. I keep from hitting her. Why'd you ask?"

I want to smash him. It's not a pleasant feeling. I used to have fantasies about fucking men. Now I want to smash them.

"I asked because I want you to look at this quilt from over here." I pull him back from it. He looks at my hand on his arm. It's a rebuke and a promise. He didn't know what to make of it. Men always make the first touch. Your elbow, your wrist, a palm on your shoulder and the tips of fingers on your collarbone or my waist through a doorway. Gaining the upper hand.

"See. There are 8 triangles in every block, but every triangle is a different color. 6 or 7 dark ones, 1 or 2 light ones. Pink. Pale green. From over here you can see how shattered it all looks. Smashed, to quote you. That's why it's a Broken Dishes, not a Pinwheel. I'm giving it to my husband."

"You throw things at him?"

"Just this." I point between my legs.

We never fight. We never argue. I get angry but not with him. And whatever I'm angry with I don't make into him. There's so much peace there. It was never like this before. I fought with men. I disdained them. I wouldn't fuck them. I don't know what came first, the anger or the distance. I wasn't saving myself for marriage. I was just saving myself.

John was different. He was so fragile. That was his strength. He'd been worn down almost to transparency. I used to worry that he'd burn through. People are like quilts—their passions are what eat them.

We've lasted almost a year. A year is so long. It's nothing to my customers. They buy my quilts to slow down time.

But Johnny makes time stand almost still. It's so quiet around him. So peaceful.

He leads the perfect life.

Turkey Tracks

We just got back from a trip and I'm very tired. It gets harder and harder to find good quilts. But when I do find one I feel like I've entered time. Otherwise I don't feel like I'm living in time at all. The future doesn't interest me. Why should it. It doesn't exist and it never will. But a quilt is full of blood and passion and pain and art and time. It's like going for a ride on a magic carpet. You don't know what we can see, why don't you tell your dreams to me. I can read the dreams in quilts. I can touch the life.

I got Johnny interested in the history when I read to him from The Minister's Wooing by Harriet Beecher Stowe, who wrote Uncle Tom's Cabin. She had all these women sitting around in a bee. This was supposed to be 200 years ago. They talked and talked. About everything. Johnny is very interested in what people say. I read to him: "The conversation never flagged, ranging from theology to recipes of corn fritters, sly allusions to the future lady of the parish to the doctrine of free will and predestination." "They talked about free will!" said Johnny. "Just like Nietzsche!"

I always try to visit the graveyards in the places quilts were made. I look for the headstones of the makers. In Lebanon Ohio I found Emma Ann Covert. That was before I met Johnny but he likes me to tell him about it because of her name. "I should have been a Covert," he says. I tried to get the Hall family to sell me her Bouquet of Garden Flowers. I wouldn't have sold it to me either.

After I saw Celestine Bacheller's incredible embroidered scene-paintings in the Boston Museum of Fine Arts I tried to find her grave in Wyoma. If she'd put a cemetery in a quilt maybe I would have found her. When I told Johnny she'd worked on this one quilt from 1850 until 1900, he said, "That's the year Nietzsche died."

This time Johnny was with me. We ended up in Blackstrap Maine. We found Henry Thompson Leighton's grave. He was buried with his wife, Maria Josephine Bateman Leighton. But they weren't surrounded by the graves of the 44 young women who'd made Henry his bridegroom's quilt. One appliqued square each. "Were they all his lovers?" Johnny asked. "Of course," I told him. "That must have been quite a bee," said Johnny.

He wandered off among the graves. Then he called for me. Screamed for me is more like it. I ran to him. I don't know if I've ever heard him raise his voice before. I thought he might have stepped in a hole and broken his ankle. When I got to him he wasn't hurt but there were tears in his eyes. He was pointing at the grave before him. I looked down. The stone was lying flat. There was nothing on it. I knew exactly what was making him so sad. "Let's turn it over," I said. But when we did, the other side was empty also. "It doesn't matter," I said. "Yours won't look like this." "What will it say? What have I ever done in my life?" "It will say Beloved Husband."

He hardly spoke on the long drive home. He didn't listen to music. The blankness of the stone was like the silence he fears. How do you save someone from nothingness. He fills my life. I wish I could fill his.

"Promise me I'll die before you," he said.

I couldn't help laughing. "Just to get Beloved Husband on your tombstone."

"That's not it at all." He didn't say another word the whole way home.

He waits for me in bed. I can feel him watching me. Listening to my pencil move.

He has never been so quiet for so long since the moment we met. And I've never been so tired in my life.

"I'll be right there," I just said.

Please answer me.

"That must have been quite a bee."

He was laughing when he said it.

He still is.

Beloved Husband.

Delectable Mountains

Today I got married. But now it was yesterday. It's 4 in the morning and I'm sitting here on the floor in my old nightgown in the moonlight while my husband sleeps in our huge bed and I watch him while I write. This is our first night in the loft. It was ready for us last week. But we didn't move in because we weren't married yet.

Such a traditional couple.

I usually turn my back to him when I write. Now he's sleeping. So I sit here with what's left of the champagne writing and watching him with my diary on my crossed legs and his semen seeping out of me like little baby fingers.

I always wondered what happened to it when the man pulled out.

It was a great wedding. We didn't know a soul. That's how people should get married. Alone. Nothing to distract you from one another.

Johnny carried my boombox there and got permission to play some music. Bach. He says he wants to have 20 children just like Bach.

"Me too," I told him. "Each one by a different man."

He also gave a little speech. We're surrounded by strangers and he says that the minute he laid eyes on me he wanted me. The flesh said she's for me. The spirit said she's for me.

People didn't know what to make of him. Men closed their eyes. Maybe they thought they could make him disappear.

Women shook their heads.

I stood there next to him with tears in my eyes.

When we got home, he opened a bottle of champagne. It's already like an artifact. It's green and thick with flowers etched into it. Or do I mean a talisman.

We sat at one of the Seymour tables. I wondered why he wasn't carrying me to the bed. He must have known it wasn't time. How does he know? All he's had is the so-called Cosima. More than I've had. He knows more too.

At first he talked about this new place of ours. Look at this, he said. Look over there at that. The furniture looks great. Are the lights too bright? Don't forget you can lock your closet. What a fine kitchen. Granite counters. Imagine that. But we can't cut on them or we'll ruin our knives.

Then, as if he were a new home himself, some new space that I am moving into, he said, "I want you to know me. Nobody has ever known me. I have never really known myself. But if you know me, then I will find myself in you."

"No pun intended?" I couldn't help it.

He laughed. He said, "But I meant it! More champagne?"

"Fuck me, Johnny."

He undressed me. No one has ever undressed me before. That's been my job. Let alone fucked me. I love undressing for men. I love to watch them watching me. I love peeling off my layers of clothes and the more naked I get the more hidden I am.

But I figured, you're a married girl now, Clarabell, let someone else do the work.

He worships me. I sit on the edge of the bed and he kneels before me and he buries his head in my lap before he so much as takes off one of my half-boots. I put my fingers in his inviting hair and weigh his head and think how much he's got in there, all those words, all those sounds, all those questions.

He lifts his head to look at me and his glasses come off in my skirt. It's like I've got 2 men now, one looking into my eyes, one into my lap.

"Can you see without your glasses?"

"I have no idea."

I slide them back onto his face. "There's something I want you to see."

I went to my closet. The key was in the lock.

"This is from me to you. For us."

I never gave anyone a quilt before. It violates all my principles.

We spread it out over the bed. It was huge.

"Wedding rings," he said.

"Double."

"It's very beautiful. And now I understand." He held up his left hand to me.

We were ringless. I'd told him the Amish wore no jewelry including wedding rings.

Now he undresses me as I stand beside him. I fold back the quilt before we lie down.

"I thought bed quilts were for fucking on," he says.

I lie on the bed and open myself up for him.

Honeymoon Cottage

Ike just left. It was the third time this week. Plus once at the gallery. "Watch me," he says, "watch me." "I thought I was the director of this film," I told him. He laughed. "You are. But I'm the star."

Handy Andy

Johnny just asked me a question. That's something he almost never does when I'm writing in here. I know he watches me from the bed while I do this, which I don't mind at all. In fact I love to feel his eyes on my back. I sometimes wish he would just rip this thing out of my hands and expose me for what I am. Look at this handwriting. Sometimes I can't read it myself. But what if he can't. From the day I met him I thought he could. But what if he can't. Or what if he can but he doesn't. Or what if he does but he doesn't understand. What if he does understand. Will he ever know me.

"Do you think of me as someone to whom nothing has happened?" he asked.

"I think of you as someone everything has happened to. Everything."

"Thank you, Clara."

That was it. I never thought of it before. How deep you sink in life when you're careful not to move.

Mariner's Compass

Sometimes all he touches is my head. I get so used to his hands everywhere. On my shoulders with his thumbs on my nipples. The back of his hands brushing the insides of my thighs. Reaching back to grab one of my ankles when I've got my legs spread high to fit him in completely. Or under me with his hands spread on my ass and his fingers moving in my crack so my hole back there's a little mouth opening and closing saying stick your finger in, which he sometimes does and I go wild. But there are times when he almost keeps his hands to himself. He has me wondering where he's going to put them. He had to learn to do this. He was not a great lover from the get-go. He was beautiful. His flesh was golden hard just like that radiant man who's got his muscly legs spread in El Greco's Resurrection and Christ is rising up hardonically, as John would say, from in between them. His face was speechless. I mean I could look at it and not be able to say anything. Not want to. But he had no idea. He was like someone whose body and mind have never met. They lived in different countries. I don't think he would have been able to recognize himself in a photograph. So he had to learn how to touch. First himself. Then me. It was like having a baby. The idea of it fills your mind, your house, the world, but you have to bear the body. Johnny's was like that. It had to be born. He'd lie between my legs and enter me. But while he was inside me he was learning how to love. Where to hide his face. When to look at mine. How to use his tongue, his teeth. What to say. What to do with his feet. How to bounce his balls against my butt. Where to put his hands. His hands would scare me if he weren't my husband. But he's learned to play me like an instrument. And sometimes all he touches is my head. His fingers on my scalp. His thumbs rubbing behind my ears. His eyelids fluttering in my hair. I wait for his hands to move down my body. To massage my breasts or hold my waist. But he keeps them on my head. He holds my head in his hands and rubs my scalp and my mind floods with pleasure. Literally. It stops thinking. It isn't a mind any more. It's a piece of my body. And he holds it in his hands. And when I come, I come together. There is no difference between thinking and feeling. There is, for goddamn once, peace.

Log Cabin

This is my first day in New York. I bought this blank book at Barnes and Noble. It was filled with students. Barnes and Noble I mean. They were standing in line to sell their books.

Suckers! I never have to go to school again in my life! I had to go to the other store across the street to find this book. It was so ugly that I almost didn't buy it. But then I got the idea to put a little piece of my quilt on it. It was only from the corners. They were a mess anyway because I used to suck on this quilt when I was a baby. And on the bus ride here I really messed it up. I slept under it. I ate on it. I used it to hide from creeps who would stare at me. Grandma Belzidas made it for me when I was little. It just fit my bed. Now it's kind of falling apart. But just the stitching. And the filling's coming out at the seams. But the fabric's still strong. It's worn down so much I can see through it when I hold it up to my eyes. It's as smooth as my skin. It got that way from me. Sometimes I didn't know where this quilt ended and I began. I used to wrap myself up in it like a mummy. Now I make myself come with it. Am I allowed to say that? Well I pity anyone who tries to read this. They used to call me The Alien at school. Because of my writing. Not because of my looks. I never had any problem with my looks. I'm beautiful. Even my father thought so. I had lots of boyfriends. I photograph very well. My name is Carla Belzidas. I'm 16 years old. I'm from the Valley of the Moon in California. I ran away from home. And nobody's ever going to find me.

Pickle Dish

I was on my way to pick up Zach at the Jewish Theological Seminary for lunch when I bumped into the Professor in front of the Columbia library. "My wife's not home," he said. We walked out through the gate and across Broadway and cut through Barnard and I thought about how I was getting my education for free. He lives on Claremont Avenue which I couldn't remember the last time I wrote about going home with him because that was the first time and the first time with a man I sometimes miss the details because I'm picturing what's to come. His wife also teaches American literature he told me today while we were walking and he actually said "Hello Dear" up toward a window as we passed the building where he said she was holding her class. "Different centuries," he said to me and I thought he was joking so I said, "You aren't <u>that</u> much older than me." He laughed and said, "I mean she teaches the 19th and I teach the 20th." Before I had sex with him I made him give me some books. "A prostitute for learning" he called me. Well the sex is over but I've got slightly used paperbacks of Wallace Stegner, Walker Percy, and Wright Morris. Just the way he did last time he asked me to describe what was happening. "Pretend you're in one of my classes." So I went for it this time. "I see little drops of come. Wet yourself with it. Pretend you're

A key taps against the lock. Go away! I want to scream. I'm reading!

What a luxury this is. Not since college—perhaps not since the dawn I crept to my room from Cosima's and curled up with *Zarathustra*, in which philosophic argument is rendered, as George Steiner has demonstrated, musical—have I been so lost in words, so blissfully obliterated. Time has not merely flown; it has disappeared. Silence is not merely golden; it is lyric. There is no music now. There is only her voice in my head.

Again the key taps. Someone is frustrated. The key isn't going into the keyhole. It's either a stranger come with Clara's keys to kill me or it's dear old Elspeth come to clean and still too vain to put her reading glasses on to fit her key into the hole.

It is, after all, I believe, Thursday now. But surely it's not 10:00 A.M.! As absorbed as I have been in my pernoctation over and within the verdant covert (she even picks my words for me!)

271

woven from her pencils, I cannot have read through dawn and breakfast both. And if I have, then the world has ended, for I see it's dark outside and would be darker still if the city didn't rage all night.

I look at Clara's clock. It's barely after two. The key keeps tapping. I know it's lax of me not to see to it but I can't help it— I read.

inside me. I'm so wet. Go ahead. Do it." I never saw a man get so excited in my life. "Stop!" he screamed. But it was too late. Which was fortunate for me because I didn't want to keep Zach waiting. "Ah" said the Professor when he could talk again. "The power of

It's in! The key I mean. I hear it turning in the lock. Can't you see I'm reading!

I don't know if I'm afraid for my life or of it. Hoping that it is and isn't Elspeth, whom it would pain me terribly to chop in half in a case of mistaken identity (though it occurs to me, as I rise and trod stiffly through the loft, that there is no diagnosis more universally accurate), I carry with me the 2-Pound Camp Wonder. And when I reach the door, I think to smash it in, until I realize I'm the one inside.

I can hear the key slide slowly out of the lock. I can feel it like a knife withdrawn. I can see the doorknob turning in a ghostly, disembodied way.

The door opens. I grip the axe just off my shoulder and wait.

It's a woman. A very beautiful woman in a black dress.

I recognize her but I don't know who she is. Or I know who she is but I don't recognize her.

She is, in either case, a familiar stranger.

I have never seen her before. But I remember everything about her.

She's got a package in her arms. She hugs it to her like a child. I recall so well her impatience on going through a door. She fumbles with the key because she will not take the time to put her package down. She has always hated that about herself. She has said she wants to be more like me.

She steps into the loft and opens up her arms to me. The package falls. It's something soft, I note; it doesn't break.

I raise the axe and bring it forth against the back of her neck.

Actually, I don't. That's why I won't bother with fiction. You can't believe a word you read. Or you shouldn't. In my case, however, I do. So I don't. Read it that is. (What! Can it be that I'm dropping my commas just like her!)

Yet here I am standing before her, entering her arms, and I scarcely can believe she's real. She seems the very coinage of my brain. I had thought she was gone forever. And now I feel her feeling me and in her feeling me feel me. Long, I hear quodli-beting in my head, have I been away from you.

But I do want to kill her. Is this so strange a desire in a husband? (Viz., her notebook with the Tree of Temptation cover.) I think not. No matter how much you love someone, and how deeply embedded she may be in your life, in your very being, there must be times when you want to erase her from existence. In most cases this would be a means of self-preservation, not because she might kill you, though she might (viz., ibid.), but because you fear that in the midst of marriage you will yourself be erased, not through murder but through the fact of being married in the first place.

In Clara's case, I have a further motive.

She is a witness.

Not to my crime; to my life.

Men were called "free," said Nietzsche, so that they might be judged and punished—so that they might become guilty.

And if I kill her, if I kill what is closest to me so as then with fresh desire to go shuddering after it and cry out with the pain of solitude, then it is only to get her in my grasp, to hold her once and for all and to retire finally to that solitary cell, that hut where I might no longer be tormented by questions that bring my very *self* into question. Marriage causes a struggle not between captivity and freedom but companionship and solitude. No other woman, no other person, can exert so strong a desire as the wish to be alone. But we have, have we not, in Rilke's description of a good marriage, appointed each other the guardian of our respective solitudes.

I have read her diary. I know she loves me. This alone might justify the succor of oblivion if I only were who she believes me to be.

"I have so much to tell you," she whispers. "Put that thing down and hold me."

Just like that, I let it go. It falls beside her package.

"Careful," she says. Then she laughs. "What were you doing with that, anyway? It's a little late to be planning a camping trip."

"Late how?" I try to pull away, but she won't let me go.

"Late in the summer," she says, completely free of metaphor.

We embrace by the front door. She presses her face into my chest and says nothing but my name, over and over: "Johnny . . . Johnny . . . Johnny . . . Johnny . . ." I cannot distinguish its sound between relieved greeting and elegiac farewell. Is this hello or goodbye?

When I feel her arms begin to loosen their grip on my sides and her hands on my burning back, I hold her all the more tightly myself, for fear that I will be embracing nothing but decomposing air and the very sight of her will be taken from my eyes. But even as she twists and slides away from me, her right hand journeys down my back and around my waist and finds my own right hand and knits them both together as she bends for her package and then starts to walk and pulls me deeper into home.

"Let's go lie down," she says, as if there's any doubt where we are headed. "But first . . . do we have any champagne?"

"Of course."

"Is it cold?"

"I believe there's one bottle."

"The green one with the etching?"

"No. But it's a nonvintage from the same producer."

"Great. You go open it. Then bring it to bed. I'll meet you there."

If it were possible to open a champagne bottle with one hand, I'd insist she stay with me. When her hand leaves mine, I wonder if we'll ever touch again.

"So what did you do while I was gone?" she says as she walks away. "I'm sorry I took so long," she chatters. "I did call you but of course you didn't answer. How come you don't have any music on? Oh, my gosh, were you playing the violin? I can't believe—"

The cork explodes from the bottle in the same moment she screams my name. My hand is awash in prickly foam by the time I reach her.

She is sitting on the bed much as I imagine I had been, fully clothed, fully conscious, volumes of her diary cracked open and asleep between her legs.

"Did you read it?"

Her voice is husky. So I clear my own before answering. "Yes."

Each of us seems to be waiting for the other to speak.

Finally she can bear it no longer and asks like some writer who calls his editor six weeks after handing over his lifework, "So what did you think?"

"Do you really want to know?" I ask, imagining myself into the role but at the same time flattered that she would even ask.

"Do I really want to know!" She reaches out to pull me down next to her. But I prefer to stand. I even move around to the end of the bed so I can talk to her as I did when I told her of Gerald Duckworth's violation of little Virginia Stephen.

"There are no facts," I proclaim, "only interpretations, so you mustn't take what I say as truth. Consider it merely elucidation. In that spirit, allow me to tell you that while I am proud of how you succeeded in getting every name correct from our drunken, wonderful first-anniversary dinner at Bouley and the Latin too except for *Nuptias*, Pepys spelled it P-e-p-y-s, not, as it sounds and as I suppose they would spell it on one of your Howdy Doody cartoon shows, P-e-e-p-s. And, hello yourself . . . you were not spelling *philogynist* correctly—the second *o* should be a *y*. You also have no concept of how to punctuate end parentheses or how to use single quotation marks. Not to mention question marks, though I am willing to concede a strange logic in your avoidance of them. I could actually hear your voice as I was reading your words, and I realize you have a way of asking a question that is as much statement as question. It's very much like a question that contains its own answer. But most people will not appreciate such subtlety, if that's what it is. And heaven help you if you want to publish these, for then you'll surely be required to temper your punctuational anarchy. Though I should think it would be worth such compromise, given the commercial value of your confessions, not that I know much about such things—commercial literature, I mean. As for the difference between *ingenuously* and *disingenuously*, it's the difference between innocence and guilt. One more thing—you really should not use the variant spelling of *vise* when you describe being entered from behind. And before I forget—"

She has risen on her knees, crushing her diaries in the process as she moves toward me upon them, reminding me of Cosima on hers as she had approached my ingenuous member. But the reason I have stopped talking is not her attack but her laughter, which keeps either of us from being heard until finally, with her arms around my neck, she takes a deep breath and says, "Maybe you really fucking are a born diaskeuast."

I pretend to be aghast, to have my father's accusation repeated thus, but the fact is I'm rather proud of myself. There are worse things to be born, I have come to realize, than a diaskeuast, particularly for those of us who are forced to admit that for all our love of the art of language, we are not artists, only, as it turns out, interpreters.

"Now what is it," she says, her lips at my ears, "that you didn't want to forget?"

"To ask you what I should call you now."

"How about Mommy." There's a perfect example. She says something in the form of a question that I feel quite comfortable in absorbing without a question mark.

"I meant, shall I call you Clara or, now that I know your given name, Carla?"

She hooks her hands into my lapels and pulls me down with her onto the bed. "Johnny," she breathes into me, "I'm pregnant!"

3 A.M.

We dance. She has gone to her closet and thrown down her dress and underwear and put on her nightgown. On her way to me she chooses the music, and, as John Coltrane begins "Like Someone in Love," she enters me, my arms, my skin, my brain. The music fills the world, and we are alone in it. We dance as one must dance — we dance away over ourselves.

This is how we celebrate, not with sex or champagne. Given her blessed condition, I am wary of the former, though she tells me it is only the lateness of the hour that keeps her from dispelling my fear, and will not permit the latter, not to her or, because we are married and must thus share sacrifice as well as God's beneficence, myself.

She is my queen of angels, queen of confessors, queen of virgins. There was snow upon the hills of Aspasia, but how was I to know? And what does it matter now? I have never wanted her more. Or less.

And what am I to her?

"You are my grave," she answers in acknowledgment that I have endured in the triumph of the sacred *karteria* of Epictetus, both quoting her diaries and providing herself transition into what she's no doubt been dying to ask: "Why did you read them?"

I tell her the truth: "Because when I looked in your datebook you had left a blank for tonight. I thought you were gone forever."

Rather than accuse me of invading her privacy—of which there is none in marriage, secrets and lies notwithstanding—she holds me all the more tightly as we dance. Or perhaps she is thinking not of me now but of the life that grows within her.

"I was afraid to write down where I was going. If I wasn't pregnant I didn't want to look there and see his name and be reminded."

"Whose name?"

"My lover's."

I begin to laugh so hard I stop dancing. My feet adhere to the floor as the rest of me quivers joyfully. She tries to maintain a raunchy composure but cannot and laughs too at her own wicked joke.

When she's able to speak again, and we're able to dance, she says, "Dr. Leslie was so happy for me he paid for everything. Not the appointment, I mean. The food and the wine. He made me eat cervelle. He said it would make the baby smart. I told him you're my cervelle."

"Does that mean you want to eat me?" I ask and marvel at how she's taught me how to talk and freed my tongue.

"Any time. Any place."

She leads me to the bed. But it's not me that gets unwrapped. It's the package she'd arrived with.

"Help me," she says, and we open it together.

It's the Broken Star/Carpenter's Wheel quilt that she'd shown me on the day we met.

"I went to the shop after dinner to get this. I had to repair it. It took longer than I thought it would. That's why I was so late. Do you remember this quilt?"

"Of course. I also read about it." I nod toward the volumes of her diary still strewn around us on the bed.

"I've been saving it for this."

"For what?"

"For when we'd make a child. For when we knew we'd be together forever."

I know what she means. When you marry and have a child, your blood is joined eternally. It is the only resurrection.

"Help me spread it out." She pushes all her notebooks to the floor. There's a violence that makes me sense she'll never write in them again.

When the Broken Star is over the Double Wedding Ring, she climbs in between them. I undress and join her. I hold her in my arms.

Libro secondo.

There is nothing more to say, or do.

But as I'm finally ending my pannychous vigil and am embracing with eternal gratitude the irenic contours of marital slumber, I hear her ecstatically drowsy voice: "Oh, I forgot to tell you, Johnny . . . there's a bike from Take A Wok chained up downstairs . . . whoever delivered your food must have forgotten it . . . I suppose they'll come to get it in the morning . . ."

We sleep.

Labyrinth

It's 5:15 in the morning and I just got woken up by a dream that was so strange I can't go back to sleep even though I slept only 2 hours and I'm supposed to open the shop at 10. Maybe I won't open today. I'm thinking of closing the shop anyway. I'm thinking of staying home with Johnny and the baby. I want us all to live like Johnny.

Anyway I'm exhausted but I'm also ecstatic so maybe it was my excitement that woke me up so early and not the dream. But I definitely had the dream. I didn't imagine it. In it I was sleeping just the way I was sleeping. So maybe it was a dream about dreaming. I was in our bed and suddenly there was a man standing over me. He was Chinese from what I could see and was young and kind of good looking and dressed like a waiter with little glasses on the end of his nose. He was looking down at me holding a violin and a violin bow. Then he bent over and put the violin and the bow between me and Johnny. And he walked away through the loft and out the door. And when I woke up the violin and the bow were actually there!

I must have had the dream because I saw the empty violin case when I came home and never got a chance to find out from Johnny what it was doing there. Johnny must have gotten up and brought it into bed. Maybe he'll teach the baby how to play it. I keep thinking about names: Wilhelm if it's a boy. If it's a girl I don't know: Maria Barbara, Anna, Sarabande but called Sara, or maybe even Carla now that Johnny knows everything.